P9-DWT-738

ACKNOWLEDGMENTS

My thanks to...

My agent, Lorin Rees, for helping me
make the leap into fiction.

My editor, Kathryn Lye, who improves the story
without altering the point.

Red Dress Ink, for taking me on.

And my family—for their inspiration, humility,
and for being the sort of people who never give up,
nor fail to be grateful for it all.

For a guy named Michael, who knew me once,
and thought that I should write a novel.

girl most likely to

girl most likely to

Poonam Sharma

RED
DRESS
INK
TM

GIRL MOST LIKELY TO

A Red Dress Ink novel

ISBN-13: 978-0-373-89550-2
ISBN-10: 0-373-89550-X

© 2007 by Poonam Sharma.

www.RedDressInk.com

Printed in U.S.A.

·· 1 ··

"Celibacy is rotting your brain."

Cristina insisted through my cell phone, while the taxi jerked up Fifth Avenue. It might even have been true, but it was a hateful thing for a best friend to say.

At my age—and my father never missed an opportunity to remind me of my age with all the subtlety of a presidential ass-pat—my mother had managed a screaming child, a barking dog, a doting husband and a medical residency. And she did it from a three-bedroom Colonial in Great Neck, Long Island. By twenty-seven, left to my own devices, I had amassed a lucrative, yet uninspiring, seventy-hour Wall Street workweek, a telling but unintentional track record of shoving plant corpses down the trash chute while the neighbors slept, and a very large, very expensive and very empty bed. It was the latter fact that had me feeling particularly vulnerable. And of the many mistakes I made that Saturday evening, the first was expecting Cristina to understand.

"Just because I've decided to be rational and take control of my life, that doesn't mean I'm crazy." I pouted, checking my watch. Draped in my traditional powder-blue silk salwar kameez and matching satin Charles David heels, I was hurtling helplessly toward another lavish Indian wedding where my parents would be seated where the love of my life ought to be. After ten years of scouring every dormitory bar, party and young singles' mixer, not to mention checking under every rock and in more than my fair share of countries around the world, I was in no mood for honesty. If bunions were my reward for a decade of running in four-inch heels, then cynicism was my logical response to the umpteenth fix-up with a prince whose castle would eventually make me break out in hives.

"But an arranged marriage? For you, Vina?" her voice climbed. It was laced with all the straight-postured self-righteousness of a New England housewife snatching home hair dye from the hands of a teenaged daughter. "I don't think so."

I sucked air through clenched teeth.

"See? This is why I wasn't going to tell you about tonight. And it's not an arranged marriage. It's an arranged…*date,* and it just happens to be taking place at a wedding."

Ever since I met Cristina, when we were the lone female interns in the J.P. Morgan investment banking department, she'd refused to cut me emotional slack. And that was what I respected most about her. Unfortunately, she also refused to accept that merely being ethnic (Cuban, and from Miami) didn't mean she automatically grasped my situation. Convincing her that it was a good idea to be set up with the Punjabi lawyer courtesy of my parents required an appeal to the rational side of her brain. Fortunately, we were both investment bankers; I knew exactly how to put things into terms that she could grasp.

"Look," I added, cradling my cell between ear and shoulder while aiming my compact at the pinky finger I used to catch errant eyeliner, "I have thirty months left until thirty. I know your mom had you when she was, like, *forty*. But you have to understand that Indian women don't have Cuban women's genes. Sure, our hips were made for childbearing, but that's where the similarity ends. The fact is that I'm only fertile until, like, thirty-five. And anyway, to figure out ideal fertility age, you take the average age of menopause for women in your family, and subtract twenty years. That's when your fertility takes a serious nosedive. For my mom, menopause was fifty, so that means that childbirth is supposed to be before thirty for me."

"But…"

"Also…consider that it takes at least six months to fall in love with anyone and run the required background checks, another nine months to get engaged, and a year to plan the wedding. And my husband and I will need at least a year of being married without being pregnant—to screw like bunnies before gravity has its way with me. That's thirty-nine months. So even if I meet Mr. Right tonight, I'm still cutting it close."

"Where do you get this stuff?"

My logic impressed her.

"They re-air *The Oprah Winfrey Show* at two a.m." I clicked my compact shut, and noticed that one of my heels was stuck in a glob of gum on the floor of the cab. "And you know that I haven't been sleeping well these days."

In an effort to spare the hem of my salwar kameez, I leaned onto one hip and lifted my shoe. Naturally, the pleather seat beneath me mimicked a fart. My eyes collided in the rearview mirror with those of the cabbie, who, until that point, had occasionally glanced at me with the standard balance of boredom and curiosity. Suddenly he sat up straighter, spearing me with a look of moral superiority— all this from a man who had never encountered a stick of deodorant. I stared out the window.

"What kind of a name is Prakash, anyway?" Cristina finally asked.

"Um, I don't know…an Indian one?"

"Well, it's just not the kind of name that I can imagine you screaming out in a fit of passion."

"Life is not a fit of passion, Cristy." I resented her for making me sound like my mother. "And I think the point is that I'm supposed to have learned that by now. Look at it this way. Meeting a guy through my parents means that the background check is out of the way. Up front, I know that he's single, educated and family-oriented, with no criminal record or illegitimate children."

"And what if he looks like a frog?"

"He will not look like a frog."

"But, Vina, what if he does? What if he looks like a bloated, slimy frog…who got hit in the face with a frying pan…*twice?*"

"Then I guess I'll have to comfort myself with the thought of his really long—"

"Vina, I'm being serious! Have you thought this through? How much are you willing to compromise? Meeting a guy through your parents is a lot more serious than meeting him by yourself. It can't be casual. You've always told me that."

"All I know is that there are men that you date, and men that you marry." I reached into my wallet for a twenty as we turned east onto Forty-seventh Street.

"And never the twain shall meet?"

I paused. "Did you just say 'twain'?"

"Sorry. I'm feeling silly. I have a date with the cowboy tonight. Maybe I'm subconsciously practicing country phrases to put him at ease."

"All Midwesterners are not cowboys, Cristy." I signaled the cabbie for eight dollars in change.

"Yes, but this one is. Seriously. He has the cowboy hat and everything. He even grew up on a ranch."

"And what…he took a wrong turn at the Old Oak Tree and wound up in New York City?"

"Apparently. And he must have asked someone to point him toward the nearest watering hole, because I met him at Denial, a bar over on Grand Street."

"That *is* silly." I wrenched the crumpled dollar bills from the plastic, swiveling slot, and smoothed them into a pile. Then I folded them and slipped them into my purse.

"Come on! Why don't you ditch the wedding, and meet up with us instead? I'll have him bring a *fre-end,*" she practically sang, as if she were dangling a new doll before my eyes.

"As tempted as I am by the idea of playing Cowboys and Indians twenty years after recess is over, I think I'll pass."

"Oh, I get it. When you play with firemen it's perfectly acceptable, but when I try to throw a little rodeo it's *silly?*"

I fought off a mental image of The Village People performing "YMCA," and feigned indignation at Cristina. "I thought we agreed never to speak of that again."

She followed suit. "We agreed on no such thing."

"I was young." I checked my watch for the tenth time since Union Square. "It's a part of my past."

"It was last year." She paused, probably for dramatic effect. "And I believe the exact line that you used on that guy was 'If I promise to run home and start a fire, will you promise to come over later?'"

"You gave me that line." I cracked a smile. "Good times, though." And then we giggled together, like only two women who know that they will see each other from virginity to Viagra can.

"Vina, I just don't want you settling for some guy who isn't your 'Prince.'" Cristina took a typically cheap shot at our friend Pamela, who wasn't there to defend herself. "You've been way too preoccupied lately with your so-called future."

"Oh, who are you kidding, Cristina? I'm an Indian chick from Strong Island. I was *born* preoccupied with my so-called future."

"I'm not talking about your professional future. I'm talking about your personal future. It's like you're turning into, well, I hate to say it, but…Pam."

"Now that's mean," I said. "First, you make me feel more pathetic than I already do by reminding me that I haven't had sex in forever, and now you're comparing me to her. And come to think of it, you wouldn't give *her* any crap if *she* was being set up with a nice Jewish lawyer by *her* parents."

"You know you don't want to get me started on Pam."

"Agreed." I sighed as we slowed to a halt by the curb outside the Waldorf Astoria. A uniformed doorman sped over and reached toward the door handle. "In fact, I don't want to get you started on anything at the moment because my chariot has pulled up to the ball. Passionate Princes are a fairy tale, Cristy, but a Practical Prince will suit me fine."

·· 2 ··

Red rose petals littered golden tablecloths. Gleaming china settings and generous floral arrangements adorned each table. The air was delicately scented. Votives flickered on every surface, fading in comparison to the luster of the many rubies, emeralds and diamonds gliding around the ballroom. Waiters circled the tables while craning their necks to scan the room of the three hundred guests; the servers were determined not to leave any glass unfilled, any mouth unstuffed or any whim unattended. Toddlers peeked from behind the saris of young mothers, while older women sought potential daughters- and sons-in-law. Elders leaned back in their chairs, appreciating how their familiar chai seemed sweeter, and their familiar aches seemed duller in the face of so much life.

By ten p.m., there was no sign of Prakash. I speared a soggy Rasgulla with my fork and lifted the cheese-patty toward my mouth, while glaring daggers across Table 21.

"Certainly I miss living with Mummy and Papa in Delhi," Cousin Neha gushed at our tableful of captivated parents.

Nearly all of their *Americanized* children had run as amok as I—moving into Manhattan apartments alone, while refusing to acknowledge "thirty and single" as a hopeless disease.

"Those three years after college and before my marriage were wonderful, really," Neha continued, "I used to enjoy myself, having dinner and going to the cinema with my friends on the weekends. But Stamford, Connecticut, is also quite nice, although it is a bit chilly for us. Vinny and I drive to work together each morning, and then we go to one of the local restaurants in the evening, if I don't feel like cooking."

Rather than nailing Neha between the eyes, the fiery daggers I was hurling instantly transformed into plastic cocktail swords before they could make it across the table. They kept bouncing off of her matrimonial shield, and collapsing into a heap on the dessert plate in front of her. From where my second martini and I were seated, it looked as if that heap was about to topple and bury the remains of my self-esteem. My first martini had vanished instantly after the third consecutive "Auntie" (any non-blood-related woman old enough to be my mother who hasn't seen me since I was *this tall*) inquired, before asking about anything else, when I was getting married myself. *As soon as he's paroled,* I thought about saying, or perhaps, *Tuesday. But you're not invited. You can just send a gift to my apartment. I'm registered at Frederick's of Hollywood.*

"Neha darling, tell me… Have you also met any nice young couples to socialize with?" another Auntie-type asked from my right. Why everyone was so interested in my cousin was as much of a mystery to me as how *The Anna Nicole Smith Show* survived while *Once and Again* was canceled.

"Oh, yes! We have met many friendly couples," Neha beamed girlishly at her husband, Vineet, who slurped his chai and winked at me. The wink was a gesture of encouragement to persevere, despite my tragic state of spinsterhood. "But you know…there are also many single people in Stamford. There are even single girls from India. I honestly feel sorry for them, being in a different country, spending the whole day alone and then going home to an empty apartment. When I talk with them it seems like it really does not bother them at all. They work, they live on their own, and they don't even have any interest in marriage. They don't even want to talk about it. Imagine!"

A three-hundred-pound woman who lives in the middle of nowhere, and has no friends outside of her husband, feeling sorry for me, I mocked telepathically to Marty—I had decided to name my martini by that point, as a reward for all of its loyalty. *Imagine!*

The same Auntie leaned over and practically yelled into my ear: "And what about you, Vina? *Koi nehy milha?*" She must have been speaking up to steal my attention from the many voices everybody assumed were living inside my head. These were, of course, the same voices that entertained all single career women when they came home to empty apartments at the end of each day. But I wondered why she also felt the need to shake a hand before her face like a tambou-rine. Were her fluttering fingers intended to deflect my bad romantic luck before it could infect any of the happy couples in the room? *Great.* I shook my head at Marty. *Now they think I've become so hopeless that I require an emotional exorcist.*

The bride and groom swirled past us on the dance floor. Twenty-seven-year-old Nikhil and Suraya, an MIT engineer and an NYU medical resident, had met at a friend's dinner party the summer before. I spotted a number of single career women hiding behind ice sculptures just to avoid answer-ing the same question posed at weddings the world over. I wondered if there was ever an appropriate response to *koi nehy milha? Did I get anyone yet?* Factually, it sounded hopeless. *No, I have not.* The truth sounded sluttish. *Actually, I've had a few men. Even some I would recommend to a friend. But nobody with whom I'm interested in growing old and less attrac-tive.*

I chose to hide behind the facade of nonchalance familiar to all unattached Indian women of "marriageable age." What that means is that I lied. "Oh, Auntie, I don't have time to worry about that right now. I'm too passionate about my career."

"Vina is just being shy," my father interrupted. That man could never be accused of appropriate timing. "We are con-fident that tonight will be the night. We have found her a lovely boy."

"Oh? Is this the doctor from Pittsburgh? The one you were telling me about?" Auntie Meenakshi questioned my mother hopefully. *What doctor? Did she say Pittsburgh? How many other people were my parents discussing my personal life with?*

"No, no." My father shook his head. "We found out that the family in Pittsburgh had a history of divorces. This boy, Prakash, is thirty years old, which is suitable for Vina. He was born in New Jersey, but he lives in Manhattan now. He is an attorney, with a very impressive bio data. He is five feet eleven inches, and both his parents are engineers. We are disappointed that they are not Punjabi—they are Gujarati—but one has got to be open-minded on that point these days. And his father attended IIT in the same batch with the brother-in-law of my third cousin, Prem, who is now settled in Bombay. Everybody agrees that it is a good family. Prakash is the eldest of three brothers, and all are highly educated."

Table 21 nodded in collective approval. "Lady in Red" wafted through the air. I drained the last of my martini, and checked for emergency exits.

"Why is everybody talking about this?" my maternal grandmother (referred to traditionally as Nani) interrupted in Hindi. "We have done our part. Now we must let the kids decide. And where is this Prakash, anyway? What kind of a boy would keep my Vina waiting?"

My earliest memory is of my Nani making Gulab Jamuns in our kitchen; I watched as she deep-fried and drizzled them with golden sugar water. I must have been six years old when I dragged that stool stoveside, and quietly climbed on top. Elbows on the counter, I waited silently until she tore off a piece of raw, sweet dough, and handed it to me. I never understood how she managed to grab the right amount of dough each time, and roll it so quickly into a perfect ball between her palms. And I asked her about my grandfather, whom I had never met.

"Your grandfather was a very good man." She shook her head and reached for more dough. "*Ithna shareef!* Here they would have called him genuine, but he was much more than that. He cared for everybody. And he used to give your mother airplane rides on his shoulders. She was too small then to remember, even smaller than you are now."

"Did he like Gulab Jamuns?" I swung my heels, chewing happily on the dough.

"He *was* a Gulab Jamun, daughter." She stopped and looked at me. "He was *my* Gulab Jamun."

"Did he look like a Gulab Jamun?" I leaned my head to one side.

"He did to me. And one day, your Gulab Jamun will come to you." She caught my chin between her fingers.

"How will I know it's him?"

"You will know," she reassured me, before rolling a dozen balls into boiling oil, which refrained from splattering, under her watchful eye.

"Are you sure?"

"Yes."

"But what if he looks more like a Jalebi?"

"He won't."

"What about a Rasgulla?"

"A Rasgulla looks nothing like a Gulab Jamun. Besides, mommy and daddy will recognize him and they will bring him for you when it is time."

I paused, tilting my head. "But how will they recognize a Gulab Jamun if he looks like a Rasgulla or a Jalebi?"

She stopped, and eyed me. "You need not worry about such things, Vina. Good girls trust their parents. That is all you need to know."

With that, I had to be satisfied. My Nani was always right.

"Ma'am? Another Rasgulla?" A waiter appeared. "Ma'am?"

"Vina? Are you paying attention?" my mother asked. Everybody at the table was staring at me. Maybe celibacy *was* rotting my brain.

"Don't worry, little cousin." Neha patted my shoulder before squeezing between the chairs on her way to the dance floor. "You'll find someone soon."

I'm not worried, I agreed with Marty. *What I am is thirsty.*

I scrunched my nose at the chai-bearing waiter leaning over my left shoulder. "I think I'm in the mood for something a little stronger."

I pushed back my chair, rose to my feet and made a beeline for the bar.

In my defense, I arrived at the wedding feeling nothing-less-than-thrilled for Suraya and Nikhil. I raised my flute, alongside everyone else, in a toast to the newlyweds. I smiled through hours of idle chatter, and now I made my way rather steadily over to the bar. And that was where, as the twenty-one-year-old bartender started looking a little too good to me, it happened. I was reaching out to take hold of my third martini when I felt a warm hand crashing into my own.

My first instinct was to yank at the drink. Snatch it away and hold it above my head. To gulp it down and Take Back the Night. But I paused when I noticed that the very masculine hand was attached to a confident and sturdy arm, which had brought along an alarmingly attractive head. And the man to whom that head belonged seemed to be thinking the same about me.

"Bartender, I believe I asked for this to be shaken, not stirred," he announced for my benefit.

Oooph, he's yummy, I thought. *If it meant being closer to a smile like that, I might actually consider climbing inside the martini.* He was a cross between James Dean and Sunil Dutt (the James Dean of Indian cinema). I smiled and loosened my grip. Countless witty responses raced about inside my head, apparently bumping into one another enough to cause a massive concussion.

"Mmmhhhaaaahhaaahh," I said. Or snorted. He must have assumed this was my own personal dialect, because he smiled as if he was impressed. I cleared my throat while he replaced the glass on the bar.

"I'll thumb-wrestle you for it," he said.

"Seriously?" I blurted. I was too tipsy to play anything cool in the face of such deep, mischievous eyes.

"No, not seriously." He laughed, as if I were charming and had said it on purpose. Looking down, I noticed that our collision had splashed the martini across the sleeve of his tuxedo. Then I caught myself considering licking it off him. That was when I decided to cut myself off for the night. I must have reeked of mock-confidence and gin.

"I'm Prakash." He wiped his hand on a napkin before extending one to me. "You must be Vina?"

Honey, I thought, *I'll be whoever you want me to be.*

"Oh! Prakash!" I slapped my forehead, regretting it immediately. "Yes, my mother mentioned you. Well…it's nice to finally meet you."

Over Prakash's shoulder I spotted my mother, who was watching us from across the room. She sat with her thumbs and eyebrows raised, as if she were rooting for the lone Indian on *Fear Factor.* I assumed that that was Prakash's mother seated beside her, considering that the woman couldn't resist a nod of satisfaction at the childbearing capacity that the fit of my salwar kameez made plain. With a full belly and an expectant heart, my father napped quietly in his chair, probably dreaming of telling his grandchildren to sit up straight.

The latest version of a classic Bhangra song, which had apparently been mixed with the theme from Knight Rider, trailed off, and "Careless Whisper" picked up. DJ Jazzy-Desi-Curry-Rupee, or whatever his name was, called out to the crowd, "Can we please haw all the luwly gentleman and lehdees join us on the danz floor now for a wery special slow song?"

Hands cupped behind his back, Prakash faked a nervous glance at the floor: "Your mom told my mom to tell me to ask you to dance. So…I mean…do you wanna?"

I grinned, and he led me toward the dance floor. Crowds dispersed. Couples embraced. Prakash took me into his arms. His frame was stiff enough to let me know who was leading, even as he refused to drop his playful gaze. We sailed around the floor, almost as captivatingly as the two five-year-olds who were probably forced out there by some photo-hungry parents nearby. I didn't need a mirror to know how perfect Prakash and I looked together.

Imagine my luck, I thought. *I've found an attorney, who's adorable, and funny, and a good dancer…and Indian? Tomorrow I'll start auditioning matrimonial henna tatoo artists. On Monday morning I'll look into the logistics of renting the horse upon which Prakash will arrive at our wedding.*

A lesser man might have dropped me at the pivotal moment, but Perfect Prakash held me firmly, as I leaned into his arm and kicked back my leg. He dipped me so far that the ends of my hair touched the floor. I smiled for my parents, as much as for myself, while all the blood rushed straight to my head.

"So, Prakash…you're handsome, you're charming, and you're a lawyer," I began once he had pulled me up. "How is it possible that no woman has snatched you off the market yet?"

"Vina, there's a perfectly simple explanation for that," he

replied, watching my form more than my eyes as he spun me around, and twisted me like a Fruit Roll-Up into one arm.

"I'm as *gay* as they come!"

I unraveled. I think I would have preferred to have been dropped.

·· 3 ··

My grandparents spoke little English, and lived with us while I grew up. Their presence guaranteed my fluency in Hindi and ensured a steady supply of Bollywood movies in the house. In comparison with what they considered *morally questionable* Hollywood films, the predictability of Indian cinema must have comforted them. Because while the actors rotate, the story never changes.

Bad first impressions inspire mutual disgust between the bratty rich girl and the rebel boy from the wrong side of the tracks. This disgust evolves through flirtation into puppy love, after she offers her silk scarf to bandage his wound one day, which he earned while fixing the engine of her car that had coincidentally broken down by the side of the road right in front of his home. The pair falls in love and meets in secret to perform choreographed dance numbers. Changing outfits between the ballads they sing at river banks and on mountaintops, they end each number with an almost-but-not-quite kiss, while peasants dance spontaneously around them. All hell breaks loose when their fathers—inevitably embroiled in a vendetta which began long before they were born—learn of their torrid romance. Someone fights, someone is kidnapped and someone is warned to stay away from the girl. Girl throws tantrum, mother shares wisdom, and after more fighting, someone is nearly killed. The parents decide to forget about the past, agreeing that love matters most, and throwing an enormous wedding, with more dancing, much singing and still no kissing.

Basically, it's *Romeo and Juliet* with more choreography and less sexual content. And unlike *Romeo and Juliet,* Bollywood lovers always have a happy ending. My parents had an arranged marriage in India approximately two weeks after their parents introduced them. They don't use a word like love, but my father cannot sleep when my mother is ill, and I have never seen her sip her morning tea without him. To say publicly that they loved each other, my father once told me, would be like taking out a press release to announce that water was wet.

No man had ever understood why I cling to the idea of a happy ending, even as I claim to have accepted the slim chances of it. These guys told me that I made no sense, or that my fixation on how things *ought to be* could easily mean I'd end up alone. Lately I worried that if they turned out to be right, I would have no one to blame but myself.

Well, that will teach me not to use an eyelash curler, I thought, blinking rapidly while I ran toward the coat check. Judging by the expressions of the hotel guests I rushed past, I must have looked a mess. Conveniently, the eyelash which came loose as I fled the dance floor had settled across the inner rim of my eyelid. And barring a knuckle to my socket, nothing was gonna pull that sucker out. With mascara streaming down my quivering left cheek, I fought off the beginnings of a facial spasm. For anyone who resents our shiny, flowing locks, let me assure you: What Indian women save in trips to tanning booths and melanoma clinics, we lose in the battle against our follicles. All that waxing, plucking, threading and tweezing could reduce a grown man to tears.

I banged on the courtesy bell while leaning into the coatroom, searching for some hint of a coat check girl.

"Vina." My mother grabbed me by the arm and yanked me around to face her. "*Vot* are you *dewing hir?*" When her voice developed the Punjabi twang, it always meant I had stepped out of line.

"Looking for a coat check girl." I avoided her eyes.

"*Vee thot* something had gone wrong." She overgestured. "You just ran off and left poor Prakash standing like a dummy on the dance floor! Papa thought you had an upset stomach, but I assumed you were feeling sick from those ten martinis."

"It was three martinis, Mother." I rubbed my right arm below the shoulder. For four feet and ten inches of relatively sedentary maternal mass, she was actually freakishly strong.

"And this is something *forr a vooman* to be proud *off?*"

"No." I banged not-so-courteously on the bell, and noticed that my throat was feeling tight.

"Oh, *beti*." She softened, her face melting into concern. "Are you all right?" Clearly she had misinterpreted the state of my face.

"Yes, Mom." I took a breath and faked a smile. "I'm fine."

"Come here." She produced a handkerchief from behind her bra strap, and proceeded to dab at my cheek.

"Mom." I jerked my head away, like an adolescent avoiding a maternal spit-shine. "I'm fine."

"If you are fine, then why are you leaving?" Her eyebrows arched. "Did he do something *wrong?*"

"No, Mom." I shook my head. "It's nothing like that. Prakash was a total gentleman."

"Then explain your behavior, Vina." She gathered up the pleats of her sari, and reflung it over a shoulder, before settling a hand on each hip. "Why are you behaving this way? Don't you know how much of an insult this is to his family? In front of everyone?"

"Mom, trust me. We're not a match."

"*Vy* not, Vina? Tell me *vy* not? You are both Indian, and professional, and he is very handsome, and he comes from a good family. *Vot* more do you *vont?* And please, Vina, don't start talking about your so-called Chemistry and Love. You are not a child, and you know that these things take time. Your father is going to ask me why you are being so unreasonable." She cocked her head to one side. "Or…wait a minute. *You* didn't say anything wrong, *did you?*"

I gritted my teeth.

"No, Mom. Of course not. Of course I didn't say anything *wrong*." I couldn't stop blinking, or cursing myself for choosing this nightmare over Cristy's rodeo. "The problem with Prakash is that he's…"

"*There* you are!"

"Oh! Hello, *beta*. How are you?" my mother cooed at Prakash. It was a frighteningly instant transformation.

"Hello, Auntie. You must be Vina's mother. It's very nice to meet you. That's a lovely sari you're wearing. Is it organza? It must have been made in Delhi, right? My mother says that you can't find such good quality anywhere in New York, Jackson Heights or otherwise."

He was shameless. She was beaming. I was at a loss.

"Thank you, *beta*. Thank you. I'll go and say hello to your father." She smiled. I tugged at my eyelid, which made a sucking noise. Glaring at me before she spun on her heels, my mother bounced giddily away. I rolled my eyes and gave up on the coat check girl, opting instead to search for a concierge.

Prakash whispered, while he watched my mother depart: "Vina, we have to talk."

I paused, and twisted my neck toward him. "*We?* There is no *we*, you lunatic. Meanwhile, you and I have nothing to say to each other." I pivoted away from him.

"You have to listen to me!" He grabbed my shoulders and pushed me backward through the doorway of the coat-room. My cheek spasmed, my eye twitched and I struggled for breath. Being half-blind, half-drunk and immobilized by my four-inch heels, I forgot all my fight-or-flight instincts. So rather than reacting I chose to hyperventilate, while trying to remember the protocol. *Was I supposed to poke him in the groin? Knee him in the eyes? Kick him in the gut? Twist and pull? Scream for help? Stop, drop and roll?*

"Vina, you don't understand!" he said, cornering me in the small room.

Hoping for an emergency exit nearby, I lost balance and fell into a pile of coats. Prakash collapsed on top of me. The snapping of my left heel was practically expected, but the groping by the coats I landed on was most certainly not. Rolling Prakash off of myself, I struggled to my feet, and sprang into a defensive judo-stance. (Note to self: Stay away from *Austin Powers* reruns on cable.)

From below the pile of coats, a giggle and a pair of heads emerged. And one of the heads had something to say for itself. "Heeeeeey baby, don't be like that. There's always room for one more person at this party."

I blinked to confirm what I was witnessing: the missing coat check girl grinning over a bare shoulder while straddling the bartender, who raised an eyebrow as soon as he noticed that I wasn't alone. And I could've sworn I heard him add, "Or room for *two more,* should I say?" as I darted for the door.

With one hand to my forehead, I sprinted across the lobby, slowing only to throw the broken shoe into the trash. Soon enough I tripped on the other one, and crashed into the lobby's glass doors, badly skinning my knee. Rather than taking the moment to feel sorry for myself, I remembered that Prakash was close behind. I clambered to my feet, threw open the doors and leaped into a waiting taxi, with just enough time to hurl my other heel out the window before the cab driver gunned the gas.

"My parents don't know that I'm gay," Prakash yelled at the window as the cab began to pull away.

"I don't know why he thinks that's my problem," I told the cabbie, who grinned and whisked me safely home.

·· 4 ··

"*Chica,* who has time for a four-hour Sunday brunch and still manages to pay their rent in this town? That's what I want to know." Cristina dragged a chair over to our table at Starbucks. She paused to lay her cell phone and her Black-Berry beside my own, and then checked her pulse on a wrist sensor before acknowledging Pamela. "Oh, no offense, Pam."

Cristina had an obsessive relationship with her physical fitness, but she also had a point. She and I had spent the better part of our Sundays during the last four years hidden in our offices, catching up on work before Monday morning. In our industry, that didn't make us competitive; it made us competent. And in an effort to burn off some of the resulting stress, Cristina had become a genius at self-defense. She mastered everything from model-mugging (assault scenarios simulated by mock-attackers in padded suits) to Krav Maga (hand-to-hand combat training based on the principles of the Israeli national army). An even more unfortunate habit of hers was using Spanish words and phrases when trying to convince me of something. She was reminding me of that additional camaraderie all ethnic women supposedly shared. It was unforgivably manipulative. Sure, I had thrown in the occasional *Schmoopie* or *Honey* when trying to steer a steak-loving boyfriend toward a Thai restaurant (because the variety would make him a better man), or to convince him that rubbing my feet could stave off the effects of carpal tunnel (I swear, I had read that some-where). But I would never have stooped so low as to use any of these tactics on my girls.

Pam, on the other hand, hailed from a very different school of thought; a school that didn't bear the burden of rent. Her father—still guilt-ridden over leaving her mother for an au pair twenty years ago—bought her a one-bedroom apartment on the Upper East Side as a college graduation present. The arrangement kept her in clothing that Cristina and I wouldn't dare buy for ourselves, even though we each earned roughly three times Pamela's salary. But I guess Pam needed it more than we did; Chanel, Gucci and Polo were standard dress code at Windsors, the devastatingly upper-crust art auction house where she worked for pennies, and the occasional invite to some of the swankiest social events this side of the Riviera. It was a good arrangement for Cristy and myself, too, since some of those invitations trickled down to us. Each event held the promise of champagne and the company of international aristotrash who probably assumed that our presence meant we were royalty ourselves.

"None taken." Pamela waved the comment away like so many pesky fruit flies, and then scrunched up her nose and peered suspiciously into the whipped cream covering my Caramel Macchiato. "Is that *decaf?*"

"Yes. It is." I stirred the caramel carefully, trying not to risk whipped cream deflation. Then I realized I should probably have resented the judgment in her tone. "So what?"

Despite the god-awful preppy clothing Pamela had seemed to know it all nine years ago, when she strolled into my freshman dorm room. It was day two of the fall semester. She breezed in, made herself comfortable among my unopened boxes, pointed to a literature textbook and asked if I was taking the Friday class with Professor Feineman. I nodded. *It was a bad idea,* she told me, *unless I wanted to miss out on Thursday-night parties just to be awake in time for the only 8:00 a.m. class requiring attendance.* As effortlessly as she said it, she lifted a heap of Ramen noodles neatly into her mouth, using chopsticks. Never having seen anyone my own age handle them properly before, I naturally assumed this was a woman from whom I could learn. Time cured me of that misconception, but Pamela's perspective had narrowed while her opinions had sharpened with age.

"*So*…you never drink decaf." Cristina sided with the enemy.

"Yes, I drink decaf." I scrolled through old messages on my BlackBerry.

"When?" Pam asked, picking imaginary lint off of my shoulder. "When do you drink it?"

"I don't know...sometimes. Who cares when I drink it? Why does it matter?"

"*Hijole*...because you've been acting weird lately, and we're worried about you." Cristina thrust her chin out at me.

"Why?" I asked. "What's the problem? Maybe I don't want to get myself all riled up."

"All riled up...with coffee? Most of your blood has already been replaced by it, Vina. And do you even hear yourself? You sound like you're about sixty years old."

"Decaf is not like you, Vina," Pam interrupted, "any more than letting your parents set you up on a blind date is. And you know that I don't have anything against you meeting potentially compatible guys. However, we want to talk about what's really been going on with you. You've been frazzled lately."

Frazzled? I thought. *If they had any idea what I had gone through before I arrived at Starbucks that morning, they would consider me incomprehensibly composed.*

Three hours earlier, I was feeling even more exposed before a larger and more sympathetic audience. I probably could have been better prepared, but who would've guessed that there were so many "Closeted Claustrophobes" in New York City?

"I, umm...my name is Maria," I had stuttered when thirty pairs of eyes collided upon me. "And I'm a Closeted Claustrophobe. It's been about eight hours since my last attack." I cleared my throat, making a mental note to make sure none of these weirdos tried to follow me home.

Admitting that I had a problem was difficult enough. I didn't see the need to share my name with the motley crew who had gathered in the basement of St. Agnes' 13th Street Church that Sunday morning. I could just imagine being outed when I bumped into one of these lost souls while strolling through Bergdorf's with my mother. *You wouldn't have to struggle to fill your time with such silly things if you were married and settled into life,* she would explain, before shaking her head at whatever heels I was considering, and strolling off in search of a Talbots.

Emotional problems, according to my parents, were a luxury of the lazy, self-indulgent American. I had learned this early about my parents, and decided around the same time that the best way to maneuver my Indian and American cultural identities would be to keep certain things about myself to myself. I knew that I had overreacted in the coatroom. And I was as sure that I needed help as I was mortified to have finally come looking for it. Twisting in my plastic seat, I cupped the bruise on my knee while committing the Five *C*s of the Closeted Claustrophobes to memory: *Check for exits, Close your eyes, Count to ten, Calm your nerves, Center yourself.*

Delilah, the middle-aged receptionist who spoke before me, teared up twice while describing the torture of her cramped bus ride. Arthur, the elderly man preceding her, explained how his frustration over claustrophobia had resulted in an anger management problem, which was magnified by his Tourettes, and had effectively ended his acting career. Already I was glad that I had come, since I didn't have it nearly as bad as any of these freaks. Things were going smoothly, especially in comparison to my first attempt at one of these meetings. Three months earlier I stopped short of entering the doorway when I overheard the Rage-aholics director threatening the Claustrophobes director with physical harm unless he surrendered the larger, first-floor room to the Fear of Heights support group, whose director was his ex-wife.

I was wondering how the albino to my left could call himself claustrophobic, given such a determined oblivious-ness to my right of personal space, when I saw a familiar figure coming through the door. It was my cousin, Neha.

"The government stole my shoes!" Arthur announced without warning, startling everyone, including himself.

I was halfway to the Starbucks before my seat had prob-ably gone cold.

"He's gay?" Cristina blurted out, nearly choking on her drink. "Wow…I knew your parents were a little out of touch with what you're looking for in a man, but that's ri-diculous!"

"Obviously they didn't *know* he was gay." I spoke up to dismiss the uninvited pity rushing at me from our neigh-bors.

"Do *his parents* know?" Pam leaned in and whispered, as if the topic were a reflection on her.

"Of course not."

"Que locura," Cristina decided. "That's pretty twisted. So much for counting on those underground, Indian-network background checks."

"There is nothing underground about the Indian network," I tried to explain. "And it has nothing to do with the background check, anyway. As far as the background check went, everything was perfect. Generally, Indian parents don't consider, or even think about, their children's sexualities or sexual preferences. Some things are just assumed."

"Seriously." Pam shook her head at Cristy, ignoring me entirely. "You said he was thirty, right? Talk about living in denial."

Was she referring to Prakash's parents or to him? In a way, I felt bad for the guy; I could relate. Our parents grew up in a culture that rejected the concepts of premarital sex and romance. Non-arranged marriages occurred so infrequently among their generation that they were referred to as "love marriages." Like most first-generation Indian-Americans, I had come to accept that my parents could never acknowledge my *premarital sexuality* any more than Prakash's parents could comprehend his *homosexuality*.

My theories on the value of self-discovery through romantic misadventure were lost on mom and dad, so I kept my mouth shut about my relationships, especially the fifty percent that involved non-Indian boys. And somewhere around age fifteen I decided to take the same stance on my claustrophobia.

"Look, I'm not pissed off that he's gay." I concentrated on my empty cup. "I'm pissed off that he led me on."

"What a tease." Cristina grinned.

"Basically," I said, sitting up straighter. "But it doesn't

matter. Prakash was only a blip on my radar. An irrelevant data point. My plan holds."

Two blank pairs of eyes stared back at me.

"Oh, God. Are you still talking about that 'thirty months until thirty' garbage?" Cristina practically yelled.

"First of all, it's not garbage. Ignoring my biological clock won't make it go away. And I'm finished wasting time. I have to be honest with myself." I raised my chin toward Pamela. "And I know *you* can at least understand where I'm coming from."

To Pamela, *thirty and alone* was roughly translated as *homeless and afflicted with a disfiguring, terminal, sexually transmitted disease.* She had been engaged-to-be-engaged with William, a Harvard-educated lawyer of the lightly pinstriped variety, since the beginning of time; or at least since the beginning of college, when she woke up in his bed on the morning after the Head of the Charles regatta. Although it never occurred to her to question his claim that his parents' divorce made him maritally gun-shy, I was sure that it also never occurred to her that there was anything wrong with treating the search for a mate like the search for an apartment. A good deal was a good deal, period. And the potential for long-term appreciation far outweighed momentary attractiveness.

"You're right, Vina. I do understand where you're coming from. And I do not want to see you single at thirty." She eyed me like a child who had lodged a marble up her own nose. "I also agree with you that we *should* all be honest with ourselves. So let's be honest...let's talk about what this is really about. Jon."

·· 5 ··

I once broke up with a man for asking if I spoke "Indian." He wasn't kidding, so I asked him with a straight face if he spoke "White." He didn't get it. That was my cue to leave. On the other end of the spectrum, I once dated an Englishman who had me groping desperately for my can of mace the moment I entered his apartment. He had collected more Indian paraphernalia than was probably ever assembled outside the Subcontinent by anyone who was not, in fact, Indian. He acted completely nonchalant when he struck up a conversation at the bar, made no mention of his fascination with the country, yet he had filled his apartment with everything from statues of Ganesha to an old-fashioned Jhoola chair to wall-hangings depicting village women dancing while balancing water pots on top of their heads.

He offered me some chai without even a hint of irony, and that was when I decided I wasn't sticking around to hear his Hannibal impersonation. Perhaps he was a perfectly normal guy, and perhaps he merely liked the Indian designs. (And perhaps I'm actually a natural blonde.) Though if that were true, he should have told me before we got to his place. Surprises are not acceptable in New York City. And as all interracial daters already know, or will soon find out, Ethnic Fetishizers cannot be trusted. I cannot tell you whether or not he knew that Bollywood wasn't an alternative to Sandal, or if there was a shrine to Indian women in his bedroom. What I can tell you is that I was out of there faster than you can say *Samosa*.

Little things are always symptomatic of a larger emotional disconnect. Of course, none of this was ever a problem with Jon. He didn't expect me to belly dance or snake charm or glide into physically impossible sexual maneuvers, which I presumably picked up from the Kama Sutra classes I'd attended while the other kids were in Sunday school. The men who believe that sort of thing are easy to spot; they're the same ones who claim that "all women are three margaritas away from a lesbian experience."

Jon asked me questions about me and my family, and he seemed genuinely interested in my answers. Without consulting me, he bought a *Hindi for Beginners* book and began working choice words and phrases into our everyday conversation. But he also spoke Spanish, French and Italian to me. For all I knew, he was calling me his *Little Subway Token* most of the time. But if you had seen his smile, you, too, would have gladly answered to anything from *Microwave Oven* to *I Can't Believe It's Not Butter*, wagged your imaginary tail and drooled all over his Armani shirt. And you, too, would have ignored all the logic against falling in love with a man who was so totally wrong for you. When we met, he was a former chef who owned his own restaurant. Being with him made me feel sophisticated, as if I was physically incapable of spilling anything on myself.

If it hadn't been for his not cluing in to the fact that my eggs were expiring by the minute, we would probably still be together. Well, that, and if I hadn't mistaken his cell phone for my own on that godforsaken morning two weeks earlier.

The day had started out like any other. I was running late for work and cursing myself for hitting the snooze button so many times. The twist that morning was an unexpected visit from my neighbor, Christopher, who flamed so brightly that he sometimes threatened to set the building on fire. His natural sense of style and inability to keep his couture judgments to himself made me feel like less of a woman, and left me no choice but to ignore his prior attempts to befriend me. So you can imagine how surprised I was to find him waiting outside my door at eight o'clock with a story about a last-minute business trip (Did accountants really have those?) and a wheezing, unimpressed Boo-boo in his arms. Agreeing to cat-sit may only have been the first in a number of suboptimal choices I made that day, but as it turns out, it wasn't just me. The entire city was off-kilter that day. Without thinking, and because I was then running even later for work, I agreed, despite my chocolate-brown sofa, to take the fluffy white Persian into my home.

The time it took to get the pudgy little boarder settled precluded my Starbucks stop, so I was at the mercy of the Krispy Kremes, which materialized in our conference room before each Monday-morning team meeting. Sarah, the only other woman on our team, shot an irritated look at me for the crime of inquiring if there were "anything choco-late" left in the box. A former professional golfer who'd gone back to her MBA after an injury, Sarah had recently joined our company in Equity Research. While she was a nice person, if you asked me, Sarah was completely ill-equipped for the world beyond sports. She cursed like a sailor, slapped indiscriminant high fives, and called everyone Dude. Some women believe that in order to compete with a man, you must essentially become one. But then again, some women refuse the epidural.

Question: Wouldn't you like to be more like a man?

Answer: Why would I want to be hairier, lonelier and more confused than I already am?

The rest of the team shook their heads at my request, but Sarah made her opinion clear. Even in an office where most men had their shoes shined, their backs waxed, their suits tailored and their personal trainers on speed-dial, my obses-sive culinary peccadilloes made me a disgrace to feminists everywhere.

"It's not easy being you, is it?" she said, pouting in my direction.

Peter, a fellow Associate, looked up from his copy of *The*

Economist; Denny, a lowly Analyst, swallowed half of a jelly doughnut and Wade, the eager Intern, stopped midsip of his coffee. All eyes around the conference table focused on me, but before I could respond the overhead lights flickered off. Everyone glanced up at the ceiling, and the lights flickered back on for a second, before flashing out again. The digital wall-clock followed suit, as did the Bloomberg terminal.

Dropping my honey-glazed, I swung the door open and stepped into a darkened office. To my surprise, my otherwise narcissistically-hyper-functioning, Type-A-personality colleagues stood dumbfounded, searching one another's faces for answers. United in temporary paralysis because of the loss of our Internet connection, we huddled around a secretary's CB radio. That's when the crackling voice of a lone CNN reporter explained that through a series of technological mishaps at grid centers across the northeastern United States, the juice had been sucked out of the region.

Within minutes we were headed for the darkened stairwell, since elevators are not an option when someone turns out the lights in New York City. We made our way down each flight single file, relying solely on the sounds of each other's footsteps to avoid a collision. As my forehead began beading over with sweat, I swallowed hard and chose to rely on the Closeted Claustrophobes' mantra to keep my mind in focus: *Check for exits, Close your eyes, Count to ten, Calm your nerves, Center yourself.* My team's co-managing director, Alan, walked before me, and my partner Peter followed close behind. With our palms on the walls and railings, we made it down the first twelve floors without incident.

Clearly, it was too good to last. Thanks to my batlike auditory skills and my nearly four-inch alligator pumps, it was the tenth-floor landing that did me in. I must have miscounted the stairs because my right leg stopped short and sent me doubling over. Knees buckled and back bent, I thrust my arms out before me and grabbed instinctively for something that might break my fall. I won't mention which part of Alan's lower anatomy did the trick, but I will say, *Thank God I didn't squeeze any tighter.*

That blackout was proof positive that New Yorkers cannot be trusted in the dark. They're almost as mischievous as Australians are in the light. Once we made it outside, I apologized profusely for sexually harassing my own boss, who refused to make eye contact with me.

"Ahem… Never mind, Vina… Let's just forget about it, okay?" Alan mumbled, before disappearing into the hordes surrounding our building.

I waded through thousands of ornery businesspeople boiling in their suits and trekked the five avenues and ten blocks toward my apartment. Along the way, I arrived at the surprising conclusion that an alligator pump is in fact the most appropriate shoe for a crisis situation in this city. Because the most effective way to express your discontent when someone gropes you in a crowd is to jam your heel into that person's foot as hard as you possibly can and twist it, like you're putting out a cigarette.

It took all of my strength to complete the final stretch: the ten-flight hike up an unlit stairwell to my place. It wasn't until I stood before the comfort of my front door that the mounting tension in my neck began to drain out of me; here I would be safe. As soon as I was through the door, I wrenched off my shoes and I promptly flung them across the room. That was the moment I remembered my little house-guest, because I nailed him right between the eyes. Booboo let out a squeal that made me wonder whether there wasn't a small child hiding in all that fur, and darted straight under my bed.

I spent the next half hour lying on my belly, peering under my bed and pleading with Booboo to come out. He stared at me maliciously, blinking away the dust bunnies, and yawning or repositioning himself occasionally on top of my shoes. Eventually, I gave up on the niceties and decided to make a grab for him. Taking a deep breath to prepare for what should have been an elegant gesture, I lunged at him. I shoved my entire arm in his direction, until my head banged against the bed frame.

"Raaaaaargh!!!!" He growled what I could only imagine was *Booboo* in cat-speak, and scratched my forearm.

"Shit!" I yelled, and recoiled from the bed, with my eyes watering.

This was the problem with being Super Woman's only daughter. With thirty months to spare until age thirty, my mother had fine-tuned the balance of home and career, secured the illusion of waking up with meticulous makeup, and mastered the art of willing my pancakes down off the kitchen ceiling mere moments after I threw them up there. I, on the other hand, at the same point in my life, was reverse-sexually-harassing my way out of a career I didn't honestly enjoy and while swooning over one homosexual man, was failing miserably in my attempt to win the affections of the wheezing, fifteen-pound cat of another. Honestly, it was a wonder that I could even feed myself.

Whether or not I look the part, I hail from a long line of loan sharks. My father has planned to make this one of his sound bytes when the *New York Times* interviews him in ten years, for a two-page spread about his daughter, the globe-trotting financier. Betel-chewing, bindi-wearing, and almost always below five feet tall, most of the women in my ancestral tree had arrived at their careers in high (or more accurately, low) finance by way of necessity, rather than choice. Practicality rules when you are widowed young in parts of Punjab where remarriage is as much of an option as a sex change. The tradition was to borrow against what little land their husbands had left them, and then loan to the poorer of their villages at three times the banks' normal rates. Pragmatism is what we know. So it was probably less than incredible that, despite my skant affection for the industry, I had managed to thrive on Wall Street.

Most people in my life had no idea what I actually *did* for a living; nor did they care to find out. And I didn't blame them. They were better off clinging to some airbrushed notion of what my days as an investment banker were really like. Essentially, I did the research that helped my bosses decide which stocks to invest in, and when. Sometimes it involved speaking with the management of public companies, who either eyed me like an Omaha Steak or dismissed me entirely. At other times it involved combing through mountains of reports on an industry to develop a reasonable opinion about where it was headed.

Typically, I would spend a week researching before I presented a conclusion to my bosses, who often patted me on the back, or otherwise told me the reasons why they believed that I was wrong, if they felt like explaining themselves. Soon thereafter, the market would always prove them right. Apparently, this was good training for the day when, if I was lucky, I would become one of them. It wasn't being corrected that bothered me so much as it was being wrong. Regardless, my plan was to stick with the job, act like I enjoyed it and apply to business school within a few years.

After earning my MBA, I could start thinking about what I really wanted to do with my life. I would have been a supermodel, but the six-inch heels I'd need just to reach up to the average model's elbow ended that fantasy. Thanks to the same genes, I was far better suited for sneaking under turnstiles than for strutting across runways.

And I would have been a novelist, but there were other genetic predispositions to consider. My father hadn't come to this country with eleven dollars in his pocket thirty years ago, mopped floors at a supermarket, begged for an entry-level engineer's position, tolerated racism and ignorance and decades of struggle, started a business and saved enough to send his daughter to an Ivy League college, only to watch her give up a career of which he could only have dreamed all those years ago.

Another reason why I survived in investment banking was

because early on I had learned the folly of questioning the judgment of the people in control.

"This is a waste of her time," I can remember overhearing my father telling my mother, when she mentioned my excitement over the prospect of entering a poem in a fifth-grade writing competition. "It is not practical, and we should not encourage her in it."

"Oh, don't be so serious, Sushil," my mother replied from the kitchen, while I squeezed my head through the bars of the banister to get within closer earshot. "It's just a writing contest."

"It is not just a writing contest, Shardha. It is a signal. And it is a waste of her time. These are important years. She should be working on her Math Olympiad, or on the Spelling Bee. Why should we train her to care what these so-called judges think? Her teacher is no Professor of Literature. He is there to teach her Mathematics and Science and History. Anyway, writing is something where there is never an absolute score. It cannot get her into good colleges. It is a waste of her time."

"Sushil, be reasonable. I cannot tell her no after I have already told her yes. She's very enthusiastic. She wrote some poem about Reality, and I think it's very clever for her age."

"That is all fine. Yet I do not agree with it. You and I both know that the world does not value these things. They value success that can be measured. We know this. We have seen this. Why should we send our daughter into such a struggling life?"

"Teekh hai," she agreed. "Perhaps you have a point. Though we cannot do anything about it now. And keep your voice down. She just went up to bed."

"*Chuhlow,* fine. But my daughter will not be a writer."

"And I will not reheat your Rotis if they get cold while you are prolonging this discussion. Let's eat in peace, okay?"

To my eleven-year-old ears, the distinction between a father's protectiveness and dismissal of my interest in writing wasn't exactly clear. What was clear was that he had tried to prevent me from doing something, so I had to do it anyway. I proudly entered my poem "Is This Reality?" into the contest. Based on a dream I had, the poem was made up of questions about what proof we had that our world wasn't some other child's dream, and whether or not that child could end our world just by waking up.

The next day, Mr. Kronin called me over to his desk to tell me that it was all right to feel angry and confused about the world, and to ask if I was interested in speaking with the school psychiatrist. Obviously, this was not the response I had hoped for. *You talk to the psychiatrist,* I screamed, before running to the bus and crying all the way home. If this was what writing would lead to, I told myself, I wanted no part of it.

"Sometimes it's not the best thing to share these kinds of feelings," my mother tried to console me. "Because it is not always guaranteed that everyone will understand it. And that can hurt your feelings. But I'm sure that Mr. Kronin didn't mean it. Not everybody knows what a special girl you are, *beti*…like we do."

Burying my head in my pillow, I scooted closer to my Nani. Mom and Dad took the hint and left us alone.

"Vina, you must not be angry with your parents."

"I hate it that they were right," I told her defiantly.

"*Beti,* they don't want to be right. They want you to be successful."

I pulled the covers over my face.

"Try to understand.... This is the way that it is in India. Boys and girls must choose which line they will take in the eighth grade…either science for medicine or math for engineering. They start preparations for college early. And your parents want to make life easier for you. It's the same way as they corrected your hands."

I came out from under the covers. "What?"

"You don't know this, but you were naturally left-handed as a child, so they corrected you."

"How?"

"When you were very small, they told you 'No' every time you used the left hand. They wanted to make your life easier because the world is built for right-handed people. See? You don't even remember being left-handed."

I didn't know what to say.

"*Beti,* good girls trust their parents."

I stood corrected, again. And this time there was no point in arguing. It was better not to waste time questioning those who knew more than I did about things like school. They were clearly more intelligent than I was or ever would be, at anything. On that particular lesson, it turned out, I was a pretty fast learner.

·· 6 ··

On the afternoon of the blackout I was still sitting on the floor, examining the wound from Booboo's outburst, when I heard a familiar voice.

"Vina? You okay?" The voice came from the hallway outside my apartment.

I knew that it was him by his footsteps, and by the way that he left out the verb to save time. Jon had used his elbow to prop himself against my door frame, so his palm obstructed my view when I swung the door open. I was always a sucker for *breathless and brave.* But he was also sweaty. I imagined him running the twenty blocks between his restaurant and my building, and the ten flights up to my door. Love is the only thing in life that is not anticlimactic; and as much as I hated to admit it, seeing him in my doorway made me feel like I was home.

Jon was tall, dark and Sicilian, in that broad-shouldered,

olive-complexioned sort of a way, so I often told myself that we looked good together. We met in his restaurant, Peccavi, eighteen months ago when I requested a rare vintage of Chateau Cabrieres for myself and my girlfriends. He complimented my choice while personally delivering the wine to our table, and stayed to chat us up and steal a glance down my blouse. I'm the first to admit that I was not above doing whatever I could to make it easier for him. I've got to use these puppies while they've still got the inclination to stand and salute.

Eventually, he gave me his business card with the following scrawled across the back: "Bella, I would love to continue our conversation alone, some other time."

I called three days later (sending the message that I was interested, but not desperate), and refused a Saturday-night date but agreed to an early dinner on Sunday (making it clear that while I was far too fabulous to have a Saturday night unbooked four days in advance, I wasn't dating anyone exclusively enough to have my Sunday evenings reserved).

He wooed me expertly from the start, which naturally made me uncomfortable; would Chinese takeout and a rental of *Say Anything* be too pedestrian for him? After our first dinner, he draped his jacket around my shoulders as we strolled through Central Park. Then he kissed me, after holding my face in his hands, looking into my eyes and smiling in a way that asked for my permission.

"Do you think he's embarrassed?" he had asked me, as we passed by a dog who stared at us with one leg raised, peeing against a tree.

Emotional risk-taking never came easily to me. My plan was to have a few months of fun with the big, sexy man, and *(All together now…)* "to keep it casual." A year later, I was drafting speeches that might dissuade my parents from disowning me for bringing home an Italian and an engagement ring. Since I had already ventured so far outside my original romantic parameters, I even surprised myself by deciding to end our relationship over his disinterest in my ticking biological clock. One of the few things I knew I wanted for sure in this life was a child. So I had broken up with Jon in a no-fault sort of a way. He got *Anne & Marie,* the CD we purchased from the band we saw in Vermont on our inaugural weekend getaway. I got David and Melissa, the couple we met at the weekly Latin Dance class he had suggested. And I thought we had split the regrets right down the middle. I thought a lot of things back then and I ignored his attempts to reach out and get back together. A clean break, I reasoned, was the best way to end something that was never supposed to have begun at all. I was the picture of restraint: totally successful in ignoring the chocolates, the e-mails and the phone calls day and night. What I mean to say is that I was totally successful, until he showed up at my door in the middle of that blackout.

"I just wanted to make sure you were okay, I guess." He gasped for breath, wiping his face like the fireman had in that movie Cristina gave me last Christmas.

"Thanks, Jon." I smoothed the hair off of my face. "That's sweet of you. Come in."

"You were at work when it happened, right? You okay for food and water here?" he asked, scanning the inside of my fridge, and the rest of my apartment, as if for intruders.

"Yeah, sure… I walked home from the office and I've got a bunch of water bottles, anyway," I cleared my throat, "Listen, we might run out of water pressure in the bathrooms, and you're pretty sweaty. So if you want, you can take a shower. There are clean towels in there." It was odd to hear myself sound so casual with him.

"Thanks, I think I will. And you know," he hesitated, "It's good to see you. I mean, I miss you."

Pamela refused to accept the breakup. Cristina suggested that I jump back on the horse, or at least the occasional cowboy. The thing was, I never gave Jon an ultimatum. I simply realized that he wasn't interested in more than what we had; therefore, I figured I should look for someone who was. That was when I finally agreed to be set up on a blind date by my parents. I tried to explain all of this to him, but Jon insisted on believing that I was "going through a phase or something," and still made numerous attempts to reconcile. He just wasn't ready to take that step, he told me, but he was even less ready to let go of me.

Now that he was naked in my shower, I wondered if maybe he had been right. Or maybe I had been right; maybe if we got back together, he would acknowledge that he wanted me to bear his children and make an honest woman out of me.

Damn. I wanted to rip off all my clothes and climb into that shower after him. I laid a hand on the doorknob and closed my eyes to imagine it. I'd strip down and sneak into the bathroom, tapping him on the shoulder. He'd turn around and grab me, pulling me close. We'd devour each other, making love against all the slippery-wet walls of my bathroom. My hair and makeup would remain perfect. Steam would rise seductively to prevent anyone from seeing anything less than a completely aroused couple. The camera would fade out.

Of course, I reminded myself of the reality before taking that big step backward. Meaning, this scenario was nearly impossible to pull off without someone slipping, or banging against the faucet or dropping someone else on their ass. And even if none of those things happened, someone was sure to wind up with soapy water shooting directly into their eyes, or their nose, or both. Not sexy. I took my hand away from the doorknob—it was all for the best, I decided. I had no business following Jon into the shower, or anywhere else for that matter. I should be sitting on my couch and looking forward to that promising Indian lawyer my father had mentioned.

Yes. Exactly. But that shower did sound inviting. Oh, why not? What was stopping me? I was young and horny and nobody had made love to me in as long as I could remember. And I loved him. And he loved me. Why wasn't that enough? Why did I always have to be so logical? Oh, all this emotional Ping-Pong was exhausting. I was not going to think about it anymore.

I grabbed some candles from my drawer, along with a set of matches, and left them by my bed. On the couch, I immersed myself in a staring contest with Booboo, who had found a stack of papers on my desk that seemed likely to hatch if warmed long enough. He had decided to oblige with his pudgy body, having already taken care of establishing dominance over me. Deciding that I could not drop Booboo's gaze without somehow forfeiting total dominion over my apartment, I made no effort to acknowledge Jon's emergence from the bathroom. He sat down on the couch beside me, and pulled my arm straight, to get a better look at Booboo's handiwork. After disappearing again into the bathroom he returned, and knelt by the foot of the sofa. Then he unscrewed a tube of Neosporin and began dabbing it gently onto my wound. I looked over and couldn't help being moved by how hard he was concentrating. And he must've sensed my gaze, because he looked up.

He brought my palm to his face, and kissed the middle of it, before tilting his head to rest his cheek inside. He had already parted my lips with his stare by the time his fingers grazed my jawbone. He laid the gentlest kiss on my lips, holding my face lightly in place, like a house of cards he was sheltering from the wind. He searched my eyes before letting his cheek glide along mine and finally burying his face in my hair. The familiar chill set in as he yanked my hips up and around so that I was straddling him.

We sat face to face and I admitted to myself then that I had decided to give in. It was one of those moments you wanted to savor, almost more so than the act, especially when you find yourself back in the arms that used to hold you. And that was how it went…as we wrapped ourselves around each other. As we pressed ourselves together, trying to merge. As his arms resettled among the familiar curves of my back, and his hands dove in and out of my hair, grabbing a clump firmly, and yanking backward to expose my neck for him. As we consumed each other, we took our time because there was nowhere else we would rather have been. He rose to his feet and I tightened the grip of my legs around his waist and allowed him to carry me toward my bed. And lay me down. And climb on top of me. And take me.

He crawled in through my eyes while repeating how much he had missed me. How glad he was that we were together again. This was how it was supposed to be, and he told me that I knew it. As we tumbled around fighting for control and for more of each other, I felt adored and completely, totally open. And even though it was my first, I kept thinking *best blackout ever.*

·· 7 ··

At the end of our second date so many moons before, Jon had invited me to his apartment.

"For a cup of coffee," he had explained, "or maybe a glass of port."

"Sorry." I shrugged. "I can't do it." I avoided his eyes while my heels dodged the cracks in Prince Street.

"Why not?" He stopped, took my hands in his and smiled down at me. "You got another date comin' over at midnight?"

"No, no. It's not that. It's just that I barely know you."

"Well, if you come back to my place," he said, cocking his head to one side, "then I might let you *get to know me.*"

"And also perhaps find three heads in your freezer," I completed his sentence.

He smirked and raised an eyebrow at me.

"I'm sorry, but I mean, you could be a cannibal...or a

Republican. And my instincts are to trust you, but it's too soon. This *is* New York," I concluded. "I don't make the rules."

"Who does make the rules, then?"

"You know what I mean."

"Why can't you make your own rules?" he asked, tucking my hand into his elbow as we continued walking.

"Because that's not how it works. You wouldn't understand. You're not a woman." I leaned my head on his shoulder as we turned a corner onto West Broadway.

"You got that right." He tilted his head upward toward the moon. "And I like it that you've got morals. It's a good thing. It's refreshing."

"Besides," I added, "think of it this way—maybe I'm the crazy one. Maybe I've saved you the trouble of waking up alone, tied to your bed, feeling used, trying to decide whether you're more insulted by the fact that you're covered in raspberry jam, or that your flat-screen TV is missing."

When he arrived to pick me up for brunch two days later, Jon brought along a bouquet of white lilies. Pinned to the cellophane was a Polaroid of the inside of his freezer, containing only two frozen lasagnas and a copy of that morning's *New York Times.* This was a man I had every reason to believe I could trust.

It was the morning after the blackout, and I nearly tumbled out of bed to grab my cell phone. I often slept closer to the window than to the bedside table, but since Jon had already slipped into the shower, the ringing jolted me out of my comfortable state of goofy-grinned, post-coital malaise. He had sprung out of bed muttering about how the lack of electricity for the alarm had caused him to sleep late. As he scrambled around the apartment in search of his clothes, I grabbed his watch off the bedside table, squinted and announced that it was eleven a.m. Since the city was still shut down, I told him, there probably wouldn't be any customers lined up yet for lunch outside Peccavi. Then I settled into the spot where he had been sleeping, and drifted back into my dreams. In the moment between waking up and opening my eyes, I could smell him on myself. The walls were red, the air was still and I was back in love—that suspension of disbelief, borne of instinct, nursed on hormones, cloaked in a warm, blinding light. I grabbed and flipped open the cell phone.

"Hello?" I chirped as if I was the lady of the house, savoring her rockin' tan the morning after she had had her way with the pool boy.

"Hello?" the caller asked.

"Um, yes, hello. Who is this?" I sat up in bed, pulling the sheet over my breasts even though I was alone, and began to finger the knots out of my hair.

"Who is *this?*"

"Well," I joked, determined not to let the caller's attitude ruin my morning, "you called my cell phone, so you probably already know who I am."

"No," she explained as if I were riding the short bus, "I called *Jon's* cell phone."

Assuming she was a salesperson or an investor in the restaurant, I chose not to accept the negative energy. I would kill her with kindness instead.

"Oops, I'm sorry. I must have thought that his was mine. His phone, I mean. We have the same cell phone. Anyway, he's in the bathroom. But I can give him a message," I cooed, scrambling naked around my apartment in search of a pen, and feeling like the Lady of My Own House again. "Who may I say was calling?"

Booboo watched my stumbling from underneath the desk chair, tentatively, as if preparing to pounce.

"*Lissette.* The mother of his *son,* that's who. Who the hell are you?"

I doubled over.

Have you ever seen a photo of someone you used to belong to, and wondered if that's really how they looked? So strong was my faith in the decency of this man that I might have been less shocked if advised by my pedicurist that she had discovered an additional toe. I was aware that the sentiment made me a cliché, but all I could take in at that moment was how much I *hated* that I had no idea.

His what?!?!?! Whose son? Wait a minute…"son"? Wait… What? Even as my throat was swelling shut, I kept trying and failing to swallow.

"Hello? Hello?" she asked again. "Who *is* this?" She sounded like someone who might punch me in the face over a pair of shoes on clearance at Macy's.

"I, um…this is Vina," I managed, eyeing the bathroom door and wondering if I should tell her anything else. Feeling dizzy, I had to take a seat.

"I…I didn't realize he had a girlfriend," I continued, squeezing my eyes shut. "Or wife? Or, um…look, I'm sorry. I don't want to know. I mean, I'm not sorry…I didn't know about you or the…the baby? Believe me. I'll give Jon your message. And I'll throw him out. But can I just ask you something? How old is your kid? I mean, I know this is awkward. But I need to know."

"Two months," she replied after a pause. And then all I could hear was a dial tone ringing inside one ear and the *glub, glub, glub* of my own blood pulsing inside the other. Booboo yawned and stretched across the window sill, having had his fill of me. I thought that blood was supposed to be rushing right now, although I wasn't sure what it was supposed to be rushing toward. Mine seemed to be draining out of my head like beer from a bottle turned upside down.

I curled up naked on the couch, the cell phone pressed to my face. With my lips apart and a hand to my throat, I listened to the torrent of water from the shower, and speculated what would come next.

I always loved waking up in Jon's bed to find our cell phone lights blinking in unison. It was as if they were dreaming the same dreams on the nightstand, of a charger for two plugged in beside the four-poster bed, in the master suite of our country home. My parents would complain about the lack of spice in the meals Jon conjured up from the ingredients in our backyard garden. An Amish hand-woven straw mat, which was far too quaint for our Manhattan apartment, would welcome visitors at our door.

I missed waking up with him wrapped around me like a teddy bear, so that the hair of his forearms danced with my breath. I missed how he would tighten his grasp and pull me closer when I tried to get out of bed. When he slept, he looked like an angel to me, and when he woke, he would tickle me relentlessly. Grabbing my ankles and kissing my feet, he would ask how I managed to balance on a pair so small. When we went to bed angry, with our backs facing one another, his foot would search out my own during the night, coming to rest once it was wrapped around my ankle.

Jon was inside another woman when he was supposed to belong to me. So why did the thought of it make *me* feel so disgusting?

By the time he emerged from the bathroom the lights were back on, and I was determined not to let him see me cry. An hour ago I had belonged to him, but now he was a trespassing dog. And I was getting ready to fire a warning shot. I could get through this if it was quick; I would have to rip him off like a Band-Aid. I would not give in or attempt to rescue him when he squirmed. I would not give him the satisfaction of reacting to the knife that was sticking out of my heart.

"I don't need anything from the store," I told him flatly, while avoiding eye contact by feigning interest in Booboo's attempts to scratch his way into my closet.

"Am I *going* to the store?" He cocked his head, perplexed.

"Well, I don't know where *else* you're gonna get diapers for your son." I was as matter-of-fact as all hell.

He stood frozen with that idiotic smile erased, as if I had slapped it right off of his chin. Stupidly, typically, maternally, I felt sorry for him. Old habits linger even after they die. I bit my lip to stifle a tear, though I wasn't sure which one of us it was for.

"Oh," I added, my voice beginning to shake, "and Lissette called while you were in the shower. Don't worry. I told her the lights are back on in midtown."

The look on his face said the wind had been knocked out of him. The pain in my gut said it hadn't been knocked hard enough. For a second I wished I were another woman, a woman who could take him back, or perhaps a woman who could ask for details that might make a difference. *Was it a one-night stand or an actual affair? How did they meet? Was he in a relationship with her now? Did he love her? Was he really, really, really sorry?*

Secretly I knew none of that mattered. I reminded myself that the baby was conceived while we were a couple, and I wondered if I was the last to know. Did everyone at the restaurant know? Had they been keeping it from me this entire time? Had Lissette known that I existed? I felt like Jon had tattooed his name on my butt while I was asleep, removed all my clothes in the middle of Times Square and invited a crowd over to point and laugh. In fact, that was exactly what he had done. Suddenly, I went into self-preservation mode, and I knew that I had to get him out of my home as soon as possible.

I opened my door and leaned against it. I felt sorry for him because I knew I could have loved him better than anyone. I hated him because of the fool he had made of me. I wanted to get tested for STDs, and to kick him until he cried. I wanted him to feel what he had done, to see my hurt and to want to comfort me, and to not be allowed to try. I wanted to see this woman, and to know if she was prettier than me. I wanted to travel back in time to the first night he was ever with her, to shake him and make him understand what he was beginning to throw away. I wanted to forget that I ever loved him. I couldn't look him in the eye before I slammed the door behind him and hurled the leftovers of our relationship into the toilet, but I did manage to force out a whisper.

"Get out."

·· 8 ··

By the time I escaped the clutches of the "Hispan–iddish Inquisition" at Starbucks (as I referred to Pam and Cristina's irritating attempts at emotional intervention), I was, of course, running late for work. While there was no expected time of arrival on a Sunday, I fully believed I'd find that Peter and Sarah had been at it since ten a.m. What I didn't believe I'd find, however, was the following e-mail from Jon.

Sunday, March 27, 10:30 a.m.
From: Jon
To: Vina
Re: Us
Baby,
   You have to know that I'm sorry. I deserve a chance to explain.

We deserve a chance to try to work it out. Please
give us that.

                                                    Jon

In an electronic folder named "Handsome" I had saved
every e-mail I had ever received from him. I had planned to
print them out one day, tuck them into a shoe box and hide
it in our closet. I had planned to pull them out to embarrass
our children during their Thanksgiving vacations from
college. I had planned to call on them for strength when Jon
spent half our savings on a luxury RV. And I had planned to
refer to them for proof, ten years and three children into our
marriage, when he began to forget that he had ever been
romantic.

But now? Now they meant about as much to me as a mug
from last summer's company picnic. Of all the goddamned
nerve. How dare he continue to refer to me as his baby? He
had a baby, and it sure as hell wasn't me. And if he had to address
me, I would have preferred that he use the title "Ma'am" while
dressed in rags and begging me for change. He would have
lost everything, you see, after some food critic became ill from
his meal, forcing him to shut down the restaurant and downgrade from his Soho loft to a cardboard box in a doorway on
Second Avenue. Naturally, I would pass by his new home each
morning on my way to a better job, and a better man with
more…stamina…and a bigger…wine collection.

I added his last e-mail to the folder and twisted my finger
through the air above my head, like a plane in some miniature
air show before thumping ceremoniously on the Delete key.

"You have permanently erased all of the messages in the folder marked: Handsome."

I leaned back in my chair, inhaled and clasped my hands behind my head. I imagined myself strutting toward Grand Central in a shiny gray DKNY skirt-suit, with my choco-late-brown Manolos barely avoiding his spleen as he lay prostrate across my path. My salon-perfect hair would flounce in the wind, synchronized to the beat of my foot-steps and the tune of "Who's That Lady?" being pumped through some invisible speakers in the sky.

I don't know if the electronic age has made relationships easier or more difficult, although I can testify to the unique sense of comfort inherent in a digital gesture of dissociation. It was especially soothing to execute it from a cocoon of prestige and privacy so many floors above the rest of New York. I comforted myself with the fact that there was at least one aspect of my life that was under control: my career.

Perhaps the only thing more annoying than a company that's an old boys' club is one that is but believes it is not. Mine considered itself *progressive*. My colleagues used phrases like "We're all fired up" and "I'll shoot that right over" and "Let's find a way to leverage that." Everyone wore suits or Brooks Brothers office casual wear, played squash on the weekends and looked like a WASP even if they weren't. At least Alan and Steve, my mentors and our team's co-Managing Directors, treated me like one of the guys.

There were only two ways to win respect at a company like that: either act as if you're thrilled to have the honor of being part of the team, or encourage the impression that you know everything about the business and are therefore an irreplaceable asset to the firm. Early in my career I chose the latter tactic. My method involved a careful blend of carrying myself as if I had it all figured out, and intimidating people from asking me questions I didn't know how to answer. Being a self-assured (translation: inherently scary) woman among the type of men who self-selected New York finance in the first place didn't hurt.

Instead of causing you to want to poke out your own eyeballs due to the mind-numbing details of what I actually do at work, I will share the stuff that's interesting. I'll talk about what went on between the people thrown together in a place like that, which is always far more compelling than how the money is made.

My neighbor, Christopher, had apparently decided that he was my new best friend. He was standing at my door not five minutes after I got home from work that Sunday evening, with a presumptuous smile and a blender full of peach margaritas. With Booboo in tow, he barreled right past me and began to make himself comfortable. Having also decided that we were too close to bother ourselves with formalities like *Hello,* he simply waved the blender in my face, kicked off his flip-flops, and bounded into my kitchen.

"If you turn me away, I'll become that pathetic queen who lives alone down the hall, drinking margaritas and talking to his cat," he said. "*Please* don't turn me into that guy. I may be getting old in gay-years, but I am still *way* too cute to be that guy."

I watched from my doorway as he sat on my couch and began pouring into my mismatched coffee mugs. After re-arranging my throw pillows and settling himself among them, he held a mug out toward me. He motioned to the easy chair, and I sat myself down.

"So tell me." He smiled, propping his heels onto my coffee table. "Why won't you give Jon another chance?"

Booboo busied himself in my closet, probably trying my best heels on for size. After leaning on my apartment buzzer for about a half an hour the night before, Jon had apparently realized that either I wasn't home, or I wasn't planning on letting him in. Since he was drunk, he decided to buzz all the other apartments until he found someone who was willing to hear him out. In the end, he found Christopher, who was all too happy to listen to his side of the story through the intercom. Which leads us to Christopher, reclining on my couch that evening, expecting me to justify myself. The annoying yet endearing thing about gay men is how they assume instant emotional intimacy with almost any single woman whom they meet. That, combined with the fact that I babysat Booboo, probably meant Christopher and I were family.

I took a gulp of my margarita and made no attempt to respond.

"Don't you at least want to *hear* his explanation?" he asked, lifting and sniffing each of the candles on my coffee table, and scoping out my copies of *The Economist, Newsweek,* and *Jane* magazine. He was probably looking for the *Vogue*

I didn't have. For a new best friend, his loyalties were all wrong.

"Not really," I answered, grabbing a package of double-chocolate Oreos from the cupboard. "I think the child speaks for himself."

"Does he? How old is he?"

"That's not what I meant." I kicked his feet off my coffee table before putting down the Oreos.

"I know."

"Look, I just don't think he should have the right to explain himself. He forfeited all of his rights when he cheated on me. And made a fool out of me by keeping it a secret. You have no idea how humiliated I am." I swallowed one cookie, and twisted off the top of another.

"Wait a minute. You mean your friends knew about this?" he stopped.

"I don't know if they knew, or if they didn't. The point is that he's got me *wondering* if any of them knew. He made me look like a naive, trusting idiot!"

"To who?"

"To myself."

After a moment of silence during which he contemplated the inside of an open-faced cookie, Christopher decided, "I don't like double-chocolate."

"What?"

"The Oreos. They're double-chocolate flavored. I don't like 'em."

"Oh, okay. Well, me, either." I sucked down the rest of my margarita and then refilled my mug.

"Then why did you buy them?"

I huffed, rubbing my forehead. "Because it was all they had. You know, you're not a very good houseguest."

He placed the offending Oreo on the coffee table and lifted Booboo to his feet, before returning his attention to me. "So you're really gonna let your ego rule your life?"

"That's not what I'm doing. I'm cutting my losses. I'm being practical. Doesn't anybody understand that? It's what it means to be an *adult*."

Christopher shrugged, and made Booboo dance before his own reflection in my mirror. I sank deeper into my chair.

"Hmm, this reminds me of an article I was reading online," I began, absentmindedly dipping an Oreo into my margarita. I took a bite, which made me gag and immediately spit a mouthful into a paper towel. Christopher was too busy checking the reflection of his soon-to-be-bald spot in my mirror to notice, so I continued. "The article said something about the similarities between financially independent women and gay men in our dating rituals. Maybe that's why you think you know how my mind works."

"*Think* I know?" He turned around.

"Anyway, the title of the article was 'You Don't Get What You Deserve…You Get What You Settle For,'" I slurred, sliding down far enough in my chair to prop my mug on top of my stomach.

"Yeah, sure. Fascinating. Whatever. Listen, you don't think I look like an accountant, do you?"

Yes…I thought, while I shook my head and insisted, "No! Not at all."

"You must kill at poker. You're really too good at telling people what they want to hear." He smiled. "And for the record, you definitely do not look like an investment banker. Anyway, I'm sorry about Jon. But I think you should seriously consider sleeping with him at least one more time. For me. He sounded sexy over the intercom."

"You probably think I should sleep with everybody."

"Well, thank you for the blanket presumption that all gay men are promiscuous," he said, trying to act offended. "Besides, not *everybody,* honey. You're far too sweet for that, even though you try to act like a hard-ass. You leave the skanking to me. For you, just the men you love."

"Lov*ed,*" I corrected him.

With one hand on his hip, he concluded, "Oh, honey, who do you think you're kidding?"

"I really don't want to talk about it anymore. It's turning my stomach almost as much as these margaritas and Oreos."

"Then let's talk about your weekend. How was that wedding? Did you meet the man of your dreams?"

"No." I tried hard to focus on Christopher's face despite my blurring eyes. "But I think I might have met the man of yours."

·· 9 ··

Hung over, lying on the floor of her apartment, spooning a severely obese cat while being spooned by its gay, balding owner, with the remains of margaritas and Oreos plastered to the roof of her mouth is no way for a respectable Desi girl to wake up.

I struggled to my feet after shaking Christopher awake. And when I noticed a new stiffness in my neck, I thought to myself, *Something has got to change.*

Coffee was a priority, but as usual on a Monday morning the line at Starbucks stretched into oblivion. Of the three grocery stores within a four-block radius of my office, only one wasn't out of my way. Unfortunately, it was also the one that was open twenty-four hours, and where personal space was a luxury. I particularly avoided that place before nine a.m. on weekdays, since the middle-aged Indian man working that shift had a habit of eyeing me like a plate of

Chicken Tikka Masala while asking suggestively if I were from Punjab. I expected better from my own kind.

I was approaching the register when I noticed a man matching my pace and coming from the opposite aisle. He stopped short and extended an arm, offering a flirtatious smile along with an *After you*. He was attractive, in a *Magnum P.I.* kind of way. Normally, I might've taken the opportunity to get my own early-morning-flirt on, but the light of recent events helped me see the situation more clearly. He was probably using me to cheat emotionally on the wife he had waiting at home. And if not, then like most men in this cesspool of a city he would probably just as soon hit on me at a bar if I were wearing something low-cut as he would steal my cab on the street if it were raining. I denied him my smile, slammed a dollar on the counter, and headed for the door. I was making a statement on behalf of women everywhere. Without saying a word.

Outside I noticed something over the tilted rim of my coffee cup, which made me stop. I caught a glimpse of a rosy-cheeked, double-chinned woman on the opposite side of Lexington Avenue, dancing gleefully for commuters' loose change. I crossed over to find "It Had To Be You" booming out of her battery-powered radio. Judging by the wisps of white hair peeking out from underneath her bandana, she must've been about sixty-five years old. A self-styled Gypsy, she shut her eyes tightly while twisting in delight, like a schoolgirl crooning into her hairbrush. A small crowd had formed around her, and I found myself staring as much at her as at the people. A man dropped a dollar into the shoe box by her feet, tipped his hat and continued down Lexington.

"Keep dancing!" she yelled.

"I'm not dancing," he replied over a shoulder.

"Then find a reason to!" She seemed to be looking directly at me.

The crowd snickered, shook their heads and dispersed.

The first thing I saw when I sat down at my desk after our Monday-morning team meeting was a bouquet of flowers. Logically, I assumed they were from Jon, so I drop-kicked them into the trash. The second thing I saw was an instant messenger chat request flashing on my screen. Taunting me. Winking at me. Blowing in my ear. "IM" is the modern equivalent of passing notes in class, except that it is sanctioned by the powers-that-be, leaves little chance for some other kid to swipe a note, and is (for most professionally unsatisfied young career-types) slightly more addictive than mediocre sex. I had no choice but to respond when I saw the following prompt from Cristina.

CristyInTheCity:	Meet me tomorrow night.
IGotYourMasala:	This is all so sudden. What will the neighbors think?
CristyInTheCity:	It's too early in the morning for jokes, *chica.* Meet up with me tomorrow.
IGotYourMasala:	Why?
CristyInTheCity:	What do you mean *Why?* Because I said so.

IGotYourMasala: What's in it for me?

CristyInTheCity: I don't know…I'll give you a surprise.

IGotYourMasala: (Smile icon.) Is it bigger than a fireman?

CristyInTheCity: What?

IGotYourMasala: My surprise. Is it bigger than a fireman?

CristyInTheCity: No.

IGotYourMasala: Is it a fireman?

CristyInTheCity: No.

IGotYourMasala: Worst surprise ever.

CristyInTheCity: *Hijole…* Where do you come up with this stuff?

IGotYourMasala: (Angel icon.)

CristyInTheCity: Meet me at the gym. 8:30. We're doing a yoga class. You need it.

IGotYourMasala: Nobody told me there would be sweating.

CristyInTheCity: It's not about sweating. It's about de-stressing.

IGotYourMasala: This better not be another one of your sneaky attempts to make me healthy. Or at least there better be a fireman waiting in my locker…

IGotYourMasala: …with a bow on his head.

IGotYourMasala: …and my name on a tag hanging from his neck.

CristyInTheCity: Grow up.

IGotYourMasala: (Shakes her fists…) NEVER!

CristyInTheCity:	Stop masking your pain with humor.
IGotYourMasala:	A priest, a swami and a Krispy Kreme donut walk into a bar.
CristyInTheCity:	Then at least wear something sexy for me.
IGotYourMasala:	(Puts her hands on her hips...) ALWAYS!
CristyInTheCity:	Tomorrow. 8:30. No excuses.
CristyInTheCity:	Logged off at 10:03 a.m.

Any time a coworker found me using IM for fun, I felt as if I'd been caught eating my crayons. Looking up from my screen I saw Peter waiting silently for my attention. *For a minute? For a week?*

"Ready to explain the Luxor deal to the intern?" he asked. Then he noticed the petals sticking out of my garbage can. "Oooh...I heard somebody got flowers delivered this morning. I didn't know it was you. Are they from Jon? Is he still trying to get back together with you?"

"I assume so," I replied flatly.

"Does this mean that he's patching things up with you and planning on whisking you off someplace to bear his many, many children?" Peter mock-punched me in the shoulder. *Which part of my office resembled a locker room?*

"Why? Are you writing a book?" I asked.

"I guess I'm nervous," he replied, grinning as he motioned for Denny and Wade to claim a couple of chairs. "Because if anything ever took you away from the firm, I don't know how I'd live without your witty retorts to my weekly team e-mails."

Peter was essentially my partner—the other associate on our team with whom I worked most closely. Born and bred in the Bronx by an African-American mother and a Puerto Rican father, he was the product of a full scholarship to Tufts. He mentored inner-city schoolchildren, ran marathons whenever possible, and seemed genuinely excited to be a part of the team. As if all of that weren't disturbing enough, he was also afflicted with the need to send uplifting weekly e-mail messages to our group.

That morning's read: *Happiness is fulfilling more than one's fair share of the teamwork.*

I had responded (and cced everyone) with *Happiness is a mutually consensual game of grab-ass.*

Honestly, you couldn't have found a straighter arrow. Peter's cheerleaderlike enthusiasm for the company made me want to shoot him with a tranquilizer dart. Or myself. Anyone, really. There was no reason to be that pumped up about something like Equity Research.

"You have nothing to worry about, Peter. I would never dream of neglecting my responsibility to the team. I'll tell you what—if and when someone does make an honest woman out of me, I promise to still fax a retort over to you from my Mommy-And-Me classes every morning. Somebody's got to temper your hideous and unnecessary optimism with some good-old-fashioned cynicism. Otherwise you'll blind us all. Really, Peter, that kind of Little-House-On-The-Prairie crap will get one of our interns mugged."

"Ouch! Someone's claws are out today! I like that, I like

that," he laughed like a mental patient at his own jokes. "Maybe you can bring some of that enthusiasm to the all-nighter we're gonna have to pull to finish up the research on that Luxor deal. You know we have to make our recommendation by tomorrow morning. Now, let's get young Wade here up to speed."

The call came from inside the house. As usual, they used separate phones. As usual, they assumed I had an hour to waste in the middle of the day. And as usual, my parents caught me wide open and defenseless at my desk when they decided to attack. Only this time, Peter, Wade and Denny were seated in my office, so they, too, got caught in the crossfire.

Peter reclined in his seat across from my desk while Denny took notes beside him. Wade sat on the edge of his seat below my framed SUCCESS poster of a rock-climber reaching the peak of a mountain. That poster, like the two of them, came with the office, along with its mahogany desk, glass door, and many walls of gray.

"This week, we've been poring over the past five years' worth of financials from a software manufacturer in Taiwan," Peter explained to Wade, through a mouthful of chicken Caesar salad. "We're finally making an investment recommendation to Alan and Steve tomorrow morning. However, we thought it might be helpful for you to understand how the research fits into the larger picture."

Denny nodded enthusiastically for the coach, biting off a quarter of his sandwich and chasing it with some French fries from my plate. *What gave him the impression that the fries were communal? Maybe a football field had sprouted beyond my office door and I had missed the e-mail?* Since he had joined us a year earlier, Denny had become like a little brother to the team; he was somebody we could mock openly and use for target practice. I was an associate and he was an analyst, which meant that I outranked him by one level, four years and miles' worth of respect within the firm. But his good humor in spite of the constant reminders of his low ranking on the corporate totem pole had forced us to develop a soft spot for him. Wade was even brighter-eyed and bushier-tailed than Denny. He had joined us as an intern the month before, and his brown-nosing knew no bounds. Wade was an intensely red-headed and predictably rosy-eyed second-year economics major at Columbia. Though he got the internship through his father's connection to a partner at our firm, Wade actually seemed intent on proving that he deserved it.

Brrrrring!

I saw my parents' home number on my caller ID, and against my better judgment I decided to answer the phone.

Dad: Hi, beti! Hold on while your mom picks up on the other line… Are you there?

Mom: Hello? Yes, I am. Hello, sweetheart.

Me: (Motioning to Peter to continue.) Hi. Listen, is it important? Because I'm kind of in the middle of something.

"So here's the deal," Peter continued, while Denny sucked on a soda and Wade took notes, "Alan and Steve have been looking at a new investment. A company called Luxor, which makes software designed to help small-business owners protect their networks from Internet-based security breaches."

Mom: No problem, no problem. This will only take a minute. So, did you hear that Meena and Avinash's daughter Parul is pregnant?

Me: Who?

Mom: You know. She was that girl from Connecticut you met during that summer when we sent you to The Hindu Vishwa Parishad camp.

Me: Mmm-hmmm.

Mom: Yes, yes, her husband is also a doctor. They met while doing their residency at Johns Hopkins. Anyway, she is due in six months!

Me: That's great for them. But I'm at work. Can we talk about this later?

"Luxor is considering acquiring a manufacturing facility in Taiwan," Peter continued. "This acquisition, if they go through with it, would double the amount of software that Luxor could produce each year."

I nodded in agreement, gulping down half of my iced tea, as if it might expedite the call.

Mom: Yes, and also Freddy and Sylvia's son, Mark? He just got engaged to a nice girl from Syracuse. She works in some nonprofit company with children or museums or something. Anyway, they met through one of those Internet-dating sites. Jewish-dating.com, I think. That way they can make sure they're only dating Jewish people, so it saves them time. Imagine!

"The announcement is expected tomorrow evening," Peter stated. "Everyone on Wall Street knows they are considering the purchase, but everyone also knows that it might be a smokescreen planted to inflate stock prices, so they can sell the company outright. If they buy the facility, the stock will go through the roof because investors will believe Luxor honestly expects the demand for their products to double this year. And higher sales would mean more profit for investors."

Me: (Elbows on the desk, picking at the skin between my eyebrows.) That's right. Great.

Mom: Sooooooo, your father and I understand that it didn't work out with Prakash, but no matter. We have another boy in mind for you. His name is Raj. He's a doctor, and he lives in Manhattan, and…

Me: (Trying to sound professional.) I'm not sure this is the right time for that.

"Exactly," Peter jumped in. "What Vina means is that the demand for software is always hard to predict. So we have to figure out if the purchase of this facility in Taiwan is a sound financial decision. If it is, then we'll have to evaluate Luxor's financials to see if they can actually afford to buy it."

Dad: When will be the right time? When you are forty? You cannot be so sentimental. We'll line up ten eligible boys for you tomorrow.

Me: (Wondering why I would be interested in anyone who was willing to queue for my affections.) I'm not ready to look at a lineup.

Mom: Don't make fun, Vina. We're just trying to help. If everything fits, you could be married by the end of next year!

"If everything squares away—" Peter sucked at his teeth with his tongue "—then Alan and Steve'll bet that Luxor will announce a decision to buy." Denny crunched his ice, and then turned to look at me.

Me: I don't need help. (Then, to Wade…) Not you, we do need your help.

Dad: Why? Are you married?

Me: No, I'm not. But thanks for the reminder. I'm really not interested in having this discussion right now.

"In that case," Peter concluded, "they will buy Luxor stock, expecting a positive announcement, and a related jump in the stock price the following morning."

Dad: If you both agree, then in that case we can have the engagement announced. Of course, we will need a year for the wedding preparations. I mean, if you're not ready now, then when will you be ready? This American system of 'dating' will only land you into trouble. With all of these so-called 'relationships,' everybody does the wrong thing because there is always somebody else coming along. Why is number fifteen any different from number twelve? Prakash is an educated, handsome boy, from a good family. All right, he is not Punjabi, which we would have preferred, but what more do you want?

Me: (Attempting to massage away my mounting neck stress.) Look, Dad. I already told you. Prakash is out of the picture because…

"These flowers are from Prakash, not Jon!" Peter announced. He had been trying to cram the remains of his lunch into the trash when he noticed the unopened card sticking out of the bin.

"Who's Prakash?" he asked.

Sarah poked her head into my office to see if we were ready to tackle the numbers.

"Oh," she said, when she caught us discussing my love life on company time, "never mind."

"Prakash?" I blurted. "You can't be serious! I don't know what this is about, but…"

How could I "out him" to my parents now? And more importantly, how could I do it without appearing unprofessional in front of my colleagues?

Mom: Flowers? From Prakash? Oh, how wonderful! Vina, you were just being insecure! Even despite your behavior on Saturday night this boy has seen how wonderful you are and he is sending you flowers? I knew he was a good boy. So we can forget about Raj. All right, I'll smooth things over with Raj's family. And you'll call Prakash to thank him. Bye-bye, darling!

Me: Wait, no! I mean…just because all the criteria are met doesn't mean that it will necessarily fall into place. There is more to it than that! Trust me.

"Vina is absolutely right," Peter concluded before heading for the door, with one hand on Denny's back and the other holding a folder that was overflowing with numbers in need of crunching. "We shouldn't simplify things too much for you guys. We'll make you think this is a science. It's not. We can play with the numbers until they look like gibberish, and spend all our nights in the office until we forget what our apartments look like, but the market is still gonna do whatever it wants. The truth is, without inside information, we're basically screwed."

Peter and Denny laughed and walked out. Wade remained because he reported directly to me. I dropped my half-empty cup into the trash. Wade was aware that he was too junior to recline, so he waited tentatively on the edge of his seat, with his back erect, his smile eager and his khaki-panted legs planted firmly on the ground. I held up a finger and made eye contact.

Mom: Okay, okay, Vina. We won't push. But we don't want to see you unmarried at thirty. Give Prakash a chance. You are not getting any younger, sweetheart.

Me: (Logging back on to my computer to begin downloading the financial statements.) I'm not?

Mom: Don't be sarcastic.

Dad: I don't understand it. When we were your age, we could not wait to begin our lives.

Me: Silly me…I thought life began at birth.

Dad: Vina, we all know you are very good with words, and very highly educated, but that does not mean that we are wrong. Wisecracks will not delay reality. You need stability in your life. And you keep avoiding the topic of getting your MBA, also. I don't know what else to say. It is only for your good that I say these things. Just give it a chance. And you have to get over this idea of chemistry. It is something which you build over years of sharing your lives. It does not happen overnight.

Me: Okay, Dad. I'm sorry. You're right.

I replaced the receiver and rubbed my throbbing earlobe, as if their perception of my life might have literally been infectious. Wade had been entertaining himself with my copy of the day's *Wall Street Journal*. Swiveling away from my screen, I addressed him.

"Find anything interesting in there?"

"Well, certainly nothing as interesting as that phone conversation," he began, and then caught himself. "I'm sorry. I mean, I tried not to listen, but…"

"No, no. It's okay. Go ahead. What do you mean?" I leaned back in my chair.

"I was taught that life began at conception."

I had to smile. "Well, Wade, I was taught that beauty was on the inside, but I've got a closet full of six-inch heels and a $200 monthly facial appointment at The Bliss Spa that say otherwise. So anyway, listen, we've got a very long night ahead of us. Don't say we didn't warn you. For us, it'll be lots of research and financial modeling. For you, it'll be lots of typing and photocopying. Grab that pen. Once I print out these financial statements, we'll be able to get started."

·· 10 ··

In our awkward years, as much as in the others, self-perception is what matters most. Aged ten, I considered myself to be approximately as swanlike as a bullfrog. The notion was cemented for me at a fateful dinner party hosted by my parents. After clearing my plate, I rose from the sofa and headed for the kitchen. Surely, I would impress my mother and her friends with the stainlessness of my white dress. They would shower me with praise and admonish the other children to learn from my example. But on my way to the kitchen I was sidetracked by an uncle who beckoned me to solve the following riddle.

"Darling Vina, tell me." He overacted for the benefit of a circle of adults. "What has a big mouth but never speaks?"

"Auntie Neela?" I replied. It was one of my earliest demonstrations of an inability to censor myself.

A roar of laughter erupted around me, like icy snowballs

being hurled from every direction. The correct answer, my uncle would explain after recovering from a belly-grabbing, knee-slapping fit of raucous laughter was "A Jar." I felt my throat getting hot, and my eyes welling up with tears. For the first time, I was aware of a tightness on the right side of my neck that felt like the tugging of an invisible noose. When I turned to run, another adult drew everyone's attention to the stain across my backside. Without noticing, I'd been sitting on a plate of food. It took all my strength not to dissolve into a puddle of Vina on the floor. I didn't know whether they were laughing because of what I had said or what I had sat in. I did know that by the time I reached the safety of my room, I noticed I had peed myself.

They say that the universe will keep reteaching a lesson until the person is ready to learn it. The first time I ignored this lesson about the importance of self-censorship, I wound up wetting my pants. This time around, I feared, the consequences could be much worse.

New rule: On less than six hours' sleep, I am no longer allowed to speak to anyone.

Maybe it was the fact that we had been crunching numbers until three a.m. Maybe it was that triple shot of espresso. Whatever the reason, first thing Tuesday morning, I marched swiftly into Alan's office, threw my shoulders back and jammed my foot directly into my mouth.

"Not that you're gonna need this, *what with your inside source in Taiwan and all,*" I blurted while raising an eyebrow suggestively, "but here's our report on Luxor's proposed acquisition of that facility. It's not a sound investment. Needless to say, therefore, I don't think that we should buy the stock."

Alan motioned toward his speakerphone.

"Hello? Alan? Are you still there?" a heavily accented voice leaped forth.

"Yes, Yokuto. I'm still here," Alan replied, taking a deep breath and glaring me out of the room. "Our line must have gotten crossed with someone else's for a moment. I'm with you now…"

I'm sorry, I mouthed. I placed the report on his desk, then backed slowly out of the room like a jewel thief who'd been spotted coming in through a window.

Just after the close of business that day, Luxor made their announcement. They had finalized an agreement to buy the Taiwanese facility. Since there wasn't enough space underneath my desk to accommodate me, I sat perfectly still, trying my best to camouflage into my chair, when Denny appeared in my office. Palms pointed outward, he leaned across my desk like a perched seal, smiling.

"They made the investment anyway," he said. "At nine a.m. today. The stock is gonna soar at the open of the market tomorrow!"

I sank deeper into my chair. Did this mean that they would fire me because I made the wrong recommendation? Or would they be in too good a mood to fire me over something as inconsequential as a recommendation which they were obviously smart enough to ignore?

"How could I have misread the financials?" I said almost to myself. "What did I miss?"

"It's not your fault, Vina. We all worked on those statements."

"Yes, Denny. But I was the one who made the final recommendation. Dammit! What did they see that I didn't?"

He looked me in the eye. "They must have seen something that convinced them it was a good call. But…"

"But what? I've been working here for a long time, Denny, and…it's just that…I could have sworn I had gone over every damn number in those reports! I rechecked all of the calculations in our Excel spreadsheets. I reran every single financial model. You know what? Maybe it's a big picture thing? Maybe I was too focused on crunching the numbers, and I missed some larger theme? Did Alan mention anything? Was there some industry-specific news, or some outside factor that I failed to consider?"

"Who cares, Vina? The firm made money! You'll probably get a little static about it. But as long as our portfolio's up, everybody wins. You are an asset to the firm. It's not like you'll be fired over this, so why don't you forget about it, and come out with the team for celebratory drinks?"

"You don't understand, Denny. It's not about getting fired. Just making money isn't…well…it isn't good enough."

I shook my head. If I wasn't any good at this job, and I wasn't any good at relationships, then what exactly was I doing with my life?

★ ★ ★

The ladies' room in a male-dominated office is usually a great place to hide. From your coworkers. Your clients. Yourself. And I would have gotten away with spending the next two hours in there if Cristina hadn't called.

"You know," I explained to Cristina, leaning closer to the mirror to investigate the unfortunate state of my pores, "I'll look far worse at fifty than my mother did. And that much more so than her mother before her. They were far too busy pulling the gum out of their children's hair and the stains out of their husbands' ties to think themselves into the wrinkles that I seem to be capable of."

"I take it that your recommendation didn't pan out," she replied. "You're always ridiculously articulate when you're depressed. *No te preocupes*. They didn't have Botox when your grandmother turned fifty. And by the time we turn fifty, they'll have much better stuff than that. Maybe even in the form of a smoothie."

I clenched the tip of my nose between a thumb and forefinger, and inched perilously closer to the glass. Two years earlier, that first hint of a laugh line had crept its nasty way down my cheek. Since then, I had developed the habit of experimenting with at least a dozen facial expressions before my mirror, to see which ones minimized, and which exaggerated, God's way of keeping me humble. Sometimes I would scrunch my brows or pout my lips to examine the skin-shifting properties of my smile. With or without parting my lips, with or without raising my eyebrows. Other times I would pull in my chin to see how taller people perceived me. Intellectually, I recognized that this probably did me more harm than good. In the act of searching for an expression that minimized my wrinkles I was almost certainly generating new ones by the minute. Even if I was only headed out for dinner with the girls, I would devolve into some pimply, nervous teenaged boy, practicing my *best James Dean* before leaving for the junior prom.

It wasn't really age that I feared, so much as the drying up of my opportunities. Kept to myself, such a personal peccadillo would have come to nothing. I would be no worse off than any man who checked for uncooperative nose hair, or winked and lusted after himself in his mirror, just to confirm that he's still got it. The problem was that Pamela had caught me a year earlier flirting with myself, as she put it, in her bathroom mirror. A sensitive friend might have laughed with me, or joined in to make me feel less absurd. Pam, however, had taken every opportunity since to remind me of the incident. And that evening's call-waiting bathroom sneak-attack was no exception.

"Hold on, Cristy... Hello?"

"Vina, you're late," Pam accused.

"That's not possible!" I mocked her, "You haven't made love to me in months!"

"Be serious, Vina. I'm talking about yoga class."

"I'm not late, Pam. I'm going to the gym with Cristy at eight. And it's only seven-thirty."

"Yes, but I know how you are."

"Oh *yeah?* How am I?"

"You're fabulous. And also, you're running late. I'll be

joining you ladies in yoga class. I…Ughh, look at me! I have no right to leave the house looking like this. *No right!* Dammit, my ponytail is lumpy. Now I'll have to redo it. Anyway listen, we need to talk. And getting a cab at this time in your area is murder. So if you don't leave now, you won't make it in time to get a good spot or a clean yoga mat."

"I know, I know. I'm just finishing up, umm, some paperwork."

"Vina, stop seducing yourself."

"What are you talking about? I'm in the office. I'm in my office. I'm not even anywhere near a mirror."

She huffed impatiently. "Then why did I just hear a flush?"

I looked up. Sarah was emerging from a cubicle behind me, heading toward the sink.

"Okay, fine," I relented, "you win. I'm in the ladies' room. I'm a geek who can't stop blowing herself kisses in the mirror. And I'll see you at the gym. At eight. But listen…I've had a long day, and I really don't want to talk about Jon tonight."

"Vina," she replied, "I said that we had to talk. Not that we had to talk about Jon. Honestly, not everything is about you."

When I switched back to Cristina, she had already hung up. I dropped my cell phone into my suit pocket and managed an unenthused smile at Sarah's reflection in the mirror. She pivoted to face me, and plunged her dripping fists into a scrap of paper towel. Then she tossed it over a shoulder into the wastebasket as she was heading for the door.

"It's nice to see that you take your time on the job so seriously," she stated smugly.

And before I could reply, she was gone.

·· 11 ··

"So last night—" Pam looked over at me while we started to roll up our mats "—my therapist broke up with me."

According to Cristina, weekday evenings were peak cruising time at The Health & Fitness Club, New York. But after yoga class I was way too concerned about the state of my own muscles to notice anyone else's. I thought I had pulled something. Cristy thought the yoga teacher had been flirting when he deepened the arch of her back during *downward facing dog*. Pam was thinking about other things entirely.

"I didn't know you were sleeping with him," Cristina replied, tossing her mat onto the pile. "Is *Good Old William* having trouble getting the job done?"

"What? No! Of course not! And of course I'm not sleeping with my therapist," Pamela huffed. "All right, fine, then… He… I guess he fired me as his client."

"Pam, your therapist can't fire you. He can only refuse

to keep counseling you." Cristina smoothed her hair into a ponytail before taking a swig from her water bottle. "And only if he's got a damn good reason. Like if you refused to take your meds. Or if you were too psychotic for outpatient treatment. Or if you kept trying to mount him during therapy sessions."

"Are you crazy?" Pam fired back as we headed for the door. "Or are you just filling your water bottle with Stoli again?"

Cristy rolled her eyes and took another sip.

"Ladies, can we please move past the bickering, and on to more important things? Like plans for Girls' Night?" I pleaded, limping behind them and lowering myself gently onto a bench just outside the door.

I rubbed my throbbing calf, and wondered if my third-grade teacher had finally been proven right. Maybe I had hurt myself during yoga because I was "too competitive for my own good." Or maybe it was that gym-rat in the weight room who had obviously been eyeing my poses through the glass walls. He was cute enough, but such a direct stare could make a statue come off like a stalker. Cristy wasn't lying, I thought. With all those pheromones flying around the gym at that hour, ricocheting off StairMasters and bouncing off Botox and boob-jobs, it was a wonder somebody hadn't lost an eye.

"I'm serious." Pam dropped her gym bag by my feet and sank onto the bench beside me. "He said that I was living in denial of the so-called 'fact' that William is never going to propose."

"Pam," I said, after pausing to share a pained glance with

Cristina, "Have you thought about looking for somebody new?"

"You're right. I'm sorry." She shook her head. "I'm just… I know it makes me terribly *unliberated,* but sometimes I worry that I'm wasting my time. I've invested a lot of years in William. What if he *never* proposes?"

She broke into tears, and to my surprise, Cristina was the first to jump in. She crouched before us, took Pam's hands in her own and looked her right in the eye.

"First of all, I'm sure William is going to propose. Eventually. When he's ready. And you don't want to marry anyone who's being forced into it, anyway, right?"

Pam dabbed at an eye before nodding, like a puppet on a string.

"Or, if you're not so confident," Cristina continued with a twinkle in her eye, "you could always go off the pill."

Pamela stopped. I flicked my gaze at the ceiling and adjusted the strap of my sports bra.

"I was *kidding*, of course," Cristy added.

Reminding Pam that I saw relationships as more than just an investment toward marriage would have come off like an attack. It would be like telling Cristina that being in perfect shape was not my idea of a top priority. So I bit into a stick of gum in lieu of my tongue, and offered another suggestion instead.

"Okay, Pam. I agree with what she said. I mean, except for the part about the pill. And also, by the way, when I suggested that you find somebody new, I was talking about finding a new *therapist*. Not a new *William*."

Pamela managed to smile and pull herself together while Cristina rose to her feet.

"Maybe we're all just a little too high-strung lately," Cristina decided. "Which brings us to the recreational portion of our program. Let's talk about Friday. The good news is that Reena's coming into town! I made reservations at Son Cubano, in the meatpacking district. And you know she's really been on a dating rampage since her divorce. So I'm sure it'll be a blast."

"Ladies, I'm actually in pain here," I explained while they readied themselves for the showers. "I'm not sure if I can make it on Friday. I might have pulled a muscle."

"No excuses, Vina," Pam ordered. "You didn't pull anything. And you're not getting out of this."

"How would you know whether or not I pulled anything?" I pouted.

"If I have to go, you have to go," she marched forward, telling me. "And don't worry about it. If you didn't already pull something in that yoga class, I'm sure you'll pull something trying to keep up with Reena on Friday night."

I was too preoccupied to fight. In exchange for my promise not to bail on Girls' Night, Pam and Cristina agreed to leave me alone with my pain. Girlfriends, like used car salesmen, take every opportunity to exploit your weaknesses in their favor.

And men, like hyenas, take every opportunity to feed on incapacitated prey. I was hunched over, rubbing my calves and begging the fitness gods to restore my muscle in exchange for six months of penance at the altar of the tread-mill. Naturally, that was when the last thing I needed in my life came looking for me.

"Do you think maybe you overdid it?" a husky voice spoke from above.

"What?" I looked up. "No. I'm fine. I've got it under control."

I resisted the urge to laugh at the cliché who stood before me. It was the peeping-gym-rat. With his legs planted at shoulder width and his arms crossed before him, he pulled his chin to one side and smiled. He must have dipped his teeth in White-Out. But I reminded myself I was in no mood for another brawny misadventure. My *drive-by-dating* days were over.

"You don't look like you've got it under control." He knelt before me, reaching out toward my leg. I jerked away.

"I don't remember asking for your opinion."

"And I'm not offering it. What I'm offering is my advice." He paused. "My professional advice, as a personal trainer. Trust me. I know a lot about sports medicine. You'll need to ice it, and you'll need to apply pressure, like this…"

"Oh. Well, thanks," I gave in, offering him my damaged limb.

"It's my pleasure." He rose to his feet, then took a seat beside me. "I'm Nick. I didn't catch your name."

He had to be kidding me with this.

"That's because I didn't pitch it." I slipped into a sweater, and zipped it up to my chin.

"You're quite the spitfire, aren't you?" His eyes twinkled. "And with a sharp tongue. I like that."

"How nice for you," I began, and then thought better of it.

There was no need to take my issues out on him, even if I knew he was wasting his breath and his energy coming on to me.

"I'm sorry," I continued. "My name is Vina. And I have just had a really rough day."

"Happens to the best of us." He waved it away. "But I'm surprised that the yoga didn't help. I thought you were supposed to be really good at that stuff. You know, really flexible?"

There was an audible screech of the needle on the record in my brain. It wasn't as if I had never heard a similar comment before, but I had no patience for it that day. I jumped to my feet and swung around to face him with narrowed eyes.

"You mean because I'm Indian? And we all snake charm and belly dance and twist ourselves into pretzels during sex? You've been watching too much porn, buddy. And you know what else?"

"Watch out, Nick. You don't want to lose any fingers," Prakash said, appearing from nowhere. "This one's hard to please."

"You have got to stop sneaking up on me like that, Prakash!" I snapped. "It's getting tedious."

"I apologize, Vina." Nick stood up. "It was a stupid thing to say. I didn't mean any disrespect by it."

I was momentarily distracted by the flecks of gold in his deep green eyes, but managed to shake it off.

"All right. Fine. So, I guess you two know each other?"

"You could say that," Prakash replied.

"Okay. Whatever. Apology accepted." I nodded at Nick, who raised his palms to show that he was unarmed. Then he smiled sheepishly before backing up and walking away.

I turned my attention toward Prakash. "But what's the deal with the flowers?"

"Am I going to have to apologize for sending you flowers, too?" he asked. "See? This is why I date men. Or at least it's one of the perks. Women make no sense. And their breasts are always getting in the way."

I crossed my arms and refused to blink. The grin slid off his face like caramel and oozed onto the floor between us.

"Look, I was sorry that I sprang things on you the way that I did, at the wedding. I thought about it. I see now that I should've told you up front, when we met over the martini. But it's not easy to trust people at face value these days."

He had a point. I hoisted my bag onto my shoulder and exhaled loudly.

"Forget about it," I said. "I'm over it. Anyway, I've got much more important things to worry about. It's fine. It's over."

"So you'll do it then?" He beamed.

I paused. "Do what?"

"You…er…didn't read the card, did you?" he asked, puzzled.

I arched my eyebrows and shook my head.

A constipated expression crept across his face. "Vina, I know that I have no right to ask, but I need a favor. I need you to play along. I need you to let our parents believe that we've gone on a few dates. It'll buy me some time before my next family setup."

"Yeah. Sure. No problem," I scoffed, shaking my head as I turned to walk away. "I can do that. Hey, while we're at it, why don't we just tie the knot? And better yet, I can spit out a coupla babies! That should keep you in the clear for about eighteen years! Just to make it look more believable, right? You're *insane.*"

He yelled at my back. "Vina, please think about it!"

"No, you weirdo!" I barked. "You're thirty years old! Grow up and be honest with your parents!"

"Coming out of the closet to your parents is not that easy, Vina. Don't you have any gay friends? Haven't you ever had to hide anything from your family in order to protect them?"

Every boyfriend I had ever had flashed before my eyes. And so did Christopher.

"Fine. I'll do it. But it better not require any actual effort on my part. I'll play along for a few fake dates. We'll say we went out for lunch at Cipriani, and then again for dinner and dancing. Let's say it was at that new Cuban place, Son Cubano, to keep our stories straight. After that, we can tell them we just didn't feel any real connection. And you'll owe me one."

·· 12 ··

Yet another biological design flaw. I thought this of my calf the next morning while forcing myself into the swamp-water-green Cole Haan flats that I normally reserved for audits and jury duty. Unfortunately, they were the only shoes I could comfortably walk in considering my state. Since my calf had joined my ego in a serious state of disrepair, I was in no hurry to get to the office. Reena called as I was waiting in line to pay for my coffee at the "Creepy-mart." She began by apologizing for having been out of touch.

"You know how busy I get in the hospital. Crazy hours and everything," she explained. I bit my tongue about my typical seventy-hour workweek. "And listen, I'm sorry for not getting in touch about Jon, but you know I'm not too good with that stuff."

"It's okay. I understand." I singed my tongue with my first sip of coffee.

"And anyway, you know my motto. There's no use crying over spilt husbands, or Italians or cowboys, as the case may be."

"So you heard about Cristy's rodeo?" I laughed.

"There's my girl. I miss that laugh, you know." She paused, and then her voice rose. "Wait a minute, could that be a girlish giggle? Could this mean there's someone new in your life?"

"No. I mean, not really." I stepped closer to the register, blowing on my coffee.

"Meaning?"

"Meaning that there's a guy, named Prakash, who my parents tried to set me up with. But the problem with him is that…"

"What?" She inhaled sarcastically. "You mean there's a problem with the perfect guy that your parents picked out of the Indian catalog for you? I cannot believe it! I simply *will not* believe it!"

Reena was not a big believer in the power of parental instinct. A mutual Indian friend of ours, she had recently reentered the dating world after finding the courage to divorce the thoughtful but uninteresting man to whom her parents had arranged her marriage. *She had never grown into loving him like her parents had promised she would,* she explained to us. Then she signed the divorce papers and moved up to Boston in pursuit of a fresh start and a lucrative medical fellowship. It was around that time that she found out about the recent marriage of her college sweetheart whom her parents forbade her from marrying because he was of a different caste. Reena was as determined never to look back as she was dead set against settling for anything less than true love. While she was waiting, however, she had turned into a total Cougar, routinely amusing herself with the more-than-occasional younger boy toy. Since her divorce she had refused to discuss it. Instead she laughed at herself whenever possible, referred to her breasts as "man-catchers" and wore shiny, dangling earrings almost all of the time.

"What can I say?" I asked for her benefit. "I'm difficult." She snorted.

"Enough with the armchair psychoanalysis. More importantly, what does your Nani think about Bachelor #1?"

"I'm not sure she really thinks much of anything about men, especially the ones in my life."

"Then she's a smart lady," she said.

"Do you think we'll get smarter as we age?" I asked, while the woman before me poured the contents of her purse out onto the counter, and scoured for change.

"God, I hope not. Can you imagine how much less fun we would have if we had any idea what the hell we were doing? Oops, I gotta go. I'm being paged. I'll see you on Friday."

Reena was thirty-one going on nineteen, and I loved that about her.

"Dollar ten."

I blinked. The woman standing before me had disappeared. I had been fixated on something outside the window, and was holding up the line.

"Dollar ten," the cashier repeated, drumming his fingers on the counter.

"Oh. Sure. Of course. I'm sorry." I fumbled with my wallet, while the people behind me cleared their throats for my benefit.

"*Vy* are you always *stering* at her?" the cashier asked, as I handed over two dollar bills.

"Excuse me?"

"That *crezy vooman,*" he said, motioning to the dancing Gypsy across the street, and then stirring the air near his ear with a finger. "She's insane...*pagal*...you know *'pagal'?*"

"Yes. Well, I guess I don't know if she's crazy or what. But I think I'm staring because she always looks so happy."

I tucked my change into my wallet and then looked up and smiled at him. He lowered his chain, raised his eyebrow, scanned my body and leered. "You from Punjab?"

Later that morning, Peter slumped into the chair across from my desk. I rejected the eleventh instant message request from Jon since nine a.m. and gave Peter my full attention. That was when I noticed something that alarmed me.

"Peter, where's your BlackBerry?" I lowered my voice, as if appeasing a child with a knife. "And why have you loosened your tie?"

"You haven't heard, have you?" He ran his fingers across his forehead and then back through his hair.

"Heard what?"

"About the annual bonuses. We're all getting screwed."

"What? But the fund is up! I mean *my bonus* is debat-able—in light of my recent ineptitude, and how obvious it probably is that I don't know what I'm doing, or even want to do, anymore—but not *yours*. No way."

"Way." He leaned forward to correct me. "And for the record, even though I know you've been unfulfilled with the industry, I don't think it has affected your performance. I definitely don't think that Alan and Steve think so, either. But then again, those bastards can do whatever they want. In an economy like this, where else are we gonna go? They know we can't quit our jobs over lower-than-expected bonuses."

"Wait a minute. How bad is it? What have you heard? Will everyone be disappointed?"

"I heard it from the security guard downstairs. He overheard some of the company's board members talking this morning. This is torture." He rubbed at his eyes with the heels of his hands. "But think about it, Vina. They were scheduled to discuss the performance reviews and annual bonuses with us last week. Why would they keep us all waiting if it was good news? I'm really pissed off. The rumor is that they were discussing my bonus, and it didn't sound good. And since your bonus is usually about the same as mine, my advice would be to forget about the thirty grand we were hoping for. We'll probably be looking at less than half that much…if we're lucky."

"Well, thanks for the warning. But I wasn't feeling too optimistic to begin with. It's been a pretty disappointing couple of weeks."

Not five minutes later, Alan summoned me into his office. Any effort to remain calm leaped right out the window when he closed his office door behind me for the first time in the five years that I had worked for him. And then I spotted Steve sitting in the corner. Why were they double-teaming me? Normally Alan discussed my annual performance review alone. Would I be fired for my incompetence on the Luxor deal? *Had Alan's office always been this cramped?* If Steve made eye contact with me, I decided, it would be a good sign, like the jury returning to the courtroom after finding me guilty of a lesser charge. I took a deep breath and tried to ignore the fact that the room was slowly shrinking.

"Vina," Alan began, taking a seat behind his desk, "Steven and I have got some bad news. We called you in here because we want to make sure that the matter is handled…er…in the most tactful manner possible."

I nodded without blinking. Steve had yet to look directly at me.

"We're hoping that we can count on your discretion," he continued.

Oh my god oh my god oh my god. They'll make me clean out my office overnight. By morning they'll be denying that they ever knew me, and I'll be banging a tambourine alongside that crazy Gypsy for spare change outside Grand Central. Or I'll be forced into the Wall Street Protection program people whisper about! They'll give me a new identity, an itchy wig and a job waiting tables at a diner in New Mexico. Oh, dear god, I'll have to start dating a trucker with a pot belly and only one tooth!

"We take sexual harassment very seriously at this firm," Steve went on, "and we take great pains to hire people who demonstrate integrity, whose core values align with those of the firm. Unfortunately, a serious situation regarding a member of our team has come to light."

Krishna, help me now! I thought Alan understood that what happened during the blackout was an accident! I knew I should have insisted on explaining myself. But I couldn't believe that I was actually being fired because I accidentally groped my boss! How was I going to explain this to my parents?

How did that damn claustrophobes' mantra go again? *Check your nerves? Close the exits? Count your eyes? Dammit, how could my collar be so tight when I don't even wear a tie?*

"Wade has been accused of sexual harassment by a secretary," Alan elaborated.

My jaw dropped open.

"Hhhunnhhh?" I blurted, partially because I had been holding my breath for the past two minutes.

"I'm sure you can understand that we are going to have to let him go," Alan started, with his arms crossed and his brow furrowed beneath a well-wrinkled forehead, "and for the purposes of team morale, this must not seem as if it comes as any surprise to you. Since he is your direct report, the three of us must maintain a united front."

"I'll have to concur with Alan, Vina. It could be very bad for the firm if we allow the situation with Wade to get out of hand," Steve added. "Very bad."

I was perplexed, having generally come to see Wade as a little brother. I couldn't imagine him doing anything like that. Had he asked her out one too many times? Had he sent a lewd e-mail? It just didn't seem like Wade. But then again what did I know? Acquiring a Taiwanese manufacturing facility with poor financials didn't seem like something that Luxor would do. And having sex with a woman who wasn't me didn't seem like something that my *boyfriend* would do, either.

"Gentlemen." I cleared my throat, after the temperature under my collar fell to a more manageable level. "With all due respect, why is this the first time I'm hearing about this? And who made the accusation? And is there any proof? I mean, I'm not disputing it. But I've got to say that I'm overseeing Wade's work here every day, and he just seems like a good kid to me. I'm stunned."

"We anticipated that you would be," Steve interjected. "And I can appreciate that you feel the need to go to bat for your subordinate, but management has made its decision. And our judgment supersedes yours. Obviously. We don't want this to become a big deal within the company. Business as usual. And we cannot tell you which secretary it was. It all has to be kept confidential, as does this conversation. You will not discuss this with any of your colleagues. Getting him out of the workplace immediately is the only way that we can ensure we will not be sued."

"But, Steve, I…"

"Vina, we have no choice!" Alan insisted, "The firm cannot afford a lawsuit. With all the bad press surrounding Wall Street lately, we cannot take that chance. Some of our biggest clients have parked more money with us recently *because* we are one of the *only* firms left with a clean reputation."

"All right." I gave in. "If you're sure that he did this, then what can I say? I'm disappointed, but I'll let him go today."

"You will tell him that it's a budget issue, but that we will cut him a check for an additional two weeks' worth of pay. As a form of severance. You cannot mention the charges against him as the reason because he might challenge them. And we simply cannot afford that kind of publicity."

I was far too embarrassed about the Luxor debacle to even ask what they noticed in those financial statements that I missed. The bottom line was that their combined forty years on Wall Street trumped my less than ten years any day. So, how could I possibly question them about Wade? The universe was making it clear to me that they knew more about everything than I did. Or ever would.

Back in my office I had taken to banging my head on my desk as a way of testing if perhaps it were hollow. How could I have missed the fact that one of my subordinates was capable of behavior like this? Why did I feel as if I was missing everything lately? Did the other women in the office think I would condone this sort of behavior? How could Wade have thought he would get away with it? Maybe he thought his father's connections entitled him to more than just a foot in the proverbial door? Ultimately, I didn't have much time to process it all, since there was a knock at my door.

"Come in, Wade." I rose and looked out the window.

"Alan said you wanted to see me?"

"Yes. Please have a seat. And um…close the door behind you." I swallowed and began pacing my office. "Look, Wade, there's no easy way to say this. I'm very disappointed about it, but we're going to have to let you go. Budget issues have come up, and…"

"Are you *serious?*" he cut me off, for the first time since I had known him. "You're really doing this? I mean, I can't say I didn't know this was a possibility, but do you really think they'll get away with this?"

I didn't like this color on him. It was way too aggressive and self-righteous for an intern, especially a sexually-harassing-intern. Perhaps Alan and Steve had been right. I couldn't believe that Wade expected to stay at the company after what he had done. I took a seat so that we were eye-level, and fixed my sights on him.

"Wade, it's better for everyone at the firm for you to leave. It would be your word against theirs. Think about it. And look, they're offering you a little something extra in your final paycheck…like a severance package. I don't know all the details, but I know as much as I think I need to know. You should cut your losses and leave quietly. That's the best advice that I can give you."

"You really do have a way with words, Vina," he spat.

"This is not about me," I fired back.

Wade took one final, deflated look at me. As if *I* was the one who had let *him* down.

"So you wouldn't believe me even if I tried to explain? Don't you want to hear my side of this?"

"No, Wade. I'm sorry. I'll have to side with my bosses on this one."

"This is bullshit," he decided, before slamming the door on his way out of the room.

·· 13 ··

"Before you say anything, I'm borrowing your blue purse. And you only have an hour to get ready for Girls' Night."

Cristina's butt, wreathed in the light from my fridge, was the first thing I saw when I walked into my apartment.

"I don't understand how you can live on this stuff," she continued before I could respond, speaking to me over her shoulder. "Not a piece of fruit or a drop of milk or juice anywhere."

She held my refrigerator door open, displaying the lamentable contents: Three Hostess pink snowballs, a six-pack of Pepsi, two Chinese food delivery cartons and a half-empty bottle of Absolut.

"Who let you in here?" I asked, dropping my jacket onto a chair and heading for the bathroom.

"You gave me the key. Remember?"

"Vaguely." I examined my bloodshot eyes in the mirror. "I don't know. Long week."

"What's with this?" She waved the Absolut bottle at me.

"Pam probably drank it." I shrugged.

"And since when does she store her alcohol in your fridge?"

"She's practicing. For when we have neighboring summer houses in the Hamptons. And she comes over to my place to drink away her sorrows because William works too much."

"And where will I be?"

"You'll be at the gym," I snapped.

"Ouch!" she said.

Cristina and I weighed exactly the same amount, but she always managed to look better in my own clothes than I did. It might have had something to do with her six extra inches of legs. We were both olive-skinned, dark-haired, and just shy of the age when we expected our metabolisms to begin to go to hell. But that was where the similarities ended. Five years earlier, when we became investment banking trainees, we both swore we would quit the business as soon as we figured out what else we were qualified to do. Or once our loyalty started to cost more than the annual bonuses our firms kept baiting us with. That day had yet to come.

To compensate, she had developed an unhealthy attachment to the gym, while I had developed an unhealthy resentment of myself. Lately that resentment had taken the form of an ulcer, which I had decided to call "Fred." Its namesake was a sports agent whom I dated briefly when I was new to the city. He made inappropriate jokes and expected me to "high-five" him afterward. He was late for every date we made, and was under the impression that Speedos were acceptable. At times it seemed like he deliberately waited until his mouth was full before speaking, just to force me to watch. He had one ridiculously long nose hair which he never managed to notice, while I, on the other hand, could often see little else. In the story of my life, he was like a dried-out zit; although you resent it, you derive a certain comfort from knowing that it will be there when you need something to pick at absentmindedly.

"Sorry," I said, turning back to the mirror and trying to ignore the burning in my stomach. "I had to fire my intern today. Things are frustrating at work. Honestly, I don't even know what I'm doing sometimes. I'm not sure I'm up for going out tonight. I feel like I'm just not in control anymore."

"Who told you that you ever were?" she asked, and then twisted on her heel when she heard a knock at the door. "Listen. Just forget about it. Whatever it is, you need to put it out of your mind. Girls' Night will cheer you up. It's gonna be like old times. By the end of the night, you'll forget Jon's name, and I'll forget my own! Voila! We're meeting Pam and Reena at the restaurant in an hour, and then your ass is ours all night. Unless you find someone hunkier to offer it to, that is. Well, if you can manage to let go of your control issues for long enough to let someone seduce you."

Massaging the tension in my neck, I sulked toward the closet.

"Va va va voom!" Christopher gasped at the sight of Cristina.

"Cristy, Christopher…Christopher, Cristy," I introduced in a monotone over my shoulder.

Almost instantly the two of them were lost in each other. I left them to share eyelash-curling techniques, and turned on the shower. I was still undressing when the phone rang outside. I should've locked the bathroom door. I should've hid inside the medicine cabinet. I should've done a lot of things differently that night.

"Guess what your Nani and I are making for dinner tomorrow night?" my mother bubbled through the phone, after Cristina came into the bathroom without knocking to hand it to me. "*Moong Khee Dhal* and *Masala Bhindi!* Your favorites!"

"Great, Mom. Listen, I've got friends over. Can I call you in the morning?" I pinched the skin at the top of my nose. I was in no condition to play the dutiful daughter.

"Why? Did you want us to make something else? If you did, then you have to tell me now, so that I can tell your father to stop at Pathmark on his way home to get whatever ingredients I'll be needing."

"No, Mom. I'm really excited about the *Dhal*. And the *Bhindi*. Really."

It was an admittedly weak attempt at enthusiasm.

"Did you forget about dinner tomorrow night?" her voice narrowed, "you said you would spend the evening with us."

"Of course not, Mom. Of course not. I'm looking forward to it," I gushed to overcompensate for the fact that it had completely slipped my mind.

"Sweetheart," she coaxed, "you seem distracted. I don't want to do anything to make you fly off the handle. I know how sensitive you can be. I also know how your father's anger always gives you stress. And you know how you get those dark circles below your eyes when you worry too much. Have you been moisturizing? Have you been eating right? You are not your normal self these days. You know that you can talk to us about anything, right?"

A lifetime of my parents' injured expressions at even the mention of any male who wasn't Indian had taught me otherwise.

"Sure, Mom." I prayed for her call-waiting to beep.

"Then what is the problem? Is it Prakash? Are you feeling insecure about his interest?"

"No, Mom. I'm not." I clenched my teeth. "I know exactly where his interest lies."

I eyed the half-naked, bleary-eyed, limp-haired woman in the mirror.

"Because you know sometimes a girl can make an impression by being quiet. *You don't always have to be so funny, Vina.* Sometimes it is a good idea to let a man feel like a man. Let him lead the conversation. Also, try to be a little bit more…soft. And I wasn't planning to tell you this, but I also got a call from his mother and…"

Oh no no no no no! My mother was trying to teach me about seduction! I had to put a stop to it before I literally crawled out of my own skin.

"Mom, it's not him. Trust me. Wait, did you just say you talked to Prakash's mom?"

"Yes, Vina, but it was nothing really. Just a small chat. Go on."

I took a chance. "I'm frustrated, Mom. With everything. And work isn't going so well. I'm just generally unsatisfied."

"Vina—" her voice lowered "—you have a wonderful job, good friends and a nice boy in your life. What more could you want?"

"I don't know. I'm just…I'm not really happy these days." I took a deep breath. "You know, there's this homeless woman who dances outside of Grand Central station. I pass her on my way to work every morning. And I…she just looks so peaceful, and I started thinking that…"

"So now you cannot bear the thought of taking advice from your mother, but you can take advice from this *pagal* homeless woman?"

"No! Mom, I…I've never even spoken to her. I've just been *thinking* about her."

"Well, stop thinking then. And start doing. These ideas are a phase. Don't you think I also used to have these cloudy thoughts while I was in my medical residency? Everybody has these feelings sometimes. But those who are successful waste no time on these indulgent thoughts. Try thinking about more important things. Like marriage. And getting your MBA. And don't tell Prakash about any of these ideas, either."

Cristina banged on the bathroom door to announce that she had invited Christopher along, that they were stepping into his apartment to pick out his ensemble and that I had twenty minutes left.

"Okay, Mom." I dropped my towel. "I'm sorry. You're right."

"Fine. Good. We will see you tomorrow night."

"So he looks me right in the eye." Reena squinted across the dinner table an hour later. "He's really intense, like he's supposed to be James Bond or something. And he says, 'Reena, I have wanted to be inside you since the moment we met.'"

As usual, Pam, Cristina and I hung on her every word. As usual, we were afraid even to blink or swallow lest we miss a beat. We leaned closer to hear over the din of clinking glasses, drunken laughter and live music. Son Cubano was the most popular Latin restaurant "slash" bar "slash" club in the meatpacking district.

"And I'm thinking, 'I know, you geek. Why else do you think I take my man-catchers with me wherever I go? And why are you talking so much?' He's all 'blah blah blah,' and it's making me want to gag." She mimed an unstoppable talking hand puppet. "I mean, shut up and let's get down to business. If I wanted conversation, I wouldn't be dating a model, especially a twenty-one-year-old model. Why do men always wind up ruining a perfectly good seduction scene by saying something stupid?"

"Gay men don't," Christopher offered, a Cheshire-cat grin on his face. "We don't usually waste too much time talking."

"I think that *straight* men are programmed to think they have to keep trying to impress us," Cristina suggested. "They think we all want a relationship out of them, so we won't put out until we feel like they really care."

"Relationship, my *ass*. I wouldn't be in a relationship with him for all the Botox in Bombay," Reena confided, to the applause of everyone at the summit. "He was sexy, and it had been a while, so I might have played with him for a few weeks. But it was really because I was guessing from the proportions of the rest of his body that he might be able to…shall we say…make an impact?"

Reena was magnificent. Sometimes I wished I were able to be as take-charge as she was…*outside* of the operating room.

"And was he?" I had to ask.

"Not so much. Average, really. But what's worse is that he didn't know what he was doing. And when I asked if I could tie him up, he said, 'No.' That it was *too kinky* for him. The big baby. The only reason I even asked was because he was moving too fast, and wouldn't really listen to me when I said, 'Slow down!' So I figured if I could control it, everybody would win, and I could go the hell to sleep and actually take a nap before catching my flight."

"How much Botox *is there* in Bombay?" Christopher asked, slurping at the dregs of his mojito.

"Not enough," Reena answered.

"Okay. Of course what he *does with it* is important. But there is such a thing as *too big,* right?" Cristina posed.

"How would I know?" Pamela slurred, having gulped down her second mojito in a half hour and assuming the question was aimed at her.

Whenever Reena was around, Pam became more sensitive about the fact that William was only the second man she had ever slept with. But she traded her sourpuss pout for a beaming smile when William's name popped up on her caller ID. She must've been drunk by that point, because contrary to her usual attention to etiquette, she flipped open her cell phone at the table.

"Hi, honeeeeeeeeey!"

"Well, I haven't found anyone too big yet." Reena grinned like a sailor on shore leave, downing her Apple-tini and signaling the waiter to bring over another round. "But then again, women do come in different sizes, just like men. Maybe *I'm* well-endowed, too."

"I don't know," Cristina reasoned. "I had a friend who said she had a friend who slept with a guy who was way too big for her. She went along with it anyway. And the next day she was out at a restaurant, and she had gotten her period. And when she sneezed, she sneezed out her tampon!"

My eyes widened into saucers and my hands flew from my mojito to my mouth, which was now stretched open in a mixture of horror and humor overload.

"That's gross!" Reena yelled.

"Not in comparison to the disgusting things that men say and do!" Christopher wasn't really defending Cristina, as much as he was defending a woman's right to say something disgusting. "For example, ladies, the other day I was walking down Lexington when I saw this man at a stoplight, watching porn on his in-car television! In the middle of the afternoon!"

"No way," Cristina challenged.

"Seriously!" He raised an eyebrow. "Do you think I could make up something like that? I mean, he had his windows opened completely, so that anyone walking by could see the screen! I know this because I almost walked into a garbage can. Once I saw it, even though it was hetero-porn, I couldn't look away. I mean, come on! Could you? In the middle of the day? Ignore porn-without-warning!"

"Yes, I absolutely could." Reena turned serious. "I think that porn is disgusting. And I don't want any part of it, watching or otherwise."

"*You* have a problem with porn?" Cristy nearly choked on a mint leaf. "This, coming from a woman who refers to her breasts as *man-catchers?*"

"Well, have you *seen* my breasts?" Reena raised a prideful eyebrow.

"Everybody's seen your breasts," Pam said.

"Um, yeah. Everybody to whom I have chosen to show them," Reena defended herself, to everyone's surprise. "You know, lately I get the impression that you ladies think I'm too aggressive, but I like the way that I am. And because I go after what I want in the operating room as well as the bedroom doesn't mean that I don't have standards. I take control of my life and responsibility for my happiness. I realize now that I'm the only person I have to answer to. And I'm having fun. I may never find the love of my life, yet at least I will be able to say that I didn't sit around on my couch waiting for the party to come and find me. Men always act like dogs, and we are expected to work as hard, make as much money, and then sit around and cry that they use us for sex? Uh-uh. That's not gonna work for me."

"Well, I guess you're right," Pam conceded, while the rest of us sat silent. "I mean, personally, I need some chivalry from a man, but generally they are a lot like dogs."

"They *are* furry," Cristina offered helpfully, cracking a small smile.

"And we do drool at the sight of fresh meat." Christopher shrugged. "Gay *or* straight."

"And they will try to mount everything in sight until someone explains to them why it is not acceptable," Pam chimed in.

"And their loyalty is transferable," Cristina added.

"And they're always sniffing things they shouldn't be sniffing. Like their socks. Why do they *do* that?" Pamela asked, her pupils dilating.

"And they wouldn't bathe unless we made it clear that it was expected." Reena brightened.

"And they will follow home anything that wags its tail at them," Christopher said.

"And they almost always find a way to embarrass us at our dinner parties!" Pam laughed.

"Excuse me. That's only the heteros," Christopher corrected.

"And they need constant positive reinforcement!" Reena continued.

"And if you rub that particular spot behind their ear, they instantly forget their own name and start having unseemly, involuntary physical reactions," Pam joked.

"And they always want to hump you in public!" Cristina suggested, to collective applause.

"What's with you tonight?" Pam leaned over and whispered sloppily to me. "You're very quiet."

"I don't know. I'm tired, I guess."

"That's crap, Vina." Pam's eyelids drooped slightly. "And you know it. You haven't even touched your food. It's Jon, isn't it?"

"No, it's not. I…"

"Vina, this isn't you. Don't become one of those pathetic women who lets a bad situation with a man suck the life right out of her. Trust me." Pam looked me straight in the eye, sober for a tenth of a moment. "I might not know a lot about picking up guys in bars, but I do know something about what a difficult relationship can do to your life. Not being able to let go of one man can turn you into a woman you don't even recognize anymore. And the longer you hold on, the worse it'll get. So stop it."

Two shots of Malibu rum later, I was beginning to think that maybe I could *Stop It*. Maybe I could, as Bridget Jones might say, *do whatever I bloody well pleased*.

·· 14 ··

Soon after we settled the bill, I was helping Pamela into a cab. She had received a frisky call from William at eleven p.m. and decided, as usual, to go running. When I returned to our table, Reena, Cristy and Christopher had already made their way over to the lounge. I planted myself on a stool beside them, and was thinking about the look on Pam's face as I closed the taxi door behind her, when Christopher's voice interrupted my hazy thoughts.

"Are you ready for your second drink, lightweight? Another mojito?"

I sighed, and responded, "Well, it'll be my third, actually. But who's counting? Bring it on, Mary."

"Good. I'll go get that waiter." He perked up, smoothing his hair and, I could've sworn, adjusting his butt as if it were cleavage.

"There's a bartender right behind us."

"I know. But that waiter has been giving me the eye. So if you don't mind, I'd prefer to get my drinks from him."

Christopher disappeared, and within minutes, Reena spotted something she liked.

"Don't look now," she said, with her teeth frozen, and her eyes cleverly diverted at our drinks, "but there are three cuties at nine o'clock."

On cue, Cristy and I whipped our heads simultaneously to the left, and commenced staring directly at the men in question.

"Nice," Reena chided.

What we lacked in subtlety, Reena made up for in taste. We nodded our approval, while sharing a conspiratorial giggle, like a couple of married senators at a strip club. Christopher returned and dropped a raspberry martini into my hand.

"I thought you were gonna order me a mojito." I pouted, steadying myself on what seemed like an increasingly wobbly barstool.

"I did," he said in hushed tones. "He may not be all that smart, but he's pretty. And that's a trade-off I'm willing to make."

"Classy," I said, feeling my oats as much as my brimming bladder.

"Don't judge me," he snapped.

"Okay. Who's hypersensitive now?" I laid my raspberry-tini carefully on the bar, spilling nearly a fifth down my arm, and then licked the back of my hand. "Anyway, what do I owe you?"

"Nothing. Forget about it. Just wish me luck." He winked. "And save your money for your cab ride home tonight. Alone."

And with that, Christopher was swallowed by the growing crowd.

"Are you sure we should do this?" Cristy asked.

"Oh, what's the big deal?" I asked, feeling bolder, and gulping down a third of my raspberry-tini. "They don't look like the kind of guys who would be offended by some assertive women."

I took a moment to examine the men, who were trying to make it clear that they were checking us out, if we wanted them to. Two blondes and an African-American. The shorter blonde looked like a country mouse in city man's clothing; as uncomfortable in his slick black suit as he was in his skin, but trying to act as if he wasn't. Or, to put it in Reena-speak: he looked a lot like *lunch meat.* The taller blonde was clearly the alpha male, scanning the bar for attractive females, lightly bopping his head to the music and grinning at the good fortune of having woken up that morning as himself. The African-American sat back; he was taking it easy, taking it in and taking great care to cultivate the impression that he was thinking deep thoughts.

Cristina narrowed her eyes and stuck out her chin. "You can't tell something like that just by looking at them."

"I can do whatever I want." I was getting sick of being told what I could and couldn't do, and sicker of having my decisions made for me.

I hopped off my bar stool. Maybe it was time to let loose?

Maybe I could rechristen myself as free of Jon by taking control of tonight? Maybe Reena's skin was *just the ticket.*

"It's something about the way they carry themselves," I explained. "Some men can handle it and others can't. They're cowboys. They prefer to feel like *they* conquered *you,* that they *won you* in some grand way. But other guys couldn't care less who starts the game, as long as they get to play. I'm betting these guys are playful. And because I've been out of the game for a while doesn't mean that my radar's necessarily rusty. I mean…I'm not sure that radars actually get rusty, but you know what I mean."

They were silent. I was restless. And the rest of my raspberry-tini was already well on its way to my head.

"You don't believe me?" I slurred. "Let's make it interesting. I'll bet you, um, I'll bet you a *pedicure* that if I do something very assertive, they'll come over and talk to us."

"You're on," Reena agreed, adjusting her man-catchers and sucking her teeth with her tongue, "because if it works, I get dibs on the shorter blonde. And if it doesn't work, then I get a pedicure."

"I'm scared," Cristina shared.

"Oh, hush. Nobody asked you. Now sit there and look pretty." I grinned, and then downed the contents of my glass before setting it on the bar and refocusing on Reena. "This is purely for research purposes. And also because I'm bored. So, I'm sending them a drink each, with our compliments."

"How do you know what to send them?" Crisina asked, pulling a compact out of my purse to check her lipstick.

"I was thinking nothing says *Wanna come out and play?* like alcohol," I answered, waving over the bartender.

"Very funny," she shot at me, while reapplying some of my lip gloss to her own lips. "I meant what *kind* of drink."

"Oh, well." I fingered an imaginary beard. "I'm thinking they're not burly enough for Scotch. And they're not double-o-seven enough for martinis. And *we're* far too classy for beer. So maybe just some mojitos? We *are* in a Cuban joint, right? *When in Rome.* Or should I say, *When in the meatpacking district?*"

"That sounds good to me. They'll think we're international." Reena accepted the bet, breathing hard against her palm.

"They'll think we're escorts is what they'll think," Cristina suggested.

"Come on," I teased Cristina and started feeling like a bit of an alpha-female myself. "Where's your sense of adventure? What's the worst thing that could happen?"

The longer I live, the more I become convinced that God has someone on staff to keep record of my hubris, and find creative ways to put me in my place. Swiftly. Case in point: I specifically told the bartender to take the drinks over to *that group of three men over there.* Naturally, he walked right past *that group* and toward another group, none of whom could have been less than sixty years old, and gave them the drinks instead.

Imagine my horror when I saw our messenger saunter past our intended targets, and knew there was nothing I could do to stop him. Imagine my shame when one of the geriatrics actually lifted a pair of spectacles to get a better look at us. Imagine my rage while I explained to the bartender afterwards that (1) those were the wrong men, (2) he would have to rectify his mistake before they invited us to their next Ice Cream Social and (3) he needed to take another round of mojitos to the correct group of men. As I had predicted, when they finally received the round of green, minty mojitos, *the correct group* of men sent back over three pink, peachy Bellinis. And they raised a gentlemanly toast in our direction before coming over to introduce themselves. I was vindicated. I grabbed hold of my fruity victory drink, like the trophy that it was. I was a tigress, predatory and majestic. I spotted what I wanted and I took it.

"Ladies, thank you for the mojitos," Alpha Male said as he glided into our bar space, and made it clear with his gaze that I was the one he had his eye on.

"And thank you all for the Bellinis. Nice choice," Reena purred like a cougar in the direction of the farm boy. He took one look at her and hurled himself happily into her imaginary lair.

"Can we just tell you girls? That's, like, the coolest thing any woman has ever done. I mean, we were sitting around getting drunk and talking about how men do all the work in places like this," Farm Boy babbled, "and then you sent us these drinks! That's great. Really. Thanks. You made our night."

Alpha Male glared him into silence, before returning his attention toward me.

"So, what can we do to repay the favor?" he asked, slipping an arm almost imperceptibly behind me, and staring so hard down my blouse that I worried he might fall in.

Well, for starters, you can look me in the eye and ask me my name before you try to climb into my bra.

"Oh, it was really nothing. We thought you guys looked like you were worth getting to know. So we decided to have a little fun. And thanks for the Bellinis, by the way." I leaned on the bar for support, and felt the alcohol in my system begin to take hold.

Sometimes I worried that I might actually hurt myself while trying to act as if I were this effortlessly sophisticated. At that moment, however, I shook it off. Tonight, I would not second-guess myself. Why shouldn't I be able to pull this off? Why couldn't I decide to be this suave? Why wouldn't I simply choose to be over Jon? Or choose not to take so much of what my parents said to heart? Or take control of my own damn Friday night? Maybe I could just block things out and think about myself for once! I could forget about Jon. I could take control. *I could be funny and still be sexy! I could do whatever the hell I wanted!* I took a deep breath and shook my hair away from my shoulders.

"I'm Vina. And this is Cristy and Reena."

"And I'm Ron. The guy humping your friend's leg is my little brother Tim. And this big muscle-head over here is my buddy Daniel," Alpha Male explained.

Tim and Reena had already separated a foot from the circle and forgotten about the rest of us. She was throwing her head back and laying a hand on her throat, laughing particularly hard at his particularly witty jokes. He was convinced that she was the only woman in the room. I was watching her mannerisms, rooting her on and wondering if I looked that shameless when I was flirting with a man.

"Cristina, what nationality is that?" Daniel asked.

"Cuban." She fluttered her eyelashes, and flung my blue purse over her shoulder.

"Really?" He perked up. "Then you know that it is pronounced 'Don-yell,' not 'Dan-yul.' I was born in Cuba. My mother is Jamaican and my father's Cuban. That means you can probably dance, girl. And the band's playing salsa. *¿Quieres bailar?*"

"So Vina." Ron turned to me after Cristy and Daniel headed for the dance floor. "What do you do for a living?"

"I'm in finance." I twirled the stem of my glass between my hands. "I—"

"Really?" He smiled, cutting me off. "I'm a VP at Globecom. You've probably heard of us. We're publicly traded. So you've got beauty *and* brains. That's a pretty lethal combination."

He arched what I could've sworn was a waxed eyebrow, confident that he had me cornered.

"I guess so." I was losing interest in him fast, along with my motor skills. Living inside his own happy little world, *Ron Quixote* failed to notice my sentiment.

"So what do you like to do for fun?"

"The same stuff as everyone else, I guess."

"Do you like to party?" He wiped what seemed like an

inordinate amount of sweat from his forehead, using the back of his sleeve.

Cocky *and* sweaty. Now, *that's* hot.

"Sure. I mean, I don't go out all that much, to be honest with you, what with working crazy hours and all. But I do okay." I racked my murky mind for legitimate excuses to leave, but came up empty.

"No. I mean *party.*" He stared at me as if I were a five-year-old. "I've got some really good powder back at my place. We're celebrating tonight. I just closed a *major deal.*"

He said it in a way that made it clear I was supposed to be turned on. I wasn't sure what was making me dizzier—the five drinks I had downed, or the fumes of unwarranted arrogance emanating from Ron's pores.

"Let me be honest with you, *Ronald,*" I lied, having decided he was too slimy for my taste, but not wanting to have to explain that to him. "I'm seeing someone. I didn't mean to lead you on. I was just playing wing-woman for Reena. She thought Tim was cute."

"I don't see a ring on your finger," he challenged.

Did he think he was presenting me with a loophole that I was unable to find for myself? *Eureka! You've found the trap-door in my commitment dilemma! Now I guess I'll just have to go home and get naked with you!*

"Well, that's true." I crossed my arms before me, and speared him with my most take-no-prisoners glare. "I'm not married. But I *am* in a relationship, so I *am not* on the market."

"If he's so wonderful, then where is he tonight?"

"Ron, come on." I tried to lighten the mood. "This is

not an MTV video. You're not gonna win me over by singing 'What's Your Man Gotta Do with Me?'"

"If you were my girlfriend—" he ignored what I'd said, leaning closer, treating me to a whiff of what I decided was garlic-and-blue-cheese-infused tuna breath "—I wouldn't let you run around looking all sexy without me."

Suddenly, I felt fiercely protective of my imaginary boyfriend. "Okay, first of all, this is a Girls' Night Out. Secondly, my boyfriend doesn't *let me* or *not let me* do anything. And besides, he knows that he has nothing to worry about."

"Come on, baby. Don't you find me attractive? It's not like he would ever find out. What happens between us can stay between us. I'm like Vegas," he implored, trying to climb in through my eyes, since the lower gates were obviously locked.

I had leaned so far back as to practically be lying horizontal on the bar.

"Seriously, Ron," I reverted to the voice I used on dogs and boardrooms full of middle-aged men, "Back off. I don't want to be rude, but I'm spoken for. So you're gonna have to not be so *into my personal space.*"

I was as offended at his presumption that I would be unfaithful as I was disgusted by his borderline bullying. I had no choice but to downgrade him to leper status. And that didn't bode well for his chances of taking me home, since he had started to spit a little bit while he spoke at me.

Prakash did owe me a favor, I thought. *Maybe he could expedite a restraining order?*

"Are you serious?" It finally registered with him that he wasn't going to get what he wanted, and like any animal, he decided to let his fangs out. "I am the vice president of Globecom! I make more money than any of the men in this place! I signed a $100 million deal today to buy a software company with two hundred employees! And I look like *this!* I am the *definition* of an 'eligible bachelor.' What could this man possibly have that I don't?"

I was floored. There were so many things I could say to explain why the way he looked at the world was lopsided, but none of them would come out correctly. I was too drunk to string a sentence together. And even a coherent argument would be lost on a man like him. He was getting drunker by the minute. So regardless of what I said, he wouldn't remember more than two words of it tomorrow. Before I picked up my purse and walked casually into the crowd, I whispered into his ear the only answer that would make him sit up and take notice.

"Me."

·· 15 ··

If you're in preschool, it's expected. If you're on spring break, it's applauded. And if you're an aspiring actress, it's forgiven. But waking up alone in an unfamiliar bed was nothing for a woman in my situation to be proud of. Cristina would've slipped immediately out the closest window. Reena probably would've done a victory lap around the bed. My thoughts, however, progressed in a different direction…

Phase 1 (Blinking awake): Dizzy. Thirsty. Headachey. Who am I? Where am I? *What am I?*

Phase 2 (Sitting up on elbows): Whose bedroom is this? What type of small animal crawled inside my throat and died last night?

Phase 3 (Noticing lack of bra under sheet, and name of estranged bedmate on framed diploma):

What the @%#$*&#$%%$?!?!?!! That bas-
tard must have taken advantage of me!*

I slid out of bed and crawled toward the bedroom door
on my hands and knees like a Special Ops officer trying to
maneuver undetected around a battlefield. I sniffed and
caught a whiff of something suspiciously similar to coffee.
Then I glimpsed Nick, Prakash's friend from the gym.
Naked aside from his boxer-briefs, he was actually whistling
while he made scrambled eggs. *An empty six-pack of eggs, next
to a chiseled six-pack of abs…*but there was no time to think
about that now. My priority was an escape plan.

*But how did I get here? Where was my cell phone? If he took
advantage of me, why would he be making me breakfast?*

Clambering to my feet, I hid behind the door. *How could
I have let this happen?* I rubbed at my eye sockets, and realized
that there was no mascara or eye-makeup on my fingers, or
on the pillow. *Which meant that I must have come to his apartment by choice, and been sober enough to wash my face before falling
asleep! But why would I go home with Nick, of all people? Granted
he was cute, but he was also a complete waste of my time. Could I
really have felt that lonely the night before?*

New rule: No more drinks that end in "tini."

I leaned against the wall for support, and shuddered at the
chill as it made contact with my naked skin. That's when it
all started coming back to me.

It must have been Ron's breath that had put me over the
edge the night before; I only wish he could have been the

recipient of the results. I was less than five steps away from him when I realized that my dinner was about to repeat on me. Clenching my stomach with one hand and my mouth with the other, I had fought my way through the crowds and into the ladies' room. When I reached the cubicle, I dropped to my knees on the cold, sticky tile, and laid my purse down beside me. Pulling my hair back, I leaned over the bowl and waited.

"Hey! Hurry up!" a nasal, scratchy voice assaulted me. Its owner banged furiously on the door of my stall. "Some of us have to take a dump!"

Locked in midhurl at the time, I couldn't exactly respond.

"There's a line out here!" she hollered, "Whaddya think? That you're the only lady in this whole freakin' club?"

There was no time to ponder the irony.

"I'm not well," I yelled over my shoulder.

"That's not my problem!" she barked.

A bony hand trimmed with sharp red nails grazed my knee. She grabbed my purse, and yanked it out from under the stall. I scrambled to my feet, flushed and threw open the door. A trashy version of Maria from *West Side Story* stood smugly before me. We locked eyes. She tilted her head, smirked, and then tossed my purse right out the door of the ladies' room.

Cursing like a *Joe Millionaire* contestant who actually put out, I chased after it. A sequined hot-pink-and-mint-green clutch was easy enough to find on the black dance floor, but its contents were another story. My lip gloss and compact were the only things left inside. I swiped at the ground between bending knees and twisting torsos, but my cell phone and wallet were nowhere in sight.

Suddenly, I thought I saw something silver on the floor. But just before I could reach for it, I was hauled up to my feet.

"Vina, what's going on?" Nick asked.

"Dammit!" I burst into sobs. "It's my purse! And my wallet! My phone! Oooh...I feel sick. I drank too much...and...and that prick expected me to go home with him! And then I was nauseous and I got sick in the bathroom. And then that witch threw my purse out here...and...and...my *keys!*"

"Whoa, there. Calm down. We'll find your stuff. Where are your friends?" he asked, helping me onto a barstool, and motioning for the bartender to bring me some water.

"I don't know. I...I have to find my wallet!"

"No." He pushed me back onto the seat by my shoulders. "You're in bad shape. You stay put. I'll find your stuff."

I closed my eyes and tried to will myself sober. I didn't want him, or anyone else, seeing me like that. He reappeared a few minutes later, dangling my keys before my eyes.

"Sorry. No luck finding anything else. Are you feeling any better? Did you see your friends?"

"No." I stood up shakily, and tried to avoid eye contact. "I don't know where anyone is. And I have to get home. I should never have come out tonight."

He grabbed my arm. "And how will you get home without a wallet?"

"Nick," I said, looking directly at him. I tried hard to maintain my balance. "I have to get out of here."

"Okay." He took me by the hand and led me toward the door. "Let's go."

Before I knew it, he was helping me into a cab. And then he got in behind me.

"So, where do you live?" he asked.

And then I woke up in his bed.

Holy Mary, Mother Of God, and Vishnu and Ram and Ganesh and Everyone Else… What Have I Done? I thought, while bristles of bedroom carpet made impressions on my naked butt cheeks. *I must have thrown myself at him!*

It was bad enough to have done something so sluttishly out of character. What was worse was not being able to remember if he was any good. *I mean, he had to be! Look at that body! Wait, no. Stop it! Bad Vina. Bad, bad Vina!*

I assumed he was fantastic. I hoped that lights had been low enough to spare him the mental image of my tummy-flab. I prayed that we had used a condom. There was only one correct way to handle this: I would slip quietly out the front door and refuse to admit that it had ever happened. *After all, who would believe him?*

I rose to my feet and took a deep breath. I peeked out the doorway and noticed the he was starting to squeeze fresh orange juice. *What did he think, that this was going to turn into a relationship? That did it. He left me no choice. I had no time to waste; I had to get out of there as quickly and quietly as possible.* I crept silently around the room, recovering my dress, bra, panties and purse easily enough. I could've sacrificed my pashmina to appease the wrathful-gods-of-the-one-nightstand, but my favorite Bruno Maglis simply could not be left behind on the battlefield. And they were nowhere to be found. *Not behind his desk. Not under his bed. Not dangling from his ceiling fan.*

A-hah! I spotted the familiar pink strap trailing from inside his closet. But when I tried tugging on the shoe, I noticed that it was wedged in tightly by the mirrored sliding door. In my rush, I then must've used a little too much force because the door flew entirely open.

I blinked. And then I blinked again.

It wasn't the video camera that bothered me. It was the three video cameras. On swiveling tripods. Aimed at the bed. Surrounded by professional lighting equipment. And stored alongside hundreds of videocassettes.

Oh, my god, he taped us! And these were probably videos of hundreds of other unsuspecting women he had lured home from the gym! He was making porn at home! Oh, my god, he was a porn producer! An illegal online porn producer! And I was his latest unwitting co-star! What a freak! He was probably Web-casting his bedroom onto the Internet…live…right now! Which meant that thousands of greasy, balding perverts around the globe had just watched me get dressed! For $3.95 per minute!

This was too much for the good Indian girl to comprehend, no matter how modern I considered myself. I lost my balance, gasped for air, staggered, and knocked over a chair.

"Vina?" Nick must have heard the thud.

I was confused. I was so angry that I couldn't breathe. And so embarrassed that I couldn't speak. My temperature was rising, while the walls of my throat were closing in. No better than a celebrity whose "personal" home video ends up on the Web, but without any of the proceeds, I had been used and digitally hung out to dry. Like a rock star who takes the groupie's word for it when she claims to be of age, I had made a not-so-innocent mistake, which I feared was built to last.

Whatever had happened the night before, it shouldn't have. And whatever I may have degenerated into, Nick had no right to benefit. He was the best friend of the gay man my parents wanted me to marry, and dammit, that entitled me to a little common decency. I scooped up my shoes and what was left of my self-respect, darted out of his bedroom and down the hall. I slammed the door as hard as I could before I sprinted toward the elevator.

Walk of shame, indeed.

·· 16 ··

Having too much time on my hands has never been a good thing, because my mind tends to run amok. That Saturday evening's trip on the Long Island Railroad was proof positive. I had bitten my nails down to the stubs by the time the train pulled into Great Neck station. I had also convinced myself that:

1. The ticket collector was smiling because he recognized me from the Web-cast,
2. Nick had probably given me an STD, and
3. None of the above mattered in the end, since I was going to die alone, anyway.

In the thirty minutes since Penn Station, I had figured it all out. Actually, this conclusion wasn't random. It was right there in the numbers. And I can tell you as an overpaid number cruncher that the numbers, unlike men and advertisements for weight-loss programs, almost never lie. Like I said: too much time on my hands. So, with whatever limited knowledge of the U.S. census I could guesstimate off the top of my head, here is what I managed to come up with.

Consider the following:
There are approximately 300 million people living in the U.S.

MY REQUIREMENTS INCLUDE:

Male and between 28 and 38	8.75 million
Living in/near, or frequently visiting NY	200,000
Straight and single	100,000
Not including bi-sexual	70,000

AND MY WISH LIST INCLUDES:

And have a college degree	40,000
And make as much money as (or are not threatened by a woman who makes as much money as) I do	15,000
And do not resemble Klingons	5,000
Or frequent *Star Trek* conventions	4,000
And are interested in commitment	1,000
And are not secretly waiting for a Victoria's Secret supermodel to come around	10

So even if I were to date one new man per week, every week, only one out of every 7,000 heterosexual and single men in New York City in my age range would be a potential match. That means I had a better chance of striking oil in my parents' backyard than of finding one potentially suitable man. Even if I had started dating while I was in diapers, the sad fact was that my eggs would have long since expired by the time I found the love of my life.

And now I'm a low-budget Internet porn star with an STD, I thought. *Faaaaaaantastic.*

I'll admit it; I was frantic. But I had a right to be. It's never as simple as a quiet family dinner on Long Island. To begin with, setting foot in my parents' house instantly takes a decade off my emotional age. I leave midtown Manhattan as a fully functional, semirational, fairly-well-put-together adult woman. I enter 34 Woods End Road as a cranky, bratty and misunderstood teenaged girl. With unruly eyebrows. And perpetually un-ironed pants. Who has no idea where she's headed. And who could not, for the life of her, locate the drawer in which a matching pair of socks might be hidden.

That wasn't the worst of it. Still reeling from having stumbled onto Nick's porn arsenal that morning, I was abnormally vulnerable to my parents' good intentions. Naturally, the last thing I needed to find in their home was exactly what was waiting for me when I arrived.

I had to stifle a shriek when I walked into the dining room. "I am serious, Shardha. This Navratan Koorma is the best

I have ever eaten." Prakash's mother was kissing up to my own. "You must tell me your secret."

My jaw was spending so much time hanging open lately, that I considered leaving it that way. Especially since I'd never close it again if, as I suspected, I had just walked in on my own surprise engagement party. Cousin Neha and her husband Vineet were seated alongside Prakash, his parents, my Nani and my own parents.

"Vina," my father said, motioning to me. "Come. Sit. Isn't it wonderful that Prakash and his parents have been able to join us for dinner tonight?"

This time, the onset of my neck stress was sudden and fierce. *Why doesn't life come with a pause button?*

Prakash glanced uneasily at me, and then looked quickly away. Neha and Vineet nodded simultaneously in my direction.

Thankfully, before any of my thoughts could spill out, my Nani intervened.

"*Beti,* before you sit down, you must first help this old lady up the stairs. I am tired. I need to go and lie down for some time."

Gratefully, I pulled her to her feet, excused myself and helped her up to her room.

"Sometimes we must do things for our parents. For the good of the family," she said to her own reflection in the bedroom mirror a moment later. She massaged one arthritic hand with the other. "Even if it is only for appearances."

"Nani," I said, ferreting the bobby pins out of her bun, "this dinner was not my plan. I did not agree to this."

"I wasn't talking about you. Vina, Prakash is a nice boy." She turned and looked me in the eye. "A nice…*gentle* boy. I can see this. I can also see that he loves his parents very much. He is a good son."

My remaining grandmother is seventy-two years old. She was born poor in rural Punjab, married off at the age of fourteen and widowed with three children before she reached twenty-five. She was illiterate, but managed to ensure that her own children would graduate from college by loaning out the money she borrowed against the small plot of land her husband had left her. She suffered marriage to a stranger as an innocent child bride and the impropriety of those who considered widows free game. She survived two miscarriages and a stillbirth in a village that lay the blame solely on the woman. She endured countless hours of labor without benefit of anesthetic, and a sleepless night in 1947 hiding in a closet holding on to her children for dear life, while all hell broke loose on the streets outside their home as Pakistan was being ripped from India.

"I give laughter from one eye while I give tears from the other," she had once told me, when I asked her how she weathered everything that had happened.

Private moments with her reminded me that my life was an enormous slice of cake, with a pitcher of champagne on the side. And that I was complaining because I'd drunk myself into a hangover.

I tucked my grandmother under the covers and kissed her forehead. Taking a deep, fortifying breath, I donned a fake smile, and marched back down those stairs.

★ ★ ★

"But in order for there to be karma for us to contend with *the next time around,* don't you agree that we need the freedom to make our own choices *this time around?*" Neha pointed her fork at my father.

Uncle Ved patted the chair beside him, and I quietly took my seat. Though not related by blood, he was referred to as an uncle since he had known my family for over twenty years. A forty-five-year-old importer/exporter from Mumbai, Uncle Ved had the unnerving habit of believing that since he was single we had something in common.

"Definitely, definitely." He heaped more rice onto his plate before passing the dish to me.

I settled into my spot while my mother spooned a helping of Dhal Makhani wordlessly into my bowl.

"Yes, of course," Prakash's mother concurred, to the approval of her onlooking husband. "Nothing in Hinduism says that you do not have free will."

"So then," Neha continued, "this means that there were potentially five different career paths I could have chosen, or five different men I could have chosen to marry. Right?"

With a mouthful of Saag Paneer, Vineet stopped mid-chew to stare his not-so-blushing bride into silence. Predictably, Neha relented, removing her elbows and her opinions from the table.

"Perhaps," my father answered. "But this is why you have a family. These people are here to guide you to choose the right path. Your parents have this responsibility to you—this karma. That is why you were given to them as a daughter.

They can fulfill their obligation only by making sure that you understand which ones are the correct choices to make."

"I think we can all agree that we are lucky to have been born with parents who have our best interests at heart." Prakash defused the situation, smiling at me for everyone else's benefit.

I returned a smile, even though I felt last night's mojitos threatening to re-repeat on me.

"My parents *told me* who to marry," Uncle Ved blurted in confession. "I listened to them, and see what happened? That marriage ended in divorce!"

"Divorce?" Prakash's mother whispered to herself, dropping her spoon into her Yogurt Rehta, and splattering little dots across her shawl.

"What? Uncle Ved, you were married? Nobody ever told me this!" I practically leaped at my mother, forgetting entirely about my manners and the fact that we had company. "Why didn't anybody ever tell me this?"

She didn't so much as blink.

"Because it is not for us to discuss. It is a family matter," she said, then turned to reassure Prakash's mother of the stability of our bloodline. "And Ved is not technically a member of our family. Not a blood relative, that is. In any case, Ved, how many whiskey sours have you had tonight?"

Ved took the hint, heard the warning and quickly averted his eyes.

"Vina, nobody is trying to *tell you children* who to marry," Prakash's father interjected. "We realize that it does not work that way with your generation. It is for the children to decide. We can only introduce suitable matches."

"Well…" I began.

"Darling," my mother cooed, spooning additional Gobi Aloos onto my plate, obviously uncomfortable with any acknowledgement of the elephant in the room, "why are you eating so little? Vina always takes very good care of her figure, you know. But I hope you are not trying to become too skinny like your friend Pamela. She looks so unhealthy. Honestly, I don't know why her parents don't tell her these things."

"Mom, Pam looks fine. I just don't have that much of an appetite tonight. And her parents don't tell her what to eat or not to eat. Besides, they moved to Montana…I thought I told you that. Anyway, she's perfectly healthy. But that's not the point. I wanted to say that…"

"Don't try to explain, Vina. These people will never understand. Pass the Bhindi, please?" Uncle Ved added, shaking his head.

I huffed helplessly. Nobody paid me any attention.

"Mon*tana*? Why so far from their daughter? They might as well live in *Timbuktu,*" my father decided.

"Really, Mom," I tried to speak up, nudging away the ladleful of Bhurtha hovering above my plate, "I'm not hungry."

"Oh, Vina, you have a lovely figure," Neha said. "You don't need to worry about becoming even more beautiful, like those obsessive American women, na?"

"Oh, come on." Prakash leaned in and pierced me with his gaze. "How could Vina ever look more beautiful than she already is? And with so much charm and grace…well…I'm sure no man *I know* could resist her."

Had he also gotten into the whiskey sours? An uncomfortable silence followed, during which I stared at him bewildered. *What would possess him to say something so clearly inappropriate in front of our parents?*

My mother, on the other hand, was oblivious to anything other than the fact that an acceptable match might have been made.

"All right then, darling. Would you please get the chai started for us?"

Before I was on my feet, Prakash's mother followed suit. "Yes, yes. Prakash, *beta,* why don't you go and help Vina in the kitchen?"

·· 17 ··

"Well, you really had me fooled—" Prakash began in a whisper.

We hadn't even shut the kitchen door behind us.

"What? What are you talking about?" I poured the milk, flipped the stove onto High and swung around to face him. "It looks like *you're* the one that's got *my* parents fooled. We had a deal, you maniac! What could possibly have possessed you to behave this way?"

His nostrils flared. "I could ask you the same thing."

"What's that supposed to mean?" I hard-whispered, "And keep your voice down!"

He leaned one hand on the counter, and aimed his face so that he could meet me at eye level. "You had no right to walk out on Nick like that this morning. You know he's a good friend of mine. Did you think I wouldn't find out?"

Well, *this* was unexpected. Where was the hair-rending?

Where was the blubbering? Where was the guy who should have been lying prostrate before me, begging forgiveness for the evening's emotional ambush? *And who the hell did he think he was to judge me for being victimized by his sleazeball friend?*

My mind spun before finally settling on the obvious. "No! And wait… I didn't… How can you even say that? Why would I care if it got back to you, anyway? Listen very closely, you moron. You and I are not dating! You are gay!"

"I am well aware of that." He straightened up, crossing his arms, shifting into a distinctly lawyerly tone, "And I am also aware that you are a grown woman. The bottom line is that you knew what you were doing last night. And you know that there was a better way to handle it this morning."

"Okay, first of all, I cannot believe I'm even hearing this." I started poking his chest, backing him into a corner. "But we don't have time to argue about last night. This is about tonight. And you could've handled *this dinner* a helluva lot better, like by not letting it happen in the first place! The *bottom line,* as you put it, is that this is insanity. And you are insane for orchestrating it. I mean, what was all that garbage you were spewing out there in front of our parents? How could you let things get this far?"

He wouldn't relent. "Hey, I didn't know we were having dinner here tonight. My parents sprang it on me at the last minute, and I had no choice but to come with them. I…"

His eyes focused on something behind me, and then widened. "The pot!"

I looked over my shoulder. The milk was bubbling and foam was dripping onto the stove. I lunged for the pot handle.

"Damn it!" I yelled, jerking away. I rushed to the sink to plunge my hand under cold water.

Prakash flipped off the switch and then hurried to my side, where he proceeded to stand, helplessly.

I pivoted to face him. "You always have a choice, Prakash. And you're responsible for the choices that you make."

The concern in his eyes morphed into malice. "And what does that say about your behavior last night? Or this morning?"

"*Arrrrrrgh!* How is that any of your *business?*" I nearly yelled, and then started gesturing with dripping hands. "You know, maybe you'd be a little less quick to judge other people if you took a closer look at yourself. You…you make me sick!"

"I?" He stepped back. "I make *you* sick? Wow, I thought I was the attorney. Vina, you really know how to spin a situation around."

"This is not about spinning anything around. And I cannot believe that you think you have the right to blow up at me. You should be apologizing to me for letting things get to this point with our parents!"

His hand flew to his forehead and his eyes slammed shut. "Vina, I…"

"No, wait. You know what? Come to think of it, I take that back. I'm not surprised at all. Why should I have expected any better from you? You're thirty years old and you're still such a pathetic child that you're running circles around yourself. You're even willing to take advantage of me, just to keep hiding your sexuality from your own mother and father! I don't know how you can even look at yourself in the mirror!"

Of all the doors slamming in my life recently, that one might have been the loudest. And not just because it left me to answer to two sets of parents on my own. But ten minutes after Prakash sped off, his parents were on their way, as well, having traded their awkward goodbyes with my own. Being so much of the adult that Prakash was not, I hid in the kitchen until his mother and father were gone. I was still slumped in a kitchen chair, with my face buried in blistering hands, when I heard my father padding up the stairs.

Eventually, the silence was broken by the shuffling of my mother's tiny slippers on the tile. I looked up, and she was looking down on me.

"Mom…" a tiny voice fought its way out of me.

She held a hand before her forehead to silence me, and then flipped it around and swiped it across her face, her tired and—for the first time I could recall—noticeably aging face.

"*Beti,*" she began, with her eyes still closed, "your father and I tried to raise you with the proper values. And we gave you your freedom so that we could be sure that you could take care of yourself. But we educated you so that you could have a good life, not so that you could forget about family and tradition entirely. Normally, I try to see things your way. I know you don't think so, but I do. You have always been a very sensitive girl. You are my daughter and I recognize these things. But honestly, I don't know what to say to you anymore. Your career becomes more and more important, and you talk about these so-called relationships of yours. You know we do not approve of them, but we have learned to keep our mouths shut on the subject, thinking perhaps you know better than we do. But where are these men you spend time with? Where have they gotten you? What are the results of all this independence you talk about? At some point, the time to do things right will pass. You are enjoying your freedom, and you are working very hard, and still you are not happy. Then this boy comes along. He is educated. He is handsome. And his parents are truly gentle and kind people. Still, you find faults with him before you have even taken the time to know him. And now you have yelled at him in your parents' home. I mean, I cannot imagine that my child would do such a thing. *My* child. It must have been a failure on our part that we did not raise you better. I accept that. But what could have been so bad on his part? Your father and I only want what is best for you, Vina, but we don't know what else to do. Now I think that maybe we should just leave you to do what you feel is right."

I opened my mouth but couldn't make a sound. She turned and walked away.

Obviously that night I chose not to sleep in my old bedroom. Because like all ungrateful children who don't love their parents, I had the audacity to live alone in midtown Manhattan despite the fact that mine had offered me a perfectly good room (rent-free!) in their home on Long Island (just thirty minutes from my office!). Did I mention it comes with an early-morning cup of tea with Mommy and Daddy? I used to try to find ways to tactfully explain why, at my age, even though I'm not married, I do on occasion have company for my morning beverage. After it fell on deliberately deaf ears more times than I could count, I gave up and agreed with their version of the story. My choice to spend $2,000 per month for a shoe box in the sky had nothing to do with the fact that I was a gainfully employed, grown woman in her late twenties who enjoyed her independence. Clearly, I did it because I hated them.

Bleary-eyed and blistered by midnight, I leaned into the door to my apartment. I dropped my purse on a chair. I dropped my clothes on the floor. I dropped into the comfort of my cherished independence. The calm of my own apartment. The space to sort things out. The promise of clarity at daybreak. The chance to be alone inside my head…

Or so I had hoped. But in reality, no single woman can ever really count on being alone inside her own mind.

"Great news!" Cristina shouted through the phone after what seemed like only fifteen minutes had passed.

"I'm sleeping," I complained, blinking at the slit of sunlight slicing through the blinds.

"Well, get up. It's ten a.m. And I know you didn't have a late night, since you went to your parents' house."

"You don't know the half of it." I pulled the sheets over my face. "I really want to go back to sleep."

"Well, you won't when you hear what I have to tell you."

She was in no mood to be refused. And I was in no condition to fight. I huffed.

"Okay, so…I know you've been really depressed about Jon lately," she began. "Understandably, although you try to keep such a brave face. But the whole situation with that bastard has been really hard for you. I mean Jon. I mean…"

"Mmm-hmm." I rolled my eyes under their lids.

At that moment, Jon seemed like the least of my problems.

"And so I thought you could use some good news. Actually, it's more like a surprise. You've been *published!*"

"Huh?"

"Surprise! I got you published! I forwarded one of your e-mails to Salon.com."

"You did what?" My eyes flew open.

"You know, it's that Web site about relationships. And they loved your bit! So they published it in this morning's edition. It's online right now!"

She paused. Once again, I was speechless.

"I was cleaning out my inbox, and I started rereading some of your e-mails about how it had made you feel. The infidelity. And then it hit me: Your e-mail could be your silver lining. I mean, you're so insightful about this kind of stuff. And…"

She was waiting for my response. I was waiting for the room to stop spinning.

"I…I was thinking that something good could come out of this whole situation, you know? Vina. Vina, say something."

I sat up. "Cristina, how could you do this?"

"I thought it would make you feel better. You've been so mopey lately."

"Better! It makes me feel horrible! Exposed! Violated! How *dare* you?"

"Vina, what's the big deal? I don't understand why you want to hide your insight, your talent."

I yelled. "It's my emotions!"

"Well," she asked, "Why do you want to hide *them,* then?"

I closed my eyes, drew a deep breath, and tried to stay calm. "Cristina, I'm not hiding anything. It was private. And personal. And you had no right to do this."

"Vina, you're being unreasonable," she countered. "You can't keep running away from this."

Things were getting out of hand. I was so sick of being psychoanalyzed by people who had no idea what I was going through. So tired of having people make my decisions for me. So frustrated over never having any control over anything. I snapped, and it wasn't pretty.

"This is coming from a woman who, everyone knows, runs so hard on the treadmill because what you're really trying to outrun is the fear that any person who gets close enough to *actually know you* will wind up dumping you?"

And I slammed down the phone before I could hear her reply.

·· 18 ··

The banging I thought was coming from inside my head turned out to be the sound of someone knocking on my door a few hours later.

"Nobody's home." I buried my head under a pillow.

"Don't be so melodramatic, honey. Believing that hot pink is acceptable this season doesn't make you a nobody. It just makes you…unfortunate. Now let me in." It was Christopher.

"Why?"

"Because if you don't, then I'll tell everyone in the building that you're responsible for the potted plants that are always clogging the trash chute."

I yanked open the door. "How did you know?"

"Please," he said with a sarcastic wink and pushed past me in a terrycloth bathrobe that looked softer than anything I owned. "What kind of self-respecting plant could resist suicide when forced to live in such close proximity to that much Brooks Brothers navy blue?"

I watched helplessly while he once again made himself comfortable in my apartment. "So you've been looking through my closet while I've been sleeping?"

"Um, no." He raised a manicured eyebrow at me, reminding me that it was probably time to re-wax my own. "That would be a little loserish, don't you think? I do it while you're in the shower."

I glared at him while kicking the door shut with my heel.

"What?" He shot my coffee table a look of disdain. "It's not like you have any good magazines. I wouldn't be surprised to find a copy of *Highlights* in that pile."

I yawned and dropped onto the couch beside him, wrapping myself in a blanket.

"Did you come over here at the butt-crack of dawn to talk about my magazine collection?"

"First of all, it's nowhere near the crack. It's noon. And I came over here to check in on you. You disappeared Friday night."

"Noooo," I corrected him. "Actually, you all disappeared."

"No, we didn't. Or at least I didn't. The waiter turned out to be straight."

"'Straight,' meaning that he wasn't interested in you?" I grinned.

"Po-tay-to, po-tah-to." He waved away the thought. "All I know is that when I got back to the bar, you were gone. And straight clubs are boring without girlfriends. So I wandered around alone, and laughed at the breeders trying to dance, and laughed at the bartenders pretending to be straight. And then, *finally*…I found someone worth taking home. Someone you know, as a matter of fact…*drum roll please*…Prakash!"

He had to be kidding me. "You have got to be kidding me."

"No. Why?" he asked, looking up from his manicured nails. "Maybe I'm developing some sort of an Indian fetish from hanging out with you and Reena. All I know is that I saw that tall drink of chai latte on the other side of the floor and I had to meet him. So I went over and asked if he was lost. He laughed, and said he was waiting for his buddy. We got to talking and he's great. He's also even cuter than you said he was. Those big brown eyes, and what a body! Girl-friend, I think I've been missing out all these years. Now I know the secret. Indian men are where it's at."

"Where what's at?"

"Where I'm at." He grinned. "At the moment. Or at least, where I was that night. And where I hope to be again, very soon."

"Huh?"

"Try to keep up, sweetie. Anyway, when he told me his name, I asked if he knew you. He said yes. And as if I didn't already know he was gay, he clarified that the buddy he was with at Son Cubano was only a friend. Nick, I think his name was."

It was beginning to sound as if The Blue Man Group was rehearsing inside my skull. Louder, and louder, and louder.

"So we flirted. One thing led to another. And then he

made me breakfast." He leaned in with doe-eyes. "I mean, he actually made me breakfast. Who *does* that? Nobody *does* that anymore. He's so old-fashioned. I'm telling you, I could really fall for this one."

I jumped up and headed for the coffeemaker. "Christopher, Prakash is not serious relationship material. Trust me."

"Vina, I know what I'm doing."

"Really? Well, did you know that he hasn't come out to his family yet? Can you seriously consider a relationship with someone like that?"

I paused to consider the irony of being the one to say this. Christopher stood up.

"I know you think I deserve better, but I have my own definition of that. Nobody's perfect. People make compromises all the time. He's a good guy. I like him. It's a compromise I'm willing to make."

I poured the water into the coffeemaker and switched it on, turning around to face him. "You've only known this man for one night."

"No offense, Vina, but you knew Jon for over a year, and that didn't seem to make much of a difference. I don't need to justify this to anyone. I didn't come in here looking for your permission to date him."

"You're telling me not to be melodramatic. Well, now I'm saying the same to you," I countered. "As your friend, I am reminding you that it has only been one night. Not even a real date. Has he even called you yet?"

"That's a technicality."

I scoffed and reached for the coffee mugs.

"Did you ever think that maybe your inability to decide what you want out of your life makes you overly emotional, and therefore judgmentally impaired when it comes to people who are willing to take responsibility for their own happiness?"

I narrowed my eyes. "Did you ever think that maybe your attraction for doomed relationships with unavailable men makes you emotional toilet paper?"

He took a step back and shook his head. "This is not a good color on you, Vina."

"I'm sorry." I exhaled, and started thinking about it out loud. "I apologize, really. You're right. I've been snappy lately. And you have a right to *shtup* whoever you want."

"You know, you have a way with words."

"So I've been told." I spooned sugar into the mugs.

"And that's not always a good thing."

"So I've learned."

With Christopher gone, and no interest in heading to the office for a few hours, I realized I had nothing to do. So I scoured the fridge for anything edible, downed two cups of coffee and checked out every godforsaken eighties action-movie repeat on cable television. Then I went online, cleaned out my inbox, read my horoscope and surfed around for nothing in particular. I even scanned the *New York Times* Sunday edition. Restlessness had made me desperate. Eventually, curiosity got the better of me. I bit my lip, hunched my shoulders, and logged on to Salon.com.

There it was on the splash page, alongside a two-column

diatribe about "How And Why To Avoid Any Man Whose Smile Makes Your Clothes Fall Off."

It was my article—"When Your Prince Turns Into A Pirate."

My article. *My* article. It had a nice ring to it. And according to the *About Us* section of the Web site, Salon.com received 300,000 hits per week. I was settling into my newfound fame, not to mention peaceful morning when all was interrupted by the ringing of my cell phone. *Was it always that loud?*

"Nani," I stated with the warmth I reserved just for her. "What are you doing?"

"Me? I'm talking to my dear, sweet granddaughter."

"And did you eat breakfast yet?" I smiled through the phone.

"Breakfast? Of course! I took my breakfast at eight o'clock. Now it is already time for my lunch. Did you eat your breakfast yet?"

"Yes, yes. I'm fine. I'm doing some reading."

"Oh, are you busy? I can call you some other time, then."

"No, no. First of all, even if I was busy, I would always rather talk to you. Secondly, I am not busy, anyway."

"Where did I get such a sweet granddaughter?"

"Sweet granddaughters come from sweet grandmothers."

"*Beti,* I called to see if you are feeling a little low after last night. But now that I hear your voice with so much *shaanti,* so much contentedness, I only have to ask you what has made you so happy."

"I am always happy when I talk to my Nani."

"I know, *beti,* but today you have a different voice. What were you doing when I called?"

"I was—" I took a breath "—I was reading something on the Internet. Something that I wrote. It has been published, Nani."

"And you didn't tell me? That's wonderful! Can I read it in Hindi, also?"

"No," I said, picturing her reaction to her granddaughter's article about the importance of sexual fidelity in interracial premarital relationships, then thanking God that she would never read it.

"Well, this is wonderful news, *beti*."

"Oh, it's no big deal, Nani. It's a small thing, really."

"Not if it has made you sound this way," she began. "What is bothering you?"

"Nani—" I hesitated "—do you remember that poem I wrote when I was a little girl? Like, fifteen years ago?"

"Yes."

"This is like that. I'm not sure it's something I want to share, or maybe it's not something I wanted to be public."

"Is it shameful?"

"No, no. Well, not in my opinion. I haven't done anything wrong, but not everybody will understand, or see it the same way as I do. I mean, Mom and Dad certainly wouldn't approve of the topics."

"*Beti,* I think that maybe you should allow it to be public."

"I thought you said good girls trust their parents," I tested her.

"You are not a girl anymore, Vina. When I was your age I was a mother and a widow already."

"What are you saying, Nani?"

"Vina, a girl must respect her elders and trust her parents. Completely. A woman must respect her parents and trust herself. Completely. That is the only way. The world is a different place now, but a woman's intuition is as important as always. It is *jo undher say athha ha*…what comes from within you. That is the only thing you should trust blindly. That is the only thing we really have. Everything else is just a show."

I almost cried, thinking how impossibly special having a grandmother was, even as I reminded myself that *It's not that easy*. But I didn't tell her that.

·· 19 ··

It was enormous and inappropriate. It added nothing to the carefully crafted illusion that I was a professional. And it was right there in my office early Monday morning for everyone to see.

Who the hell did he think he was?

Technically, there were two of them. One was topless and the other bottomless, until they reconnected upon my arrival. Perhaps this was Jon's last resort, since I'd returned none of the ten messages he had left for me since the morning after the blackout.

I was not amused.

"We're a Singing Horse-o-Gram," the head shouted.

"And we're here to apologize for Jonathan, because he's been such a horse's ass!" the rear explained, to my mounting horror.

Before I could protest, they had launched into an apolo-gram or a sing-ology, or whatever other euphemism was used to disguise this auditory assault. Apparently, I had no recourse. This was some alternative version of a singing telegram company that specialized in forcing women to choose between forgiving men for their stupidity, or risking total humiliation in their workplace. The ass was finishing up its rendition of "I Can't Smile Without You" when Alan and Denny snuck in to enjoy the show.

Although it is physically impossible for someone with my skin tone to blush, I turned at least ten shades of pink. Attached to the flowers and balloons they left behind was a note.

Not so good at being subtle.
But I admit to what I am.
And even a Pirate deserves a chance to explain.
As well as the chance to be a better man.
Please?
Love, Jon

"Is it, um, safe to assume this is from that boyfriend of yours?" Alan asked, amused to death at what he mistook for embarrassment. *I was actually fuming with anger.*

"No. I mean, we broke up. He's not my boyfriend anymore. Long story. Ends with Jon being an ass."

"I'm sorry to hear that, Vina." Alan stiffened and adopted a more formal tone, "I'm sure you'll find someone else."

"Secret admirer?" Denny chimed in.

"No. These *are* from Jon, but it's over. He hasn't accepted it."

"Are you sure it's over? You seem very affected," Alan said.

"I am sure. Trust me. I might even be done with men entirely."

"Considering women?" Denny grinned.

"Considering celibacy is more like it. Take this last weekend, for example. My friends and I met these guys at a bar, and one of them wouldn't let it go, you know? Like a dog that had sunk his teeth into my leg, and I couldn't shake him off."

I collapsed into my chair.

"What happened?" Alan asked.

"I don't want to talk about it. Certainly, I don't want to bother you with it. I want…to forget about it and get my day started. I'm here to work, not complain."

But then an invitation to chat from Jon on Instant Messenger popped up on my screen. I had finally had enough. I was going to let it all out, and Alan and Denny were going to have to hear it.

"Okay, do you really want to know? Jon and I are over. Finished. *Kuthum. Finito.* Because he cheated on me. It was a long time ago, but I only found out now. And let's say that it wasn't in the most convenient way. Secondly, this weekend, this *prick* just assumed I would go home with him! He was so arrogant. And even after I lied and told him that I had a boyfriend, so that I would let him down easy…to do *him* a favor…still, he kept pushing the issue! I mean, he honestly thought he could *impress* me into cheating on my imaginary boyfriend! God! The world is a cesspool. I can't believe it took me this long to see what was right in front of me!" I declared. "Is there no decency left?"

"How did he push the issue? Physically?" Denny asked, suddenly concerned in a very endearing little-brother-who-thinks-he's-your-big-brother sort of way.

"No, no, no." I shook my head. "It's nothing like that. If it was that, I'd have kneed him in the groin. Hell, my friend Cristina would have ripped his face off without breaking a nail. It's that he was bragging about how much money he made. About how he is a 'VP at Globecom' and he wanted me to help 'celebrate' the company acquisition he closed that day by getting coked up with him."

I was now sarcastically bunny-earring my words, adding dramatic emphasis in a language that Denny would appreciate.

"As if the money was supposed to impress me so much that I would sleep with him. I mean, do I *look* like a prostitute?"

"No, you most certainly do not," Alan offered magnanimously. "Calm down, Vina. You've had the misfortune to have met your fair share of Neanderthals. On behalf of men everywhere, I apologize."

"I don't know. It would have been bad enough to come on so strong when I said I had a boyfriend, but then to assume financial status was the only thing that I was looking for in a man! What's the point of having this career, then? This wasn't what I needed right now, you know? Look, I'm sorry for venting. I just feel like I can't count on anything these days and that I've got to have eyes in the back of my head. Like I can't assume there's a decent male soul on the planet," I whimpered, and then added, pointing to the third chat request from Jon that had popped up since I'd sat down, "And now I've got this self-admitted jackass to deal with."

★ ★ ★

Less than an hour later, Peter cornered me by the coffee-maker. "So? Have you heard anything?"

My face must have looked vacant.

"Your bonus. Did you hear?"

"Oh. No, Peter. I didn't." I stirred sugar into my mug.

He looked as if he had just lost his best friend. "Well, I did. Ten grand. I expected thirty."

"I'm sorry, Peter. Fine, I'll ask them. But we already know it's gonna be bad. Probably five, if you got ten. I'll go and get it over with." I thought for a second. "And come to think of it, I *do* have an excuse to ask. Accounting e-mailed me this morning to confirm the amount of Wade's final paycheck. It was too high apparently. Probably a clerical error. I can call Alan, and ask about the bonus as I'm getting his permission to cancel and reissue the check."

"All right," he said, taking my coffee mug. "Keep me posted. I'm knocking off early. They can't fire me for that. I'm also not coming into the office this weekend. I've worked every damn weekend for the past year for nothing. And never mind about me—this will kill the team's morale. Anyway, Godspeed."

He mock-saluted me, cracked his neck and walked out of the room. I felt sorry for him. Nobody deserved a bigger bonus this year than Peter. I decided I would call Alan the next morning, if he hadn't already called me by the end of the day.

Uncharacteristically, I slipped out of the office early, and decided to walk the long way home. I had planned to make my way across Fifty-fourth Street, and then down Lexington. But I was stopped in my tracks on the corner of Forty-second Street, when I saw her. Dancing for everyone and no one in particular. After a few moments of watching her twirl, I found myself fixated on the expression on her face. So calm. So unaffected. So apart.

I don't know how much time had passed before I was jolted back into the moment by a Chinese food delivery man knocking into me. For no real reason, I ducked into the Starbucks across the street, and ordered two large iced coffees.

"Hi," I said, while holding out a cup to the Gypsy. She had just finished up a slow version of Rod Stewart's "This Old Heart of Mine."

"Well, would you look at that? And I thought I was doin' a rain-dance." She winked. "But I'll take coffee just as gladly. Thank you kindly."

She sniffed at the cup as if it held some fine wine, before taking her first gratified sip.

"You're welcome. Umm," I faltered, "I'm Vina."

"I'm very glad to meet you, Vina." Her eyes crinkled at their corners, clearly from habit. "They call me Ellie."

"So do you…do you do this every day?"

"What else would I do?"

"It's beautiful. I mean, your dancing…it's beautiful."

"Well, now *that's* a lie," she said, laughing wholeheartedly, before taking another sip. "Nobody in their right mind could see me dancin' and think it's pretty. It ain't pretty. But I'll take the compliment anyway, m'dear."

I smiled nervously while she pulled the bandana from her hair and began re-braiding her long, silver strands.

"Say, shouldn't you be on your way home from a big, important job in one of these big, important buildings?" She gestured up and around her in every direction.

"Yeah," I replied, "I guess I should, but...so...if you don't even think that you dance well, then why do you do it?"

"Because I don't care what I think. It's a side-effect of what I think *they'll* think, anyway. I care what I feel," she told me, glancing sideways. "I used to be trapped, too."

I put a hand to my chest. "I'm not trapped. What are you talking about? You don't even know me."

"Then tell me this." She leaned in. "Why did you leave the big, important job in the big, important office early, and come and talk to me?"

"I was just curious about you."

"Okay."

"I've seen you dance before."

"Umm-hmm..."

"And..."

"And?"

"And you always look happy."

"Bingo! Tell her what she's won!"

"Crazy, but happy," I explained.

"Oh, I'm not happy because I'm crazy. I'm happy because I let myself be. I care more about what I *feel* than about what other people *think*. And *that* makes me happy."

"All right." I got sarcastic. "So you're *happy* living outdoors?"

"I don't live here," she said, pointing to the ground, and then to her head. "I live *here*."

I raised an eyebrow.

"Why?" she asked. "You know anybody who doesn't?"

"I guess not," I replied and started to leave.

"It was nice talking to ya. Thanks for the java. I better get started on my next show. Don't want to disappoint the fans!"

·· 20 ··

"Alan?" I reclined first thing Tuesday morning, twirling the phone cord with my finger and twisting my chair around to face the window. "Hi. It's Vina."

"Vina. Yes. I'm glad that you called."

"I wanted to get your input on something," I began. "It must have been an oversight, but I got an e-mail from Deb in Accounting, saying that the last check we cut to Wade was for five grand. They brought it to my attention since I was his manager. I wanted to let you know about the clerical error before I told them to cancel the check. I'll have them reissue one for the accurate amount, which is something like a thousand dollars, including severance pay."

"All right," he said, then cleared his throat. "Thank you for bringing that to my attention. I'll take care of it personally. You don't have to worry about it."

I squinted at a man who seemed to be changing his clothes before an open office window across the street.

"Are you sure? Because I can do it. It's only a matter of one phone call—"

"I am aware of that, Vina. Since it was just a mistake, let's not make a big deal of it." He brightened. "So, what do you say we talk about your performance review and bonus? Is this a good time?"

"It's as good a time as any." I tried to sound perky.

The man changing his clothes caught me staring, and gave me more of an eyeful than I cared to see. Namely, a view of his red lace panties and what was inside. I cringed, swiveling back to my desk.

"That it is. That it is. Can I assume you have had a chance to read over the written performance review we sent out via e-mail to you this morning?"

"I have," I lied.

"Then you know that the feedback, both from your managers and from your teammates, has been solid. And to add to that, I do want to tell you what a pleasure it has been to work with you this year. You put in the hours, and that has not gone unnoticed."

"Thank you. It's nice to hear that," I said.

"But let's be honest," he continued, "that much is expected of every man on this team. You bring more to the table. We see you moving into management because you are a real team player. Not a 'showboater.' Steven and I believe that you understand the importance of doing what's best for the firm, and we appreciate that. All things considered, we are more than pleased with your contribution. We look forward to your bringing even more enthusiasm to your work in the coming year. We have decided to give you a performance bonus of $30,000. We want to see you take that enthusiasm to the next level, moving forward. Keep up the good work."

"Really?" I couldn't hide the surprise in my voice.

"Is that a problem?"

"No. I mean…it's just…" I stumbled over my thoughts.

"Vina…is this something that we are going to have to discuss at length? Because I would like to get these performance reviews finished quickly, and I still have to talk with some of the other people on the team."

"No, Alan. Not at all. It's exactly what I expected, or I should say, *what I hoped I deserved.*"

"You're a smart girl, Vina," he practically snorted. "You'll go far at this firm."

By seven the next morning, I hadn't slept a wink. Another restless night had left me with bags under my eyes that were so large my entire head could have fit into them. I must have spent about twenty minutes trying to make sense of myself in the bathroom mirror. Before I knew it, however, I was running late for work. So I slapped my face with cold water, loaded on the concealer and told myself to *take it like a man.* Unlike some women, I didn't have time for this crap.

The last coat of powder was what did the trick, erasing almost every hint of uncertainty and emotion from my face. I breathed deep and then smiled, and the woman my colleagues were expecting smiled back at me. The firm didn't pay me to get in touch with my inner child, I reminded myself. They paid me well enough to hire it a sitter. And I had a job to do. One more deep breath and a posture check later, I was ready to face the day.

Even though my apartment building wasn't ritzy enough to employ a doorman to proactively deny them entry, non-residents never had an easy time getting in. The sad truth is that most New Yorkers will look you right in the eye while closing a door in your face. Their defense is that they have no way of knowing whether or not you're a homicidal lunatic. So, unless you have your own key, they can justi-fiably assume you've escaped from Bellevue, tossed your medication and been attempting to recommence your stalking of someone in the building. This cynicism is normally a bad thing for me. Like when I've got two arms full of groceries and am unable to locate my key, and my so-called neighbors still refuse to open the door.

Wednesday morning, however, their unwillingness to trust their fellow man made me feel very much as if they were on my side. When I left the building I found Jon waiting outside the door. He said he had been trying to get in for an hour. He was holding two venti Starbucks Caramel Macchiatos, and wearing a tie I had bought for him.

I will not give him the satisfaction of witnessing the joy with which I usually greet a Caramel Macchiato, I decided, *but I will give him the image of my backside as I walk away from him without missing a step.*

He held a cup out in my direction and I waved it away.

"Vina, wait. You've got to hear me out. This is ridiculous."

"Oh! You had a *child you never told me about,* and *my* behavior is ridiculous?"

Apparently, I wasn't so good at the unaffected facade.

"Look, I have to get to the office." I brushed past him. "Why don't we just both try to move on."

I had no plans to engage in this, and now I was running even later for work. I walked briskly to the subway, with my briefcase held close and my lips held tight. There was no way I'd let him hear my pain.

"Wait!" he yelled, as I struggled to disappear into the crowd.

I picked up the pace, weaved my way down the stairwell, and nearly knocked over an unsuspecting preteen. *How many casualties must this relationship claim?*

"Vina, come on!" I vaguely heard him say as he faded into the noise of the city.

The 7 train pulled into the station, and I made my way quickly toward the far end of the platform, managing to board the train just before the doors closed. I sandwiched myself between an elderly woman and the doors. She made no attempt to disguise her irritation, and the sign that was an inch from my eyes informed me that I shouldn't be leaning on the doors, either. It was cramped and stuffy. I had to close my eyes to steady my breath. Though at least I knew I was safe.

But not for long. I almost had my heart rate back to normal when I heard his voice again. *I couldn't believe I ever found comfort in that voice.* He must have boarded a different subway car and been pushing his way through the other commuters. Soon enough, I found myself cornered, along with the old lady, and a smirking teenager who immediately yanked off his headphones.

Fabulous. Now we had an audience.

"Just listen." His chest heaved as he grabbed an overhead railing to steady himself. I jerked away, and banged my arm.

"You haven't left me much of a choice, have you?" I rubbed at my elbow.

"Vina, I wouldn't have to chase you into a subway if you would answer the phone, or reply to Instant Messenger or even pay any attention to the singing telegram!"

"Don't you dare make this my fault. How dare you!" My forehead was getting hot. "How *dare you* do this to me? You don't even have the right to talk to me anymore. I am on my way to work and now you've got half of New York listening to our personal business."

"Vina, I—"

"I don't want to hear it!" My voice nearly cracked. "Do you have any idea how stupid that singing telegram made me look in front of my bosses?"

"You don't even like that job, Vina. You never have. This is me, I know you."

"First of all, don't…aaaargh!" I opened a shirt button; it was getting warm. "Just because I may not love what I do, does not mean I don't plan to do it well. That stupid singing horse sucked away at my credibility! And being my ex-boyfriend, you should have known that. Obviously, you were only paying attention when it was convenient."

"Okay, I'm sorry. Now that we're here, let me explain."

"No! There is no 'we' anymore. Don't you get that? It's gone. Evaporated. If you could lie to me the entire time, then there never *was* a 'we.' And now that we're here, let *me* explain. I am a good woman, you bastard."

"I know! That's why I'm following you all over Manhattan and embarrassing myself in front of all these people."

The train's passengers had fallen silent by that point. Most were listening intently, craning their necks and shushing one another to get a better show. My throat tightened with each additional pair of eyes on us.

"You want a medal for that?" I was becoming more flustered by the minute. "Let me make this really simple for you and for all of the people in this subway car who are probably going to go tell their entire goddamned offices about this. You cheated on me. You lied to me. I no longer give a damn what you have to say."

"I didn't love her. I love you!"

The old lady, who was now separated from me only by my briefcase, searched my face for some sign that I might give in.

"You HAD A CHILD WITH HER AND YOU NEVER TOLD ME," I yelled in his face, blinking away the beginnings of a tear.

Some nearby Goth kids whispered and giggled.

"It was just a one-night stand! One mistake! I knew you would never forgive me, so I kept it to myself. She only told me she was pregnant after four months, so then I thought, 'Now how can I tell you?'"

"Oh, so this is *my fault?* I was unreasonable to expect you not to *shtup* other women?"

All eyes were on him; even the old lady was now clearly on my side. A bald and goateed man towering over us in a leather jacket shook his head at Jon. A tattoo on his neck read "Feel The Pain."

"You messed up, buddy," he concluded with the grin of a man who had been there himself.

"Okay, look, I get that I should have told you sooner," Jon said. "But I thought you would leave me."

"Well, you never gave me that choice, did you?"

"If I *had* sat you down and told you, and given you the choice, then you would have left me. I didn't want to lose you."

"Is that supposed to be romantic? What you don't understand is that the loopholes don't matter."

"Vina, you don't always have to live by the book. You can do what you want to do sometimes, instead of what you think you're supposed to do. I know that you still love me. Do what your heart tells you."

"You're right, Jon," I said after a pause that was more than pregnant—it was six weeks past due. "Maybe I should live more by my heart. Maybe I would be happier. So here's what my heart is telling me right now, more than anything else. You and I are over. And I should care less about what anyone thinks about my choices, than about how I feel."

Jon was silent. The teenagers had lost interest. For the first time, I noticed my throat loosening up.

"I am so sorry, dear," the old lady chimed in.

"Don't do this, Vina," Jon whimpered.

"*You* did this," I told him, and stepped from the train.

★ ★ ★

I went straight to Cristina's apartment after work.

"I'm so sorry," she yelled, throwing her arms around me before I could get my own around her.

"No." I shook my head. "I'm sorry. I was wrong. I had no right to talk to you like that."

"But I had no right to submit that e-mail without asking you!" She gave me a pained smile.

"It's over," I said, feeling some of the tension drain out of my body. "Can we just forget about it?"

"As long as you know that I only want what's best for you, *chica*."

"So do I," I replied. "I wish I knew what that was sometimes. It's more than Jon. It's my whole life. I'm suffocating, Cristy. And I don't even know where to go for air."

·· 21 ··

Seeing Peter in jeans was almost as disconcerting as the first time I saw my mother in sneakers. We are not an athletic people. Peter was sitting on a soggy bench near a fountain in Central Park, wearing a baseball cap and two days' stubble. The alarm bells in my mind should have gone off at five-thirty that Thursday morning, when I was awoken by his call. Peter wasn't usually given to dramatic episodes. He had instructed me, without even so much as a *Good morning,* to meet him here within the hour.

I took a seat beside him, fixed my gaze solemnly on a man selling marijuana less than twenty yards away and whispered, "You're pregnant, right? Okay, look, I'll assume it's mine. And I want you to know that I'm here for you. We can go to a clinic and have this taken care of today."

"Is that supposed to be funny?" he nearly bit my head off. "What the hell is wrong with you?"

I was taken aback by the contempt in his voice.

"Peter," I put a hand to my chest and said, "I'm sorry. I…it's all this *cloak and dagger* stuff. You pull me out of bed at this ungodly hour and tell me to come here. You don't even explain what it's about."

"I think you should be taking this more seriously." He leaned on his knees, cupping his hands before him.

"Taking *what* more seriously, Peter? What's going on?"

He tilted his head as if to force me to admit that we both knew what he was talking about. My mouth fell open. He rose to his feet as Sarah approached us, and I (feeling as out of place as if I were at church) rose, too.

"Peter. Vina. What's going on?" she asked without looking at me.

"Look, guys," Peter began, pacing on the damp grass. "I didn't know what else to do. We've all worked together day-in, day-out for a long time now. I have to believe that means something. So I'm asking you to be honest with me. I really had a lot of respect for both of you…*have*. I *have* a lot of respect for you. I hope that I'm not wrong."

Sarah and I glanced at each other, shrugging in mutual confusion.

"The reason I called you both here to talk," he said then stopped and faced us, "was to tell you what's been going on, and to see if I can get any answers from you. Yesterday I was contacted and interviewed by SEC investigators. They believe the company—our team in particular—has been making trades with inside information. It's Alan and Steve, mainly. The SEC believes that both of you knew about the trades. And they have strong reasons to believe that you, Vina, were involved."

"What? Why…why?" I stammered, the air having been vacuumed from my windpipe. "Why would they think that? Which trades? Did you talk to Alan about this?"

"I can confidently say that my record is spotless, Peter. But I cannot speak for anyone else," Sarah testified, as if before Congress.

"Vina," Peter said in a softer voice, like he was coaxing the murderer to reveal the location of the bodies, "I need to know why you fired Wade."

"What? *Wade?*" I put a hand to my forehead. "Peter, I'm not supposed to discuss that. I was…told not to. But look, if this is between us, then I might as well. I fired him for sexual harassment."

"Wade? Who was he sexually harassing? How *could* he sexually harass anyone? He was an intern." He was now talking at me as if I were insane.

"A secretary," I practically whispered.

"Which one?" Sarah demanded.

"I can't tell you." I was getting dizzy.

"Why not?"

"Because I don't know, okay? Alan and Steve told me to do it. Look, what does Wade have to do with this, anyway?"

"That's not why *he* thinks he was fired. He's a key witness for the SEC. He claims that he walked in on Alan while he was on the phone with a source in Taiwan. That's how they knew to make that investment in Luxor. Wade went to the SEC saying that we tried to buy him off. And now they have pressed charges against the entire team. You've been named in the suit, since you terminated him. Vina, as my friend, I am asking you to tell me what you know. This is my *career* here."

I could see the fear in his eyes. "Well, his last check *was* larger than usual, but I was told it was severance."

"Since when do we give interns severance?" Sarah asked. "And why didn't this raise any red flags for you, Vina?"

"It did." I sank back onto the wet bench, trying to collect my thoughts. "But it wasn't exactly severance. You see, Alan said he would take care of it."

"I need to get home and think about what I'm gonna do." Peter shook his head. "I was hoping to get some answers here. Apparently, all we were was coworkers. One last question, Vina. What was your bonus this year?"

I couldn't look at them when I said it. "It was…thirty grand."

Peter backed away from me as if he had just seen the blood on my hands.

Sarah, sensing that I was dangerously close to feeling sorry for myself, added her own two cents. "Vina, how the hell could you let this happen?"

Satisfied with the image of me dumbfounded, mouth agape and frozen in place, Sarah decided that she wasn't interested in hearing my answer. She walked off into the midmorning chill.

Like bulldozers across a crime scene before you have had a chance to collect all the evidence, time rolls most aggressively when we are unprepared. I walked the entire thirty blocks home from the park, feeling more light-headed with every step. On the way, I left a voice mail for Cristina, attempting to explain, without the benefit of a clear mind or a complete vocabulary, that the SEC was investigating me for complicity in insider trading. Real friends are those with whom you can be incoherent.

When I got home, I couldn't bring myself to take off my shoes or coat, to allow myself a seat on the couch, or even to pour myself a glass of water. Apparently, after so many years of accepting the authority of my parents, elders, teachers and everybody else, I had reached the point where I was nearly incapable of questioning it at all. As a professional woman it occurred to me that even with the best of intentions that kind of attitude meant I was a fraud. So I just stood inside my apartment, wondering at how unfamiliar it felt, wanting to be anywhere but inside my own life.

·· 22 ··

On the morning of her wedding day, my mother stood alone in the kitchen of the home where her parents had raised her. She was watching for the chai to boil and she was waiting for a sign. The astrologers and swamis had been consulted, her parents and in-laws-to-be had mutually approved and she had willingly consented to give her hand in marriage. Her groom was a tall, twenty-nine-year-old engineer from America; the son of a police chief and the pride of a Punjabi Brahmin family. During her one and only meeting with him a few weeks earlier, she had found something comforting in his ways, spied some evidence of affection in his face. Even though Hindus believe that spouses are linked karmically through seven lifetimes, this young woman, having left her fate in the hands of the gods when she nodded her consent, found herself feeling uneasy.

Motionless, she surveyed the contents of the room,

inhaling the smells and memorizing the stillness of the air in the only home she had ever known. Silently, she stirred cardamom seeds among the tea bags in the pot of boiling water, and she began to imagine the shape her new life might take. Then, in the moment before her anticipation could round a corner toward dismay, the unexpected occurred. A salamander lost its grip on the ceiling above my mother and plummeted earthward, bouncing off of her head and then onto the floor. As the lizard scurried away from her imposing presence, she smiled. And she exhaled. She was confident now that today was an auspicious day.

I had never accepted the idea that everything happens for a reason; partially because Hinduism implies a far more complex web of causation, and partially because free will is so precious to me. In my estimation, things happen and we learn to carry on. Eventually, out of some need to make sense of our lives, we cite the good as proof that the bad was necessary, since it must somehow have made way for what came afterward. But I had yet to see any sign that things were meant to unfold a certain way. There were moments when my eyes refused to refocus a situation into any other, and when it became clear that there was no longer any point in trying to deny the obvious.

There aren't too many ways for a girl to interpret waking up with her face on the cold, dirty tile of an elevator stuck between the twenty-second and twenty-third floors of the downtown office building where SEC investigators are anxiously preparing to depose her. I could say that I had no idea why all of this was happening to me, but that would be a lie. I knew that it was happening because I had the audacity to speculate aloud whether things could get any worse. And life prides itself on being ironic in only the most twistedly poetic ways. Curled around my purse on the floor of that elevator, it seemed as if for most of the morning I had been in a dream.

At six a.m. I had called my parents, hoping to explain what was going on, and to tell them I was likely out of a job.

"We know, honey." My mother's voice explained, "We saw it in the newspaper. Daddy and I are on our way to your apartment."

The lines and edges of the world began to blur. I scanned the walls and then the ceiling of my apartment, wondering how everyone could remain so calm. My insides shivered and then resettled, and everything sprang sharply back into focus. I felt nothing. Methodically, I donned my robe, unlocked my front door, bent down and reached for the morning paper. And that's when my legs went weak because there, staring back at me from page one of the business section, was a photograph of myself and all of my colleagues at last year's company Christmas party. Drunk, merry and sporting matching Santa's hats bearing the company logo, we were bloatedly toasting in front of the camera. From where I sat now, we looked as if we not only knew but were proud of what we were: cocky Wall Street fat-cats, high on champagne and corruption. Behind us stood an opulently decorated, forty-foot Christmas tree, and above us hovered a large, bold headline claiming "Their Greed Knew No Bounds."

By the time my mother and father let themselves into my apartment, I was on my knees in the bathroom, clinging to the toilet bowl as if it were a lover who was trying to leave me. While I didn't remember eating anything the night before, I felt confident that I had already vomited at least half of my body weight. But the physical reaction didn't agree with the emotional. Inside, I could have sworn that I felt nothing. My mother knelt beside me and smoothed the spit-soaked hair from my face. Looking into her kind and eager eyes, I realized the worst part of it all; that the problem with compartmentalizing parts of your life so well is that when your life falls apart those who want to help you won't even know where to begin looking for the pieces. And surrounded by people who want to help, you will wind up feeling that much more alone.

My lack of coherence stripped away my already shaky ability to censor myself. And that was when I made the mistake of challenging the gods, via my mother, by asking her whether things could possibly get any worse.

So it was fitting that after I pulled myself together, explained the situation to my parents and marched down to the offices of the SEC investigators, who had called and demanded my presence there that morning, the elevator would labor its way past the twenty-second floor before deciding that it was in no mood to go farther.

And then the lights went out.

Note to self: This might be a good time to look in to "random-anvil-falling-on-head" and perhaps "flying-pigs-inflicting-concussions" insurance.

Just after the elevator stopped, I decided that this was comical. It had to be. The universe was testing me. Perhaps this was the final hurdle, to see if I were strong enough not to lose it, right? Right. So I could beat this simply by practicing the deep-breathing technique discussed in the online chat room where I found the information about the St. Agnes Closeted Claustrophobes meeting. No problem. Piece of cake. At this point there was nothing left to do but laugh at myself.

Laugh at myself, and of course, press the emergency button. So I did. But it didn't light up. Naturally, the cabinet containing the courtesy phone was locked. Not surprisingly, I was the only person in the elevator. Predictably, I had left my purse-size use-in-case-of-emergency crowbar at home.

Wait a minute, how did that breathing technique go again? Was I supposed to breathe through my mouth, or my nose? Was I supposed to hold in my stomach? Oh, my god, my pants felt tight. In fact, everything was starting to feel tight....

My heartbeat had broken into a sprint. *Don't worry about it, Vina. Be reasonable,* I told myself. *I'm sure someone has noticed that the elevator is stuck. Help must be on the way.* The problem, however, was that oxygen was running out, and I was having trouble stifling the twitch in my right eye.

Don't lose control, Vina. You're better than that. Don't make this a bigger deal than it has to be. I backed myself into a corner, while reminding myself to remain calm. *It will be fine,* I heard voices resembling my parents' telling me. *And this is no time to be dramatic or overly emotional.*

Trembling, I clutched at my purse to rummage around inside for my cell phone. Things would be clearer, and I would be more reasonable if I could talk to people and make sure they knew I was trapped. *Trapped, but not alone.* I flipped open the phone, and then realized that it couldn't get a signal.

I was alone, and that was it.

I began banging furiously against the elevator doors, pounding and shrieking so that help might hear me. At some point, I know I must have paused to remove my shoe and used it instead of the palm of my hand, which was beginning to go raw.

After a minute, a day, or some stretch of time in between, there came a voice from above. "Hello, ma'am? Are you all right?"

I noticed that the cell phone on the floor provided just enough blue light to illuminate the reflection of a crazy-looking woman in the steel doors before me. And once I saw her, I froze. *Who was that woman?*

Whoever she was, she apparently felt the need to sound calm for the benefit of that voice from above because she answered, "Yes…y…yes. I am. It's fine. I'm fine."

"Don't you worry about a thing," he continued, "we'll have you out of there as soon as the repairman gets here."

"Um, okay," she yelled back.

I marveled at how she could sound so steady while appearing so atrociously unwell. The dichotomy was frightening. *How can you act so serene when everything is so wrong?* I wondered. *How can you function at all?*

"We're doing everything we can, ma'am. Please remain calm," he added a few seconds later.

And she did. She continued taking orders from above and proceeded to smooth her hair and take a seat there on the floor of the elevator, like a robot, never questioning anything. Never questioning anyone. Refusing even to react to the reality laid out before her, which was that breathing was getting harder, that her chest was feeling tighter and that she was beginning to feel dizzy. She just sat there like an idiot, letting it happen to her.

The lights suddenly flickered on. I blinked at my reflection and thought I looked ridiculous. Why did I take the time to match my earrings with my shirt that morning? Or my pantsuit with those damned alligator shoes Jon had always adored? Why hadn't I thrown them out a long time ago? Why hadn't I thrown them at the back of his head? Why hadn't I spoken up against my bosses' firing Wade? *Who did I think I was fooling?*

For all the effort I was willing to put into meaningless details like accessorizing this outfit, why wasn't I willing to put in the effort to prevent myself from suffocating under the weight of everybody's expectations? I backed away from my reflection, sliding along the floor, trying to suck in some air. Finally, I steadied myself against the far wall. There was sweat on my forehead and a knot growing inside my chest. The elevator jerked. And so did something vital inside me. Like any rational person whose life had already been coming apart at the seams, emotionally, professionally and now mentally at the same time, I forgot myself entirely.

"Just relax. Please remain calm. Everything is gonna be fine," the man from above yelled again. Maybe twenty seconds later, I was rocking back and forth with my face in my hands.

"Is everything all right?" the moron was now asking the woman who was trapped in an elevator dangling some twenty floors above ground. The air around her slowly depleted.

This would be the moment when she finally allowed herself to lose it. She was yelling and banging on her reflection in the doors. She kicked the walls and yanked at the neck of her shirt, with tears and mascara streaking down her face. When finally she tired, she was gasping for air. And then she collapsed from the inside out, and sank straight down onto the floor. She was mumbling about how nothing was anywhere near all right. How she had managed to ruin everything, and how she had no one to blame but herself.

·· 23 ··

I awoke to a jerk as the elevator resumed its ascent to the twenty-third floor. They were still expecting me. When the doors opened, the building superintendent and SEC investigators found me, purse in hand, crouching in the far corner of the elevator, still groggy from exhaustion and the shock of such an unprecedented torrent of emotion. Without moving I asked through a dry mouth, "Water, please?"

But the voice that responded was not one I was expecting.

"Sure, Vina. Sure you can. Let's just get you out of here first."

I turned and looked up into comforting brown eyes. It was Prakash, and he was reaching out a hand.

"What? What's going on?" I attempted.

"We understand that you've retained Mr. Shah as your legal counsel in this matter, ma'am," one of two sweaty, middle-aged men was telling me from outside the elevator.

"But we're going to have to request that he remain silent during this deposition."

I opened my mouth, confused.

"He *is* your legal counsel, isn't he?" the investigator asked, once I had risen to my feet.

"Um, he…well, yes, I think?" I questioned in Prakash's direction.

"I saw it in the paper this morning. It seemed like they had been investigating and gathering evidence secretly for months, so I assumed they would be bringing you in for your deposition immediately, before the press had the chance to get near you. I made some calls to a friend at the DA's office to find out where they would be deposing you, and volunteered to act as your legal counsel," Prakash explained, holding my arm. "I thought you might need the support."

"Yes." I cleared my throat, grateful for whatever made Prakash decide to be there for me. "Mr. Shah is my lawyer."

"My name is Thomas Segal," the older of the two SEC investigators stated, waving Prakash and me toward two stiff-backed chairs on one side of a conference table. "Do you know why we've summoned you here?"

I'm thinking it's because they've gotten wind of the message that life had been trying to impress upon me—that I was wholly incapable of managing my own affairs, and should therefore not be allowed to play with the other children. Instead of sharing all this, I answered, "You're investigating my firm. I'm here to cooperate. Completely."

"Well, that will make things easier for everyone involved,

ma'am." The sweatier interrogator picked up where his partner had left off. "And your cooperation will cause the authorities to look more favorably upon you."

"I've got nothing to hide," I murmured, sinking a bit into my seat. Prakash pressed my hand reassuringly.

"Then let's get started. You remember researching the possibility of an acquisition by Luxor Corporation in November of this year, I'm sure. What was your recommendation on that investment?" Sweaty asked.

"I…I recommended against making that investment. Nothing in the financials justified it."

"And when your bosses made the investment anyway, what did you think?" Oldie, who also turned out to be Meaney, barked.

"I thought they were better at making investment decisions than I was."

"Mmm-hmm." Sweaty leafed through some papers theatrically. "And I'm sure you recall a former intern by the name of Wade Smith, whom you fired?"

"Yes." I realized where this was headed, and began chewing on my bottom lip.

"It has been reported to us that you terminated his internship due to budgetary constraints. Is that true?"

"Well—" I began.

"In a year when your firm was doing so well—" Meaney cut me off "—it hardly seems reasonable that you would need to fire an intern to cut costs."

All eyes were on me.

"I…I can explain. Alan and Steve—my bosses—told me

that Wade was sexually harassing a secretary. I was instructed to fire him on these grounds, so I did."

Sweaty and Oldie looked at each other, smirking in a way that made me more uncomfortable than an aging rock star in a room full of women his own age.

Sweaty turned toward me. "And did you tell Wade this?"

"No." I looked down, averting my gaze from Prakash.

"Why not?" Meaney leaned in.

"Because they told me not to."

"And did you investigate these claims of sexual harassment?"

"No."

"Why not?"

"I trusted my bosses."

They paused. Oldie rose to his feet, took a few paces and stared out the window. "That's it?"

"That's the truth."

"Ms. Chopra, how long have you worked on Wall Street?"

"Almost five years." I chewed on the rim of my almost empty paper cup.

"And have you felt, in general, over that period of time, that your compensation was commensurate with the value you provided?"

"Yes, I…I think so."

"Ms. Chopra, is it true that your performance bonus is based in large part on the accuracy of your investment recommendations?"

I nodded.

"And how did the accuracy of your recommendations this year compare with those which you made in previous years?"

"This year I was wrong more than usual," I begrudgingly admitted.

"Can you please tell us, for our records, what was the amount of your annual performance bonus this year?"

"Thirty thousand." I struggled to get comfortable in my seat.

"You are no doubt aware that your coworkers have all reported significantly lower than expected bonuses this year. Did you think their bonuses were fair?"

"Well, no," I hesitated, "I didn't."

They paused. "And how did you, in your own mind, account for that discrepancy?" Oldie asked.

"I guess I didn't."

Meaney sat back, satisfied. My stomach growled. Prakash continued squeezing my hand.

"You didn't," he repeated, as if he had heard about as much as he could take from me. "One last question before we get into the specifics. Are you familiar with a company called Globecom?"

Dear God, why me?

"Ms. Chopra?"

"Um, yes. Kind of. I mean I've never researched them, but I am familiar with them, in a way. I met one of their VPs socially once," I said carefully. "At a bar."

"Mmm-hmm. And would it surprise you to hear that your bosses made a sizeable investment in Globecom two weeks ago?"

"Yes…I mean, no," I struggled. "I mean, we never researched them. I never researched them. This is the first I'm hearing of any investment in them."

"And you say you knew one of their VPs personally?"

"No, not personally. Socially. I mean…not socially, either, really."

Sweaty was starting to look more like Meaney, Meaney was starting to look a lot like a sadistic creep and I was starting to get more than a little bit sweaty.

"Well, which one is it, Miss Chopra? Did you know him or did you not know him?" he said, about five inches from my face.

"I *met* him. Once. At a bar. And he was bragging about being a VP at Globecom and having made a major acquisition and wanting to celebrate it. But…I mean, he didn't know who I was or anything, and… Oh, my god!" I sat up straighter, as if I were actually witnessing the pieces of the puzzle falling into place. "I told Alan and Steve about that night. Are you telling me that they made the decision to invest based on what that jerk told me?"

Oldie replied, "From what we can gather, they recognized that any major acquisition deal would signal a huge jump in Globecom's stock price the next morning. So they took the information you gave them, and decided to buy early and sell for a large profit a few hours later. In light of the firm's abnormal profits on Luxor, we had been watching the trading activity closely, and noticed that the Globecom shares were purchased and unloaded abnormally quickly. Your bosses knew exactly what to do with the information you gave them."

"But I didn't *give them* that information," I pleaded with everyone in the room. "I swear I wasn't even thinking about it that way. I mentioned the jerk from Globecom in passing because Alan asked me why I was upset. I mean, that guy had been such a slime. He honestly expected me to go back to his hotel room because he was bragging about closing that acquisition deal. Alan acted like he was trying to console me. I can't believe he would turn around and trade on that information."

Sweaty McMeanington folded his arms across his chest, studying me for a while. "You expect us to believe that you had no idea."

"No, I don't expect you to. I can see how bad this looks, but…I need you to. I swear I had no idea. I swear it. You have to believe me."

Eyes wide, I pushed across the table toward them, reaching out almost physically even as my head was spinning, recalling all the conversations I had with Alan and Steve, Denny and Wade, and Peter and everyone else at the firm. The pattern became so obvious. They had traded on the Luxor deal despite my recommendation because they *did* have an inside source in Taiwan. Wade must have discovered the truth, and really been fired for that reason. And then they bought Globecom stock with no regard for the rules of information. And my bonus was merely strategic because they wanted to make it look like I was an accomplice! I looked to Prakash for some sign that I was even the least bit believable, and to my surprise, he gave it to me. He nodded his head to encourage me to continue.

"Oh, you *swear? Cross your heart?* Are you kidding us with this?" Segal raised his voice, standing and planting both meaty hands down on the table so he could look down at me. "Do you expect me to believe that a woman like you, a woman who has managed to excel in a cutthroat world like Wall Street finance, where men normally control everything, a woman who is clearly as independent and aware of her surroundings as anyone, and a woman who got a bonus *three times* the size of any of her colleagues this year, after making more than one bad recommendation, would fire her own intern without investigating allegations of sexual misconduct, and take her bosses' words for granted *entirely?* You actually expect us to believe that you could have been so completely and conveniently ignorant of what was going on right in front of your pretty nose? Little girl, you can't expect us to be that naive, and you can't possibly be that naive yourself!"

I buried my face in my hands, and mumbled.

"What was that?"

"I said…" And felt the tears start to stream down my face. "Apparently…I *can.*"

·· 24 ··

After the interrogation, Prakash and I stood facing each other outside the building, alone for the first time since we were in my parents' kitchen.

I fixed my gaze intently on a gum wrapper on the sidewalk. "So, do you think I did okay in there?"

"Considering the circumstances," he said, scratching the back of his neck, "yes."

"Do you think," I added, biting my lip, "do you think that I might have to go to jail?"

"No." He looked me squarely in the eye. "I mean, not if you're willing to cooperate and give them any additional information they might need concerning your bosses' misconduct. But we'll cross that bridge when we get to it, Vina."

"Thanks for saying *we*. I know you don't owe me anything."
Silence.

I had to ask, "Don't you want to ask me if I did it?"

He smiled in that same reassuring way that let me know he wouldn't drop me at the wedding. "I don't have to ask you that. Deep down you're a nice Indian girl from Long Island, one who would never do anything like this."

"Listen, Prakash." I held his arm. "I need to apologize to you for my behavior at the family dinner on Saturday night. It was unfair."

Prakash shrugged. "No, Vina, you were right. About that, anyway. And I have to apologize for pulling you into my problems. The truth is that your outburst in the kitchen was the kick in the butt I needed. So in a way, I do owe you something. I came out of the closet to my parents the next day."

"Oh, my gosh. I don't know what to say. Look, it wasn't fair for me to judge you. And I am happy for you that you managed to take that step with your parents, but that's a separate issue. I shouldn't have lashed out at you just because your friend Nick turned out to be a pornographer. I have to take responsibility for the choices I made that night, and one of them was going home with him."

"What are you talking about?" He wrinkled his eyebrows, confused. "Nick really liked you. He told me you ran out the next morning without even thanking him."

"Thanking him? For what?"

"Wait a minute, what are you talking about? Nick's a lot of things, but he is not a pornographer. Where did you get that idea?"

"From the video cameras and videotapes I found aimed at the bed I woke up naked in that morning. But like I said, look, it's not your problem. I've got too many other things to worry about right now, anyway."

"No, I think it is my problem. And I think you misunderstood. Nick's not that kind of guy. He's using that video equipment to make a workout video that will be sold through a national distributor. It's a business idea he's been working on for a while."

I blinked.

"Was that what you thought happened on Friday night?" he asked. "No. You're way off. What happened was that your friend Christopher had left the club with me, and your girlfriends were nowhere to be found, so Nick didn't want to leave you alone since you were so drunk and upset. And when he got you into a taxi to make sure you got home safe, you passed out before you could tell him where you lived. Your cell phone and wallet had disappeared, so he had no choice but to take you to his place. Didn't you notice your wallet was missing the next morning?"

"Of course," I said. "I canceled my credit cards the next day, and was just grateful that I had enough loose cash to get home."

"Well, you regained consciousness in his apartment, saying you felt disgusting because you had vomited. So you showered to sober up, and then fell asleep in his bed. Nick slept on the couch. And he was insulted when you left without even thanking him in the morning. The thing is, he really liked you. So I was pissed off because I thought that you were blowing him off just because you were mad at me."

"You mean we didn't…"

"No, Vina. I've known Nick for a long time. He's not that kind of guy. You were completely out of it, and that's not something that he would find attractive. For god's sake, he's not some horny frat boy."

"Prakash, I guess…I guess it looks like I made an honest mistake."

"No, Vina. It looks like you made a snap judgment about a nice guy, and exercised no judgment when it came to your bosses."

"But I…I didn't know…and I didn't remember…I had no idea," I stuttered.

"There's a lot you don't know about Nick," Prakash said. "And about a lot of other things, too."

"Well, I'd like to apologize to him."

Prakash shook his head. "I think it's too late for that, Vina. You should probably move on. Try to work some of this stuff out on your own."

·· 25 ··

My strategy to cope with the crap that life dumps on me goes something like this:

(1) Make an unrecognizable and quite unladylike sound. Somewhere between a burp, a shriek and a whimper.

(2) Go home and change into more comfortable and less flattering clothes. Avoid all mirrors. Lock doors, close windows and draw shades.

(3) Curl up into an emotional and physical fetal position on my couch, insulated by heaps of blankets and pillows, and surrounded by a protective moat of take-out menus and remote controls.

(4) Blame myself for not having seen it coming (whatever it was), blame trans fat and the NRA for making the world such a complicated place to live in and long

for a simpler time when most people were decent, so women didn't always have to know better.

(5) Commence calling cheap knockoffs of The Psychic Hotline (although I would never admit this to any of my friends), while consoling myself that at least it's cheaper than calling the family-condoned Sadhus (Read: real psychics masquerading as holy men and providing birth-chart and palm readings) back in India.

This time my disillusionment took me far beyond the kind of solace that any tele-psychic or Tivo might provide. Short of actually divorcing the world, I found myself filing for a trial separation in the form of a plane ticket to Fiji. My parents weren't happy about it, and my friends were more than concerned, but I knew it was something I had to do. And nobody was going to stop me.

After a rather swift trial, Alan and Steve wound up in some white-collar prison, serving five to ten years for trading on insider information. Wade's sullied reputation was eventually re-shined and infused with a large cash settlement for wrongful termination. Sarah quit and was immediately hired by another company, and Denny decided to apply to graduate school. Peter was the only team member who was promoted, largely because they needed someone diplomatic and trustworthy enough to repair the client relationships that had been ripped to shreds by the scandal.

For my part, I hadn't been to the office in two weeks, since that day when I made my way home from the SEC investigators' offices. Thankfully, I could rest assured that my professional reputation was refortified, since phone taps on Alan's and Steve's personal lines had reportedly cleared me of any wrongdoing. Within ten days of my deposition, I was informed that I was no longer a suspect as far as the SEC was concerned, and that I would never formally be charged. Rather than celebrating, I found myself unable to pull my attention away from the question of how I had wound up in that situation in the first place. I huddled in my apartment with my thoughts and my regrets, and just when I would begin to feel like the dust around my professional earthquake was beginning to settle, my guilt over having trusted Jon for so long would resurface. Honestly, there were times when I couldn't see a way out.

Meanwhile, Human Resources had me listed as taking advantage of a "temporary leave of absence," while they tried to decide what the heck to do with me. I took a far more circuitous route back to stability than did any of my coworkers, but in truth it was because I had far more to learn. Far worse than Jon or work or any one thing in particular, it was the no longer avoidable pattern emerging in my life that I had to sit still and make sense of. I was trying to understand how and why I had let things get to that point. I was trying to find the common thread between my obliviousness to Jon's true character, my bosses' true motives and my inability to voice and to question. At the root of it was: How did all of those themes intersect, and why had I failed to protect and to stand up for myself? The weight of that question was more than frightening; it was paralyzing.

Countless voice mails from friends, family and reporters went unanswered until Cristina and Pam eventually forced their way into my apartment. Cristy threatened to shave off my eyebrows unless I would consent to a shower. Pamela cleaned my apartment even though she had never in her life had to clean her own. Then they both dragged me to a therapist for the first of three visits they had taken the liberty of scheduling and paying for in advance. I was almost jolted out of my emotional state by the disappointment in Cristy's eyes when I failed to laugh at the joke she made about my being a mustache trim and a bottle of aftershave away from being a man. But I was simply too disengaged to pay any attention to the rational knowledge that I ought to care.

During our first meeting we just stared at each other. Suzanne was the type of therapist, I came to realize, who waited for the patient to begin the conversation. She was a young-looking forty-five, wearing a deep-pumpkin-colored shirt, brown leather vest and matching pants, and a smile that made me ask if I might be wearing a straitjacket that I simply couldn't see. So I averted my gaze, instead examining my fingers as if discovering them anew, which probably made me look like I was crazy. Or like I thought I had done something wrong. That made me feel defensive. So I spent the better part of my time giving her dirty, suspicious looks. And after our first hour of silence was over, Cristina took me home.

During our second meeting, the following day, I asked Suzanne why she wasn't saying anything. Her thoughts were not important, she explained; mine were. When I asked her if she thought I needed therapy, she said what was important was if I thought I did. When I told her that my friend had forced me to come, she told me nobody was forcing me to stay. But she said it in a way that implied only a weaker psychological being would choose to leave, rather than work through her issues. Despite my monumental resentment of her and of Cristina and of everyone else in the world, I decided to stay in the chair. Somehow the prospect of being judged inferior by this complete stranger was more than I could bear.

"I don't mean to be rude, Suzanne, but you don't know me or my problems," I finally offered.

"Why don't you tell me about them? I want to know about them," she explained, and then added after the cynicism registered on my face, "I care."

She *cared*. And the hostage negotiator was always on the bank robber's side.

"You can't believe that I care?"

Well, I *could* believe it. Theoretically, I *could believe* whatever I wanted to.

"It's not that. It's just…I mean, no offense, but you're being *paid* to care."

"You don't think I would care if I weren't being paid?"

"No, that's not what I said. But you're not my friend, by the nature of this relationship. You're my doctor."

"Your problems are valid, Vina. Why is it that you feel the need to place me into only one category?"

"I don't know…I mean, I don't." I suddenly felt as if I

were trying to explain the importance of financial planning to a teenage pop star with her first record deal.

"You seem frustrated."

"Look, I'm not a mental case. There's just too much going on for me to explain to someone I don't know."

"Do you think it might help to try?"

"No."

"Can you explain why not?"

"No, I can't. That's just it. I cannot explain anything. There's so much going on in my mind right now. How can you understand my situation? I don't even understand my situation. Everything in my professional life and romantic life fell apart and I didn't even see it coming. So how the hell am I supposed to explain what happened to a stranger?" I blurted out, before bursting into sobs.

"Well, if you can't tell me what happened, can you tell me what you want?" she asked, carefully handing me a box of Kleenex.

"I want my life back."

"You want to be happy again."

"Mmmm- huhhh."

"What does that mean?"

"I want my life back. I'm sick of being so angry with myself and with everything around me."

Similar to the morning when I woke up on my floor between Christopher and his cat, I went home that night thinking something had to change. Shuttling between my cave and this woman's office wasn't going to help me; I had to find a way to help myself. The only problem was I didn't know how.

Our third meeting lasted all of five minutes. I walked into Suzanne's office, sat down, and she informed me that she would be recommending that I start taking medication. Zoloft, it was called. She felt that it would stabilize me so that I could "focus on dissecting my feelings and laying them out in a way that we could more comfortably address."

I remember watching her mouth form the words. I remember asking myself how could she think that diminishing my control over my mind would ever help me feel like I wasn't going to lose it. She knew nothing about how bad my judgment had been, and already had the audacity to want to steal from me what little of it I had left. I wanted to explain all of this to her, but that was the moment, sitting on the rubbery chair in her office that made unpleasant sounds whenever I sat, rose or shifted my weight, when I acknowledged that I was the only person who could think my way back to trusting myself and the world. My own thoughts were all I had. It wasn't a dismissal of the psychiatric process. It was a reaction to the idea of getting stock tips from someone who kept all of their money in real estate.

"I am the only person who has to live inside my own head," I explained to a surprised and concerned Cristina through the phone the next morning, while searching the Internet for the cheapest airfares to Fiji. "So how can anybody ever understand this *for* me?"

"I can accept that, Vina. But why do you have to run away?"

"This is not about running away."

"A meditation retreat? In Fiji? For two weeks? Listen to yourself, Vina."

I was listening to myself, I thought; and perhaps for the very first time. Still, I understood why it must have sounded ridiculous. To be honest, even I wasn't completely sure where all of this would take me. But I had some time off work, and some money saved up, and I had spent the previous sleepless night staring at my ceiling, racking my brain for some idea of the next step I should take. Suddenly, around five a.m., the answer came to me: Vipassana. It was a type of meditation I had heard of years earlier, which promised nonreligious guidance on the path to self-knowledge and healing. A quick Web search had revealed the rest. Special meditation centers the world over were fully funded by donations, and claimed to provide free intensive meditation guidance to those who were seeking it. While most classes were fully booked months in advance, I decided it must be some sort of sign that the only available slot within the next three months was for a retreat beginning just a few days later, and on the other side of the world.

Naturally, I was nervous, although I was far more frightened of the idea of losing my resolve. And I would rather have eaten my own foot at that point than spend one more minute with the status quo. I needed a change. And I needed Cristy's support.

"Cristy, you're starting to sound like my parents."

She wasn't about to give in. "Well, good. I'm worried about you. And speaking of them…have you told them about this yet?"

A few hours later, I did. And in their defense, few parents (Indian or otherwise) would have been comfortable with a move like this, even if their only daughter hadn't been in the middle of a nervous breakdown.

"I need to be alone, Mom and Dad," I told them through the phone while hauling out my suitcase from the depths of my closet. Attempting to explain why they shouldn't expect me to call when I was away was tricky.

"I need to be away from anything and anyone that makes me question the validity of what I'm going through. You still don't accept the reality of my claustrophobia, much less my relationships. And you don't realize that you should respect me more for trying to find help. But it's not my place to change the way you look at things, especially before I learn to change myself. Honestly, I've got to start trusting myself, and taking better care of myself. I'm tired. And maybe what you do is the best you can do, considering how you were raised. But it doesn't help me right now. I need to figure some things out for myself, without the stress of having to justify anything to anyone. So, please understand."

I tried my best as to why it had to be in Fiji. I tried my best as to why this seemed like my last chance to get a grip before I gave in and decided to blot out every thought entirely. My parents tried their conflicted best to understand, and they insisted on seeing me off at the airport.

Nani held my face between her hands before the security checkpoint at JFK.

"I'm not crazy, Nani. I am trying to figure things out."

"*Beti,* sometimes you try too hard to be a good girl. I couldn't be more proud of you. You are finally doing something for yourself. Remember, *beti*. *Jo undher se athha hai.* What comes from inside is what matters. And if it tells you to go to India or Fiji or Timbuktu, then for God's sake, go. Yes, you are a strong girl, but if that *shaanti* inside is disturbed, nothing else will ever be good in your life. And I can see that your *shaanti*, your peace, has been disturbed."

My parents mustered smiles from a few steps behind her. I smiled back and then leaned in to whisper in her ear, "Will Mom and Dad be okay?"

She bent down, lifted my backpack and held it out to me. "You let me deal with them."

As it turned out, they had already managed to start dealing with themselves. I found the following note tucked inside my backpack somewhere high above the clouds a few hours later.

Beti,

It is not so easy for us to understand why you had to go to the other side of the world, when you have a family here that loves you and only wants to help. We believe that a person should be with their family at times like this. Maybe we didn't pay enough attention to some parts of your life. Though it was not with the intention of making you feel ignored. Just remember one thing: there is a school for almost every skill in life, but there is no school where you can learn how to be a parent. It is the most important job we have, but it is also the only one thing which nobody can ever teach you. Take your time, and do whatever you need to do.

We believe that peace of mind is a choice, but perhaps it is not always so. Be safe. Find your own *shaanti, beti*. We are here for you whenever you need us.

Love,
Mom and Dad

·· 26 ··

"Observe your sensations. Do not react to them."

The meditation leader's voice came from every direction as I struggled to sit perfectly still. My right leg had fallen asleep, my back was beginning to ache and the wool blanket in which I was wrapped mercilessly tickled my left cheek. And keeping my eyes shut for any length of time was driving me insane.

Serious meditation is about as exciting as an audit, and about as easy as trying to convince your hair not to grow. But in the best of cases, it can be emotional detox. It requires patience, seclusion and a complete disinterest in returning to your actual life; and at times it felt like forcing nails down the chalkboards inside my mind. If it hadn't been for the fact that I desperately feared returning to New York without anything to show for it, I probably would have crawled out of a window by the end of the first night. Sitting still had never been my forte.

"Whenever you find your mind wandering into the troubles of the external world, simply bring it back to observations. Be aware of the emotion just as you are aware of the physical sensation. It might be tickling or prickling or hot or cold or itching. It might be anger or regret. Do not be frustrated with your mind. Simply observe your mind's behavior and laughingly bring it back to the observation of the physical sensations of this moment. Focus on the breath."

I was sitting myself into a coma in the meditation room of a secluded retreat in Fiji, along with forty-nine other seekers-of-mental-stability, all of whom were clearly better at this than I was. I knew this because, even though I wasn't supposed to, I kept opening my eyes to check if everyone else's were closed. They always were. The only person who was having a worse go of it than me had been sobbing for the past twenty minutes. The meditation must have begun to take its effect, since my auditory perception had been sharpened enough for me to deduce, without so much as looking in that direction, that she was seated two rows before me and to my left. Day One was brutal.

Group-directed Vipassana meditation was a centuries-old peace-seeking technique requiring a strict vow of abstinence, silence and vegetarianism, along with the renunciation of reading, writing, television or any other external stimulants for the duration of an eleven-day introductory retreat. The sexes were separated, and encouraged to focus inward. Even eye contact was discouraged. So by the end of Day One all I really knew for sure was that of the two sets of feet sharing my bedroom, neither had apparently ever met with a pedicure.

Day Two wasn't quite as bad as the first. Still, I wondered how I managed to land in what felt like an adult version of television's *Brat Camp*. The daily schedule was as follows:

6:00 a.m.—Retreat volunteers ring a wake-up bell. Students leap out of bed and make their way to pre-assigned spots in the gender-separated meditation hall, settle atop pillows, wrap themselves in blankets and begin meditating in total silence.

8:00 a.m.—Pure vegetarian breakfast is laid out in the dining hall also separated by gender. Students serve themselves, eating face-to-face with each other, while attempting to remain alone with their thoughts.

9:30 a.m.—Required group meditation again.

Noon—Pure vegetarian lunch consisting of vegetables and roots, steamed and boiled, plus berries and seeds, neither steamed, nor boiled. After lunch, people either nap or meditate in silence in their rooms, nature-walk or meditate in silence amongst the grounds.

2:00 p.m.—More required meditation.

5:00 p.m.—"Dinner," consisting of a bowl of fruit.

6:00 p.m.—One hour of instruction by a meditation instructor about the philosophy behind the course, including how to build on the method for the next day.

8:00 p.m.—You guessed it…

9:00 p.m.—Lights out.

Perhaps I had gotten in over my head. The purpose of Vipassana seemed to be learning how not to react. But my people are from a part of Punjab where even a heartfelt condolence can become animated enough to erupt into a sloppy boxing match. And I was raised in New York, where most of your neighbors would just as soon throw a hockey puck at your head as look at you. I grew up thinking that only druggies and Californians managed to keep a straight face when saying things like *Take it as it comes.* The rest of us reacted to life, and we did it loudly.

Thankfully, by Day Three, it appeared that my mind had called off its rebellion. It had concluded that if it continued to insist on thought, it risked being deprived of meat indefinitely. Instead of spiraling and circling and bumping into one another like many drunken hamsters inhabiting my skull, now my thoughts only interrupted my concentration every once in a while.

I am observing the sensations between the bottom of my nose and the top of my lip. It is cold…now warm…now cold….

I am observing the sensations on my chin, which feels as if it is being tickled by a tiny piece of hair…. Which I am sure is not there… Although it could be the beginnings of a woman-beard. That's gross. I should look into electrolysis. I wonder if it's prohibitively expensive. But I must focus. And that's not relevant, since no one here will look anyone else in the face. Right… There is no such thing as a permanent tickle…. I no longer feel the tickle…. I am observing the lack of a tickling sensation….

What the hell did Cristina's date mean when he described the mushroom soup as "interesting" at my last dinner party, anyway?

Everyone loves my mushroom soup. I'm so glad she dumped him. Maybe I should try making Lobster Bisque next time. But what am I thinking? I can't afford to throw a dinner party! I don't even know if I still have a job! Bad Vina. Bad, bad Vina. I am observing the sensations on my neck....

I am observing the sensations in my right arm, which is warm and surrounded in blankets at my side. I can feel the harsh wool on the skin of my forearm, which is beginning to itch. But there is no such thing as a permanent itch....

Except for the itch I have to make Jon pay for what he did! I should have slapped him in the subway when he said he loved me. I should call Alan and Steve in prison to tell them to go to hell. Why don't I stand up for myself more? Oh, what the hell am I doing in Fiji with all these freaks? Because I deserve it, that's why. I'm a mean, judgmental person who jumped to conclusions about Nick and then fled the city without even apologizing. Maybe Prakash is right; maybe Nick's better off without me. Why would Nick want to hear from me again? And why the hell won't that woman stop crying! I am observing the sensations in my fingers....

My bra strap burned, my thong was riding up, and once an hour I had to reposition my legs to prevent them from falling off from a lack of blood flow. Despite my growing resentment of the meditators who remained smugly in the same position hour after hour while I struggled, I started to work up my tolerance bit by bit. Maybe competition wasn't so unhealthy. I had reached the point where I could clear my mind of virtually anything but the sensations of the moment. The discomfort, the exhaustion, and the general lack of stability. For about five minutes at a time.

This was the point I had reached by Day Seven, when I had learned to pay such close attention to my body and to my mind, and become so attuned to the impermanence of my every itch and tingle, that the only thing left was the stillness. And in my observation during the calm, I could see clearly that what festered inside was the truth. The truth was that my inability to be fair to myself was the culprit for all of my problems. The truth was that if I had been honest and more tolerant of myself and my imperfections, I would have questioned things more. I would have noticed things sooner. And I would have sent out signals deterring the world from ever trying to deceive me. My eyes could not be open to the world in any real sense until they were open to what was going on inside me.

Now I was experiencing disappointment, observing regret and feeling the tears streak the curves of my face. There was regret for how I had treated myself. There was sorrow for how far I had let things go. And then, there was an indescribable, sweeping, physical sensation. Beginning on top of my head and showering through me, like so many tiny orbs of energy from nowhere and everywhere. The sensation cascaded warmth in slow motion through the tips of my fingers and the edges of my toes. For the first time in my life, I was able to listen to what was coming from within me because I was truly alone with my self. I recognized her, and I felt nothing but compassion. I apologized to her for everything I failed to protect her from, and I forgave her for every time she managed to let herself down. And then I sat ever so still and I held her while she sobbed and sobbed and sobbed.

·· 27 ··

At root I think we're all pretty simple. Men want to be appreciated by someone who tries to accept them. Women want to be adored by someone who tries to understand them. Lacking the patience to wait for people to ask me the right questions as a child, I had developed a habit of over-explaining myself. Not that I was the only one; the average woman uses approximately 5000 words per day in comparison to the average man's 1500. Therefore, my announcement of plans to take an extended vow of meditative silence met with less than enthusiastic support from my friends and family. Like most people, they assumed that retreats were akin to cults. Normally I would have cared what they thought, but as bad as things were by then, I admitted that when you're barely hanging on by a thread, you'll grab for almost anything.

And so it was that after what seemed like a hundred days

of battling my mind into submission in a cabin in the hills of mainland Fiji, I was exhausted and refreshed, yet unprepared to return to the sharp lines of my actual life. I had grown comfortable inside my mind, and rather attached to the idea that my judgments were the only ones that mattered. Thankfully, after spending so much time immersed in meditation I also felt resensitized to the world. I'll admit that at first, even my own speech sounded to me like the road-raging shouts of a teamster who had been cut off on the Queensborough Bridge. Each word was amplified as it bounced off the insides of my skull. But I knew that it was worth it. Sometimes letting go of everything you think you know about yourself is the most premeditated thing you can do.

When our meditation leader lifted our vow of silence on the final morning of the retreat, I met my cabinmates formally for the first time. Valentina was a Spanish woman in her thirties who was pursuing meditation as a vacation from the pressures of raising three children in New Zealand. Lindsay was an English twentysomething with blond dreadlocks and a pierced eyebrow who made her living as the voice of corporate voice mail recognition systems, asking people to *Please press "1" for the company directory.* To my surprise, Valentina waved my words away when I tried to introduce myself over the juice and cookies they laid out for us.

"Well, I've already *heard* your voice," she said. "You've been talking in your sleep every night!"

This must be how a serious actress feels when her tasteful, artistic nude photos show up on the Internet. I knew there were other people in the room, but I never really thought it would get out. I wanted to apologize profusely and beg her and Lindsay to forgive me. But I also felt a little violated by the fact that they had listened.

"Why didn't one of you just shake me awake or throw something at me from across the room?"

"Honestly? I was grateful to hear a human voice," Lindsay explained. "This is the first time I've tried anything like this. This meditation stuff, you know? And I was beginning to go batty by the third day. Frankly, I was glad to have the company at night."

"Yes, yes," Valentina agreed. "It was very entertaining."

"Oh, okay." I forced a smile. "Then I guess, you're welcome?"

"So…can I ask you a question?" Lindsay leaned in while Valentina nodded at her. I braced myself.

"Who is this Jon, and why did he give you a photograph of his freezer?"

Thoughts that need to be heard will find their way out of a person, spilling and tumbling however clumsily over one another, making a mad dash via enlightened dream-state or drunken circumstance, simply because they're determined toward some audience they are convinced will be waiting.

"So what brought you here?" asked the housefrau stuck beside me on the floor of the van. "You don't seem like the usual meditator."

Shoulder-to-shoulder in the vehicle, whose owner had offered a few of us a lift to the nearest town, I felt we were already too close for comfort. Before I could come up with an appropriately evasive answer, somebody else decided to speak on my behalf.

"I don't think she's so unusual," a man in a windbreaker with a British accent, an uncommon warmth and a head of salt-and-pepper hair replied. "Perhaps there is no such thing as a typical meditator."

"I guess I'm trying to make sense of some things." I smiled thankfully at him.

"That's garbage," my neighbor concluded. "We're all here for some reason. Some very specific reason."

"Oh, you think so?" I turned toward her. "Then what's your very specific reason?"

"Okay, I'll tell you." She took a breath and thought about it for a moment. "I was a perfectly typical housewife, living in the suburbs of New Zealand, and all was well. But when my children left home for college, I found myself feeling terribly lonely. So I started to drink. Too much. And it got to the point where honestly I frightened myself. So I told my sister, and she recommended that I try this, since a friend of hers swore by it. I came to see if it could help me."

"And has it?" Salt-and-Pepper asked.

"I won't know until I'm home." She shrugged. "But I am glad I came."

"I believe that it will," Salt-and-Pepper said, smiling graciously at her, "because if it can help me, I'm fairly certain it can help you."

"Why?" I interjected. "What's your story?"

He leaned back, and looked out the window at the countryside that was zooming by. "I should be dead. Five years ago my doctors diagnosed me with leukemia. I tried every medical treatment possible, but my body was just ravaged. It seemed like nothing could be done for me. When I was at the end of my rope, I decided to look outside of the hospitals. To open myself up to other kinds of healing. So, one day someone told me about Vipassana, and I figured I had nothing to lose. The doctors said I was too weak to get through it, but I came anyway. I've come back for an intensive retreat once a year ever since, and my doctors say I'm a miracle. By all accounts, I should be dead."

"You can't honestly believe that this cured your cancer," the housefrau protested.

"No, no," he insisted. "But it helps me tremendously, and that's all I really need to know."

All eyes were back on me.

"I...I felt like I was drowning," I blurted out. "Inside my own life. Like I had no voice. And it was all my fault. I couldn't explain myself to anyone, because I couldn't even explain myself to myself. So I felt as if I couldn't even breathe. I needed help getting back to trusting myself. I needed to be alone with myself. I'm from New York, and it's not easy to do that there. I guessed this was as far away as I could possibly get from my life."

"What are you?" she asked, then bent forward as if to sniff me. "A writer?"

I laughed. "Not exactly."

"So what are you gonna do with it?" he asked.

"With what?" I looked up.

"With what you have learned about yourself, little girl."

I paused. "Breathe, I guess."

"Are you ready to go back to your life?"

I shook my head. "I don't think so." I hugged the backpack in my lap. "At least, not yet."

"Then where *are* you going?" the woman asked.

"I guess I'll get to whichever town we're headed to, and figure it out from there. I still have some time off from work, since most of my colleagues probably think I came out here in search of my marbles."

"If it's not entirely out of line—" Salt-and-Pepper lowered his voice "—might I make a suggestion?"

I was wrong, I thought to myself the next morning after hopping out of a seaplane into the knee-deep waters off the coast of the remote island of Kandavu. *This* is as far away as I could have gotten from my life.

Faced with the evidence of a continuing struggle in my psyche, I decided to take more time to tame the cacophony in my mind. Besides, I had yet to attempt the practice of Vipassana outside of the confines of the meditation retreat, and was less than convinced that plunging right back into the chaos of New York City would do me any good. That would be like taking a flight to Vegas right after paying off your credit card debt. So when the Brit explained that fellow retreaters often rented huts on the beach of this tiny Fijian island, a sort of halfway house, to ease their way back into the world, my only question was, *When do we leave?*

The Yasawa chain of islands was about as remote as you

could get without space travel. And I'm not just talking about the absence of a Starbucks anywhere on the island. There are no paved roads, telephones, locks or indoor plumbing. An "Airport" sign above a shack on the beach marks the location of the lone daily seaplane's arrival, which carries supplies, food and up to four people who hop into the water and wade to shore while holding their belongings above their heads. To my surprise, once we made it onto the beach, Salt-and-Pepper motioned a friendly salute and started heading off in one direction.

"Where are you going?" I asked, hoisting my soggy backpack up over a shoulder.

"Up there." He pointed toward the peak of the only mountain on the island. He planned to camp at a clearing on top of it for a few days and enjoy the silence.

"What about me?" I asked his back, which was shrinking into the distance.

I heard the seaplane taking off behind me. Just as Salt-and-Pepper had explained, I was able to rent a thatched-roofed, sand-floored, hammock-furnished hut on the beach from the descendants of tribal cannibals. It came with all the fruit I could eat, and all the privacy I could hope for, so long as I didn't mind having no one to talk to, and nothing to do. Nothing, that is, for about three days, during which I wandered the beach, slept and meditated, and resented the idea of having to return and explain myself to New York. But one evening, I received an unlikely invitation to join in an evening fireside drinking ritual with the local family from whom I was renting my hut.

Kava is a native intoxicant with roughly the consistency

of muddy water, whose popularity is owed entirely to the fact that it numbs the bottom half of a person's face within minutes of ingestion. It looks like chalk and tastes like water that has been used to rinse out the insides of a cement mixer. I didn't want to appear rude or ungrateful, and I was well aware of the fact that there were no locks on the door of my hut. Anytime anyone said *Bula,* I gathered, everyone was supposed to chug it down. Then the storytelling began. So I drank the Kava and appreciated the fire, while listening to what I hoped was merely folklore about the cannibalistic prowess of their not-so-distant ancestors. As unappetizing as it was to stare into the concoction contained in the hollowed-out half coconut I held, these drinks were still a welcome departure from the predictability of their rosy-tinted, sugar-rimmed Cosmopolitan cousins in New York. I wanted to stay on that island; reality just seemed like it might have too many sharp edges. Though I resented its power, I secretly feared that the comfortable solitude of that island might be the only thing preventing me from shaving my head and jumping naked off a cliff.

"Well…don't *you* look like a postcard?" a familiar voice woke me from my nap on the beach the next morning. This was odd. Usually I was completely alone.

I had been sleeping off a sort of hangover from the previous night's Kava, hoping that the water might wash away some of what I'd taken in. Nearly a month from the day when I scraped myself up off the floor of that stalled elevator, I was baking in the sun on a beach where the only footsteps in the sand were my own. Miles removed from anything reminiscent of civilization, I savored the sun on my eyelids. Using a coconut for a pillow and allowing the warm waters to carry the powdery sand through the gaps in my toes, I was more than slightly jarred by this unexpected intrusion.

"Where did you come from?" I asked, fumbling to balance on one elbow while shading my eyes with the other hand. "I thought I was alone."

"We're *all* alone," Salt-and-Pepper replied with a grin.

"Don't be smug," I said. "You surprised me."

He shrugged.

"You know, I don't even know your name." I tilted my head to hide from the sun behind his shadow.

"Does it matter?" He dropped his satchel and took a seat beside me, facing the ocean.

"I guess not," I replied. "Anyway, how was it up there?"

"You don't look so good." He ignored my question, focusing instead on the bags under my eyes. "Are you hung over?"

"No," I protested while struggling to sit up. "Well, not exactly."

"Don't tell me you got into the Kava with the cannibals," he said, as if there were nothing out of the ordinary about our conversation.

"They're not cannibals. Some of their ancestors were."

"Oh, okay." He grinned, clearly amused.

"Did you come over here and intrude on my privacy just to judge me?"

"No, I'm quite sure you do enough of that for yourself."

"What are you talking about?"

"Look, you're scared. I get that."

"You're a nice guy, but you don't know me." I looked away.

"I think I do." He paused to remove and then re-don his baseball cap more than once. "You know, I didn't always have cancer and study meditation and camp out on mountains in the South Pacific. Let me tell you more about myself."

I gave him a look that signaled he had my attention.

"I used to be a priest. Back home, I grew up in a very religious family. I always felt as though I didn't belong. As I was told to, I grew up and became a priest like my two brothers. I thought I was happy. I saw a lot of people struggling and I was able to help them. I thought that was all I needed. Then one day I met a woman and I fell in love with her so immediately and so deeply that I didn't know what to do. Of course, I knew the church wouldn't allow a priest to marry. I struggled with it, and eventually decided to leave the church for her. My family shunned me. A few months later I found out about the cancer. After I tried every possible medical treatment, with my wife by my side, I thought about looking into alternative healers in other parts of the world. My family thought I was crazy, and forbade me to try any treatments or healing methods that might fall in line with what the church deems heresy. They said I should surrender myself to God's will. I chose to fight instead, because I couldn't see why God would give me love and then want me to die. I allowed myself to fight, and to find my own answers, rather than accept what I've been told. And I'm still fighting."

"No offense, but what does any of this have to do with me?"

"Look, life isn't a movie. Things don't just happen. You don't go from devastation to epiphany in an instant. You're not going to get repaired by meditation or anything else. You'll only see things a bit differently every day. If you're smart, you'll always participate. You have to go out and find things, places, people who will see you for who you are, and help you find what you need. Whatever it is you have been through or are going through is valid, but getting blitzed on Kava isn't going to help you make any progress. There comes a point where healing turns into hiding. Part of healing is taking what you've learned and facing your demons again. You need to accept the fear that you will fail yourself again. Some people never have the chance. I know fear because 'Fear of Anything People Will Think of Me' is a luxury I don't have anymore. I don't have the time for it. I wish I had the chance that you do."

"You don't even know what I've been through."

"It doesn't matter what it is in particular. You're walking and talking and able to move forward. That's not a lot. That's everything. Take it from a dying man."

"Did you face your demons?"

"Yes, I believe I did. But for me, like for you, part of it was my parents, who forced me to go into this life, and part of it was myself."

"My parents never forced me. They did their best, I guess."

"Well then, stop blaming them."

"I don't blame them."

He raised an eyebrow at me and then continued.

"Healing is not a process with a beginning and an end. It's a road you keep walking. You don't sit down and wait for life to come and find you again. You expose yourself to it. Truly rip off your clothes and see what happens. Because you can. Bare yourself. Let the wounds have air so that they can scab over and start to heal. If you're very fortunate, you might find someone who will recognize that you're searching, even if you can't or won't admit it, because they'll be searching in a similar way. Someone who can love you for who you are and who you want to be and how you choose to occupy your space in the world. Then it doesn't seem so much like healing anymore. It starts to seem more like life. Like being alive again."

"Why are you telling me all of this?"

"Because there's a seaplane leaving here in a few hours for the mainland."

"I'm not ready," I mumbled.

"Who ever is?"

"You're a very difficult man," I said.

"And you are a woman who is already everything that she needs to be, but insists on believing that there is something missing."

"What do you want from me?"

"I want you to want to go back. And to be grateful that you have the chance to do it. If not for anyone else then for some crazy guy you had a memorable talk with, while you were hung over on Kava on the beach of some unknown island in the South Pacific."

Looking back there wasn't that much to think about. I knew I couldn't hide out on that beach forever. Everyone else seemed to be picking themselves up, saying a prayer and facing the day without benefit of one percent of the blessings I had waiting for me. And I knew I had no right to stay down.

I shook my head, kissed my friend on his cheek and rose to my feet. There was nothing else to say, so I smiled, and he did the same in a way that suggested he knew we would never see each other again. One second later, I was in a dead sprint headed down the beach toward my hut. I had a seaplane to catch.

·· 28 ··

While I am the physical antithesis of Annie Reed in *Sleepless in Seattle,* and have lived through nearly thirty years' worth of experience to the contrary, I always hold on to the possibility of a chance airport encounter with a handsome stranger who'll change my life. Oftentimes I'm waiting for my baggage, or to check in, and I will pick the cutest stranger in my field of vision, then imagine the witty things he'll say to break the ice after we both reach for the same baggage-identification-rubber-bandy-thingy. Or how he'll smile and insist that I take the seat in the waiting area where we were both headed. Or how our eyes will meet across a sea of dimly lit airplane seats during *Casablanca* (the in-flight movie), when I get his Kosher meal by mistake.

I don't know why it's Kosher. Work with me.

I do this not because I'm delusional, but because I'm bored. And I'm a woman. And it beats eavesdropping on the almost always boring conversations of the people around me. (Maybe I should start bringing books to airports instead?) And since, on my return to my so-called life, which consisted, at that point, of a mailbox full of bills, miserably failed attempts at love and career, family and friends who had deemed me insane and a bizarrely intimate relationship with my gay neighbor and his cat, I would rather think about anything other than what the hell I'm gonna do once I get there.

I was settled on the plane and noticed a young married couple squabbling near my row. The husband of said couple begged my pardon and proceeded to ask me to switch seats with him. His wife contributed by glaring fiery daggers into the back of his skull.

"She's upset that I didn't force them to seat us together at the check-in counter," he implored me with a defeated whisper. "We're already trying to work through some marital difficulties to begin with. It would really help if I sat next to her. Could you switch seats with me?"

It was at these moments that I was glad to be single. Even though I had specifically requested the window seat, I gave it up without a fight to this sad, sad man. What other choice did I have? His wife was radiating negativity so powerful that I feared it might swallow me whole. I suspected that this might be the only negotiation that worked out in his favor all day.

Of course, I gave up my seat so the couple could sit side-by-side. I was such a Good Samaritan, I told myself. God must have seen that gesture. So as I made my way to sad-

husband's originally assigned row, I feasted on visions of the original-James-Bond-look-alike who would rise from the adjacent seat to flash me a winning smile, and insist on using his chiseled forearms to hoist my bag into the overhead compartment. Then he would proceed to entertain me with stories of his travels as an investigative reporter for *National Geographic,* which was how he was killing time while on sabbatical from his teaching position at the Harvard Business School. Obviously. Did I mention he would have a thing for short, brown women with delusional imaginations?

He would tell me that I had the most marvelous laugh, and take the liberty of asking me to dinner that night. He would invite me to Le Cirque, where he could always get a table, since his brother was the sommelier, kiss me under the moonlight outside the front door of my apartment and call me once he got home to ask if we could make an immediate promise to see each other exclusively. He would propose in a combination of English, French and Hindi, which he would've learned within a year without my having had to suggest it, in order to win over my family.

Oh, and there would be roses. Everywhere we went. Always.

However, instead of canoodling with my international man of mystery, on one side I found a severely obese preteen, who laughed so violently each time he scored a point on his Game Boy that he spat damp Doritos crumbs onto my lap, and on the other, a Mormon preacher, who thought this flight was the perfect time to teach me everything about *The Joys of Jesus*. Neither one of them would allow me the privilege of an armrest. But I wasn't surprised. The kind of touching-happenstance romance that always sweeps perky-girl-next-door heroines off their feet by genuine-but-still-doable-male-co-stars almost never happens in real life.

My maternal instincts have been in hyper-drive since approximately the twelfth grade. Three seconds is the typical amount of time it takes for me to lose my composure along with my posture, and regress to a point where I begin babbling to infants, as if I just picked it up one summer on a bike tour of Europe. Entire romantic evenings have been ruined when I, at the subtlest hint of a bright-eyed, pudgy-cheeked, round-bellied potential new playmate, have forgotten that my date was in the room. I have been known to get down on all fours, in a red dress and heels no less, just to meet a toddler at eye level.

It wasn't so much that I wanted children of my own right away; it was more that I wanted to devour everyone else's. Perhaps I envied them their innocence. Whatever the reason, I've always wanted to gobble them up. That is, of course, if they were the *cute-and-playful-and-well-behaved-and-ticklish-but-not-chronically-gassy* type. If they were the *screaming-bloody-murder-while-biting-everyone-and-throwing-pancakes-at-the-walls* variety, then I found myself leaning back and admiring my tummy. All the while I would repeat *Niiiice, flat stomach* in my mind, and congratulate myself for having wasted all these eggs.

Regardless of how many pancakes a child might have

thrown at the walls, however, I cannot abide the image of one being hit. As if the baggage claim at JFK wasn't violent enough to begin with, I was frozen in my tracks by the sight of a curious young girl who'd placed her hand gently onto the luggage conveyor belt, full of excitement at the way that it moved. When her mother saw this, she yanked the girl away and after shaking and scolding her, slapped the child across her face. Hard.

Welcome back to New York.

It could have been the sensory overload of the airport after two weeks of meditation, but I was in shock. Normally, I would have bitten my tongue. For another moment, the woman continued to scold her now sobbing daughter while a growing number of people couldn't help but stare. Finally, I decided I would have to say something. But before I could, someone else stepped in. A man walked over to the woman and her child, and carefully interrupted them with what I assumed was an appeasing smile, despite the fact that I could only see the back of his head. Then, in a voice so delicate that it was contradictory to everything about the well-built warrior, he said, "Excuse me, ma'am, I think the girl's learned her lesson. Maybe it's not my place to say this, but maybe you should take it easy on her. She's only a kid."

The moment I heard his voice, I knew it was Nick. What was he doing here? Was he here by coincidence? Or did he spend his Saturday afternoons trolling the baggage claims, looking for children to save from the wrath of their disgruntled parents? Either way, I wasn't ready to see him or to apologize for my earlier behavior. I wouldn't even know where to begin. I knew I should take the opportunity to disappear while his back was still turned to me, but I was too interested in what would happen next. So I edged myself within earshot, trying to hide behind a few people.

"You're right," the woman snapped, rising to her feet and getting within a few inches of the man's unwavering face. "It is *not* your place to tell me how to raise my daughter. Where the hell do you get off trying to tell me what I can and cannot say to my kid?"

"I was not trying to offend you. But I'm not the only one who was startled by your yelling. I can understand that you're upset and worried about your daughter hurting herself. But there is no need to raise your voice at me."

"How *dare* you!" Her eyes widened as she became increasingly aware of the crowd nearby. "This is none of your damn business!"

Nick raised his hands before him protectively, attempting to calm her. "As I said, please keep your voice down. And for the record, it *is* my business, as much as it is everyone's business to stop someone from hitting a kid. Maybe I have no business telling you what to say, but I do have every right to stop your abuse if I see it in public. And you hit her way too hard."

"F— off, buddy. I am *not* abusing my child. You have no idea what you're talking about, and you better stay the *hell* away from us, or I'll call the police," the woman concluded, before grabbing her daughter by the arm and dragging her toward the exit.

Having witnessed the scene from only a few feet away, and

being embarrassed that I failed to step in and echo Nick's sentiment, I felt compelled to pat him on the back, but didn't. I turned on my heel and headed in the other direction, not ready to deal with him yet. In moments he caught up with me and laid his hand on my shoulder. My stomach leaped.

"Nick! Hi!" I greeted him way too enthusiastically. "Listen, I saw what you did with that woman and you were totally justified. I'm sorry I was running off. I'm expecting a friend to meet me here and I don't want her waiting too long."

"I'm waiting for a friend, too." He smiled.

Maybe it *was* too soon for me to be back in New York. Because his mouth, his eyes, looked waaaaay too inviting to me. I felt self-conscious, and realized immediately that I had no makeup on and hadn't had my eyebrows or skin attended to in weeks. I appreciated the attention, but knew he was probably here to pick up someone else. Regardless, if meditation had taught me anything, it was that I didn't speak up for myself nearly enough. Maybe this was an opportunity to test out what Salt-and-Pepper was talking about. Maybe it was time to expose myself.

"Okay, Nick, I need to talk to you."

Before I could finish, Cristina bounced over and swept me into a hug which included a squeeze and a little jig. Then she draped herself across Nick.

"Welcome back, Vina! I was in the ladies' room. Oh, and you've already seen Nick!"

"Yeah," I said, caught off guard. "I didn't know you guys knew each other."

"I didn't tell you? We met at the gym. Actually, he's my trainer," she giggled.

Oooooooooh, so she had a crush on him, and he came along to the airport to do her a favor. Well, it certainly didn't take him long to get over his crush on me. And he had the nerve to flash that flirtatious smile. Not very superheroish at all. It didn't matter, though. I still needed to apologize for my past behavior and unfair presumptions about him. I would just have to do it another time.

"I was sticking my nose in where it didn't belong," Nick explained, staring at me, "and Vina here was telling me what she thought about that."

"It was no big deal, really. How ironic that you're friends," I added. "Why don't we get going?"

I headed straight for the automatic doors, determined to find the appropriate time and place to make amends. As for the rest of my thoughts, I'd keep those to myself for now.

"Okay, I'm confused," Cristy bubbled, "but I'm sure you've had a long trip. Anyway, Vina, I was going to tell you this later, but I can't wait. Prakash and Christopher are tying the knot next weekend in Vermont. And you and I are both gonna be *bridesmaids!*"

Lovely. Everyone else's life was progressing right on schedule while I was publicly humiliated, probably unemployed, and had been reduced to misinterpreting the flirtations of the crushes of my girlfriends at airport baggage terminals. Pre-Fiji, this would have had me feeling very sorry for myself. But after all that had transpired, it seemed as if I should simply be grateful that Christopher wasn't likely to be a very bitchy bride. He wouldn't expect me to wear something bright yellow or polka-dotted or covered with unflatteringly positioned bows. No, at the very least I knew that he would never do that to me.

·· 29 ··

Talk about your bitchy brides. Cristy and I were draped in layer upon layer of shrimp-orange chiffon, and bisected by a way-too-tight white bodice that matched the gloves on our hands and yes, the enormous, tacky bows in our hair. *I must really love Christopher,* I kept telling myself as I watched him and Prakash hand-feed each other chocolate layer cake with peach-infused ganache. The flavor combination, to everyone's surprise, did work out all right. But there was nothing all right about the way that I looked on the night of Chris's commitment ceremony with Prakash. We were seated on a podium in front of two hundred people, while photographers' bulbs flashed at us from every direction. Did I mention there was also a bow on my butt that was about as elegant and appropriate as a Kick Me sign?

To my right was Cristina, trapped inside the same monstrosity of a bridesmaid's gown, and beaming so brightly at

Christopher that I was afraid she might fuse. Her enthusiasm might have been an attempt to counteract the toxic fumes radiating from Pamela, who sat alongside William, and whose bitterness over yet another person getting married before her was stronger than the Kava I had tried. Directly in front of us, three rows into the audience, was Nick. And he was flashing that impossibly bright smile in our direction.

"Hey," I said, elbowing Cristina. "Your boyfriend's trying to get your attention."

"My who?" she asked, then squinted her eyes at me. "I thought you were away for too long. You got into the nose candy with those drag queens in the bathroom, didn't you? Come on. You know I don't have a boyfriend. But listen, if that guy on the end of the second row winks at me one more time, you might not want to wait up for me tonight."

"Which guy?" I asked through smile-clenched teeth.

"Gray suit, brown hair."

"Honey?" I said after getting a better look. "Um, I know I've been out of the dating scene for a while, but I'm pretty sure that man's a woman."

"Oh, come on, Vina. That meditation retreat was supposed to cure you of your cynicism. What are you talking about? There is no way that guy is a...*oh, my god! That is one mannish woman!*"

"Yes, she certainly is. Though I think the correct term is butch. And for the record, meditation was not supposed to cure me of anything. It was supposed to—"

"Yeah, sure. That's interesting. Now who did you say was trying to get my attention? If I just spent the last half hour making eyes at a butch lesbian, I think I need to reaffirm my heterosexuality. Honestly, these gowns are a nightmare. We look like a coupla frosted cupcakes. I had no idea Christopher could be so mean. The butch lesbian in the suit probably took one look at me and thought I was a man in drag."

"It was Nick."

"Who was Nick? Nick was a *drag queen?*"

"What? No! Now who's the one who's *on something?* Nick was the one who was *staring* at you," I clarified.

"Nick? Yeah, sure. He was looking at *me.* Don't be naive. Everybody can see the way he drools over you."

"Then you don't have a crush on him?"

She tilted her head. "He's hot, but I know you like him. Who do you think you're talking to?"

"But I thought, since you brought him to the airport last weekend—"

"Vina, since when do I bring dates to the baggage claim? Christopher and Prakash were fussing over wedding details at his place, and when I said I had to come pick you up, Nick jumped up and immediately volunteered to drive me to JFK. Frankly, I was surprised at the way you ignored him for the whole ride home. But I figured it was because you weren't interested in starting anything so soon after your…umm…*episode.* It's probably a good idea, Vina. You need to get stable on your own first, anyway."

★ ★ ★

"When I first met Christopher, I knew that he was going to marry Rich," a drunken cousin of Christopher's was toasting to the crowd, and I mean drunk to the point where he was wobbling about like a dashboard hula girl. "But then Rich dumped him! Or slept with someone else. Or got it annulled. I don't remember. Whatever the case, I know two things for sure: one is that laser removal really can make it look like there never was a tattoo, and the other is that what happens in Vegas *really does stay in Vegas!* Am I right?"

Nobody was laughing. Prakash's eyes were bulging so hard that it was clear they might soon pop right out of his head. Again, Nick decided to intervene and halt the carnage. Prakash clenched Christopher's hand, and Cristina clenched mine. Prakash's mother double-fisted glasses of white wine while trying to stifle her sobs, but I had to admire her for being there. One small step for any other mother must have been an ascent to the top of Kilimanjaro for her. Apart from greeting her when I first arrived, I tried to keep my distance; I thought it better than providing a constant reminder of what could have been. Prakash's father had claimed to accept his coming out at first, but then refused to come to the wedding. *One out of two ain't bad,* Prakash told me with moist eyes as I adjusted his bowtie in the Bridal Salon moments before the ceremony.

"All jokes aside though," Nick began, snatching the microphone away from the cousin, and glaring him into a chair as if he were a disobedient child, "there is very little that any of us know for sure, except that life is the series of choices we make, and that if we're lucky we come out of it without too many scratches. Or too many regrets. Things start moving so fast at a point that we forget to step back and ask ourselves what's really important to us in the first place. Like friendship. I met Prakash in college, and since then, he's been like the gay older brother I never had. One thing I can say for sure is that Prakash has been a better man since he's been with Chris than he ever could have been on his own. The whole is definitely worth more than the sum of its parts. And I think that's what a couple is supposed to be. So, to the happy couple…"

Prakash's mother groaned. Nick, I could have sworn, tilted his champagne glass in my direction. I raised my glass along with every other captivated onlooker in the room.

Nice save, I mouthed at Nick from where I was seated.

Nice dress, he mouthed back.

Normally, it was the social equivalent of a police lineup: standing before your family and friends so that everyone could get an unimpeded look at the unmarried women. Thereafter, for good measure, we would be made to feel that singledom was a prison from which we should be praying to escape, even if it had to be at the expense of the other similarly sentenced women with whom we were "competing" for the lone remaining cowboy headed out of Die Alone Creek. It was roughly two days' ride past No Children Junction. At this gay wedding, however, some rather aggressive drag queens were thrown into the mix. I'll say this. Despite the tremendous effort they put into perfecting their makeup and training themselves to saunter in a way that makes genetic women look rough in comparison, drag queens will trade their girlish demeanors for boxing gloves if it means a better chance at a flying bouquet.

I never had a shot. I caught a glimpse of Nick's gaze following me carefully across the floor and got distracted. Various thoughts were obscuring my sense of perception so I failed to react to the bouquet careening through the sky toward my head. Luckily, a chubby coed standing behind me broke my fall when a drag queen named Cleopatra body-slammed me out of her way. When I came to, all I could focus on was Cristina lifting me off the floor while I heard myself posing to no one in particular, "Why don't I ever see anything coming?"

Less than twenty minutes later I was icing the elbow I had landed on when I spotted Nick walking in my general direction. I flagged him down and decided that at the very least I still owed him an apology. Besides, given the outfit I was wearing, and the busted lip I was now sporting, it seemed a little less ridiculous to be apologizing for running out of the apartment of a guy I hadn't slept with, and then ignoring a guy I hardly knew.

"So, can I talk to you for a minute?"

"You can talk to me for as long as you like." He leaned against a banquet table.

"I owe you an apology."

"Yeah, I think you do."

I tasted a little blood, but decided that I probably deserved it. "I'm sure Prakash told you how I…misinterpreted waking up in your bed that day."

"Vina, he didn't need to tell me. It was pretty clear when I heard that door slam. I just can't believe anyone would think I would take advantage of them while they were drunk. Now, *sober* is another story…"

"Well, yes. That was part of it, and I also found the video cameras in your closet."

"Yeah…and?"

"And…I thought that you were videotaping us…doing stuff that it turns out we never did."

It took a minute to register, and when it did, his eyes widened and he let out a deep laugh. "No wonder you ran out! Wow, having an imagination like that must be exhausting. You must have been mortified!"

"So you're not offended that I assumed that about you?"

"It's not exactly a compliment…but hey, I have three sisters. I know that women can't just give every guy they meet the benefit of the doubt." He raised an eyebrow and continued to laugh out loud. "Especially if they wake up in the guy's bed, I guess."

"I know, I know. But you don't have to enjoy it *that* much." I cracked a smile. "Have some compassion. Look at the dress they've got me in. Haven't I suffered enough?"

"I'm sorry. I know. It's just not something you hear every day." He regained his composure. "But if that was all it was, and Prakash cleared the air before you left town, then why the cold shoulder at the airport?"

"What do you mean?" I feigned ignorance.

"You know what I mean, Vina. Ignorance is not a convincing look on you. We were having a nice conversation, and then you froze up and ignored me all of a sudden."

"I wasn't ignoring you." I scanned fruits surrounding the chocolate fountain behind him as if I were interested in them.

"Yes, you were. You absolutely were. And nothing changed from the beginning of that conversation, so…wait a minute. Was this about your friend Cristina? Did you think I was with *her*?"

"No." I stuck out my chin like a disgruntled teenager. "I didn't think you were *with* her."

"You must have. Why would you think that I would do something like that? After I clearly…" But then he got flustered. "You know what? Forget it."

And then, to my surprise, he stormed off. He left me with a swollen lip, an aching elbow and one big question on my mind. *Why did it matter so much to him what I thought?*

·· 30 ··

"The question is why does it matter so much to you that it matters to him why it matters to you?" Cristina further confused me in the ladies' bathroom shortly after Nick's abrupt departure. I cringed as she tried reapplying lipstick to my increasingly swollen lip.

"Sorry about that, princess." Cleopatra made her way over to the next sink. "A girl doesn't know her own strength sometimes."

"I guess that's true. Anyway, I don't want to fight with you. I've got enough problems." I turned to Cristina. "And I don't want to deal with any riddles right now, either, okay?"

"Yeah, and I don't want to go home alone tonight, but when the universe hurls a drag queen at your face, you find creative ways to cover up the bruises with some lipstick. And when the universe sends you a butch lesbian in the middle of a sexual drought, you go home and go to sleep by yourself."

"Since when are you having a dry spell?" I asked, forcing her to smudge my lipliner.

"Would you sit still?" she huffed. "It's been like two weeks!"

"Two weeks is not a dry spell. I swear, if you were a man, you'd be a walking erection."

"So?"

"Why do I even try?" I asked Cleopatra. She shrugged at me in the mirror, and continued retouching her mascara.

Just then, Pamela burst into the bathroom, her foundation striped with tears.

"Honey, what *happened?*" Christy practically squealed, as we rushed Pam to one of the makeup tables.

She gasped and whimpered almost indecipherably.

"Who made you slap Britney Spears?" I asked.

"Nooooooo!" she shrieked and then blew her nose before speaking more clearly. "He made me waste seven *years!*"

Cleopatra fished a hanky out of her cleavage and handed it to Pam. Pam used it to blow her nose and compose herself before making the mistake of catching a glimpse of her reflection in the mirror.

"I just can't do it anymore! I just…I just can't! It's pathetic! *I'm* pathetic!"

"Pam," Cristy said and held her by the shoulders. "What are you talking about? What can't you do anymore?"

"We had a fight. A really bad fight. Out there. Just now."

"You and William?" I asked, kneeling before her and taking her handkerchief since there was nowhere for her to dispose of it.

"No." She shot me a look I hadn't thought her capable of. "Me and Kevin Federline."

"Sorry! I have a slight concussion so I'm a little slow on the uptake. What did you fight about? Why would he pick a fight with you?"

I held the handkerchief out for Cleopatra to drop into the basket behind her. She raised an eyebrow, which I assumed meant she expected me to know better.

"He didn't. That's the point. It was me. *Me!* I was yelling, and screaming like some crazy woman." She seemed to be reliving it. "I…I just don't know what happened. I remember being so happy for Chris and Prakash, and telling William something about how happy they looked together. And he turned to me and he said, *Well, that won't last long.* And then I realized something. I realized that I *hate him.* I mean, what kind of a man would say that at someone's *wedding?*"

She searched our eyes for answers neither of us could provide, before continuing, "And what kind of a woman am *I* to want to marry *him?*"

"No." I started shaking my head. "Don't say that."

"Vina, it's okay. Stop protecting me. It's long overdue." We could see the wheels in her mind turning. "I don't…I don't think that I like who I am when I'm with William. That crazy woman, the one who completely lost it in front of everybody out there, wasn't me. *This* isn't me. I have to get out of here!"

"Vina, wait." A hand reached out to stop me by the shoulder while I was at the coat check a few minutes later.

"Nick," I huffed, "this is really not a good time."

"Just give me a minute. I'm sorry I overreacted. I'm a little off tonight."

"Join the club. Pam and William had a huge fight. She's a mess, so Cristina and I are taking her home."

"I know. I saw the fireworks. Is there anything I can do? Do you ladies need a ride?"

I had to smile. "No, no. I think there's a car waiting. But thanks for offering to save a damsel in distress. Again."

"Any day of the week," he replied. "So listen…"

"Hey, Vina," Cristina intervened, winking like a balding insurance salesman into his third gin and tonic at an airport bar, "don't worry about Pam. I'll take her home. You stay here and enjoy the rest of the party, okay? Okay, bye!"

She was gone before I could respond.

"I guess that's that." I took a deep breath. "So, you were saying?"

"Right, right. I wanted to tell you that I was very impressed with what you said. The point you made about how important it is to trust your instincts."

"Oh. You mean in relationships? You're talking about that piece on infidelity in Salon.com? God, that feels like it was such a long time ago."

"No. I mean, I did read that piece, but I was referring to something Prakash told me you wrote to him in an e-mail during your trip. You said the hardest thing about meditation was allowing yourself to let go, and that learning to trust your instincts through meditation was a skill that could translate into trusting your instincts for life in general. I've never seen anyone put that aspect of meditation into words successfully before. He was telling me about that phrase your grandmother uses and how meditation sort of brought you back full-circle to her advice."

"So you're into meditation?" This was too good to be true.

"I'm curious about it," he said, pulling out a seat for me at a nearby table and then taking one beside me. "Not the kind of retreat you took, because I don't think I could sit still for that long. I've tried yoga a few times and things like that. I find all this stuff fascinating. Anyway, my point was that you're really insightful…when you take the time to be, that is, instead of jumping to conclusions about nice guys like me. You should write more about things like that. I'd love to read anything else you've written."

"Thanks. I'm blushing, and Indian women don't really do that."

I couldn't help batting my eyes at him. As soon as I did, I found that I was developing a full-blown crush on him. Familiar voices clawed to the surface of my mind. *What about ambition? What about religion? What about the difference between men you date and men you marry?* I recognized them and I laughed. These doubts had as much power as I gave them, I told myself, and it was more important to be in the moment. All else evaporated the instant I registered the fact that Nick was definitely staring at me. Not only did I like it, I didn't feel guilty for liking it. *Oh, what the hell…I am observing myself sucking in my gut, and taking a deep breath, along with a leap of faith.*

"So," I began, and straightened up to give him my full attention, "how did you and Prakash become so close, anyway? You went to college together?"

Ask a man to talk about himself in any level of detail, and he'll go home thinking he had the night of his life.

"We were roommates in law school," he explained, stirring his drink with a swizel stick and paying absolutely no attention to the fact that my jaw had just hit the floor.

"I...I assumed it was college. I never knew you were a lawyer."

"You never asked," he replied. "You know, taking things at face value is a bad habit of yours."

"So I've heard. So why don't you practice?"

"I guess I got disillusioned with the law. Defending people I knew were guilty of some pretty terrible things didn't sit well with me. I come from a big family, like I said. I have three sisters, and nieces and nephews, and I didn't want to participate in the legal machine anymore. Justice is a subjective notion, as it turns out."

"Really?"

"Sorry. I get all wound up when I talk about it. I want to hear more about you, Vina. I think you're great. But first—" he stopped and stood up "—I have to apologize for not offering to get you a drink yet. What are you having?"

"A Chardonnay, please."

I leaned back, crossed my arms and watched him walk away.

I was checking for food between my teeth in the reflection of a butter knife when someone sat down in his chair.

"Can I give you a little unsolicited advice?" asked a pretty, petite redhead wearing a low-cut green dress and the plastered smile of a Stepford Wife.

"Huh?" I turned to face her, putting down the knife.

"Women who prey on men who are spoken for are an embarrassment to the rest of us."

"Come again?" I was confused, and searched the bar for Nick, whose back was turned to us.

"I'm Kat." She extended a limp and clammy hand she knew I wouldn't shake. "And I'm with Nicky."

"You mean…you and him?" I asked.

"I sleep in his T-shirts and everything." She shrugged innocently.

"Well, are you sure he knows that?"

"We've been on-again, off-again since school. He's just a flirt. That's as far as it goes." Then she leaned closer to me with a venomous glare. "Save yourself some time. Ultimately, he's committed to me."

Unfortunately, this scene started to feel too familiar. Flashbacks to that phone call and all of Jon's baby-momma-drama formed a knot in my stomach. This time, I wasn't going to fail to protect myself.

"Good luck with that," I said, before I rose to my feet and headed for the door.

How nice. He's a hard-bodied lawyer, she's his long-suffering girl-friend and I'm a colossal dork. I smiled politely at all the strangers on my way to the valet, and began to wonder if maybe the butch in the grey suit had the right idea. But on my way home in the rental car, I was feeling anything but sorry for myself. So what if he was flirting with me when he had a girlfriend? Men did that sort of thing all the time. And I would probably be better off alone for now, anyway. I had to report to work on Monday and figure out what I was doing with the rest of my life. When it came to the romantic part, at that point, I had to ask, *What was the rush?*

·· 31 ··

My first day in the office since returning from my emotional sabbatical, and HR had yet to decide what to do with me. Apparently, someone had managed to give the company the impression that I had spent the last month wearing a Superman suit and scribbling scripture all over my face with magic markers.

"Oh, hello! Welcome back, Ms. Chopra," the receptionist greeted me enthusiastically. Then she contorted her face and continued in a nodding whisper, "How are you?"

"I'm fine, Jen. Doing great. Never better. I've got a nine a.m. with someone in Human Resources."

"Yes, your appointment's with Gabe. Suite 306. Elevators on your left." She smiled, and cocked her head to the right. *"And good luck with everything."*

It was odd enough to be in the building without being treated as if I would forget my own head if it weren't attached. Then again, this wasn't the South Pacific, I reminded myself. It was New York, a place where it was best to blend in. A place where complaints over the stench from a solitary container of rotting mooshu pork, which forced the building super to let himself into my apartment, were the only interest any of my neighbors had shown in my absence. A place where nobody pays any attention to their neighbors' business, absence or history of domestic violence until some unsavory scent creeps its way into the hallway, or some unsavory character creeps its way up a fire escape. A place where I could take comfort in the fact that nobody at work would badger me for details about my time off, since that kind of inquiry might be mistaken for a sign of concern. I decided to take advantage of the indifference I expected, and to coast by on a minimal amount of work, trusting that my new coworkers would pick up the slack so long as I twitched or feigned the imminence of tears in the middle of a routine meeting from time to time.

Probably in an attempt to gauge potential hires at their most vulnerable, the Human Resources department of any major corporation is deliberately designed to avoid offering physical or emotional comfort. Small, stiff sofas face the door. Intimidating company logos hang on the walls where soothing artwork ought to be. It's always ten degrees colder there than in any other part of the building. And the staff-bots never stop smiling. I was searching for the telltale microphones and floodlights that completed any soundstage, and was speculating where the perfectly postured receptionist's "off-button" might be hidden, when someone startled me with a hello.

"Please, follow me to our conference room."

Gabe Schmidt was taupe. I was certain I had forgotten what he looked like before I stopped looking at him. He asked me to take a seat while he extended his very moist hand along with the company's sincerest apologies for the *difficulties* I had encountered as a result of the *unfortunate choices* of my managers.

"I want to assure you that the company appreciates your hard work and loyalty," he said.

I blinked. The clock ticked. Somewhere, a pudgy pop star who believed way too much of her own hype asked someone *If this dress made her look too skinny.*

"And we look forward to continuing to count you as a member of our team for years to come."

I lowered my head and raised an eyebrow at him. He smoothed his comb-over before continuing.

"There are a few options for you within the firm, Ms. Chopra. We'd like to start by finding out what *you* want."

"You mean you're not just gonna plug me into some empty spot in the company?"

"We don't see it that way. Frankly, we assumed that you would have some ideas on where you would best fit in, and on what you could bring to the table. We expected finding a place for you to be more of a collaborative effort. What do you want? Where do you think you belong within the firm? What are the unique qualities you possess that will make you a good fit for a certain team or group? What are you excited about?"

I really had no idea what I wanted or was excited about,

what I brought to the table or where I belonged. But it occurred to me that this was one of my opportunities to face a demon, to speak up and question authority. Suddenly my perspective shifted. So I made a choice.

"I want a clean slate and a second chance. In a new team. I want the chance to find out if I'm excited about the work."

"All right." He smiled unblinkingly. "I'm sure that can be arranged."

By the end of the day I was seated at my new desk in my new office on my new floor, surrounded by cardboard boxes containing everything that had been stored from my old office. No confetti and no fanfare. Corporate America was as homogenously impersonal as it was reassuringly predictable. Perhaps it had always been that way. Apparently the dust of my former career had settled while I wasn't looking, along with the stacks of documents on this new desk thoughtfully provided by my new secretary. With the documents at my fingertips, I decided to throw myself into it. I kicked off my shoes and planned to read all night long in order to get up to speed on the company my new team would be discussing the following morning. I thought of Salt-and-Pepper, and I was grateful for that chance.

Normally, to be in the position I was in on Tuesday morning would have implied a more promising sequence of events. However, it was just the fault of my clumsy new secretary bumping into my desk a few moments earlier, initiating the avalanche of previously collated files, which she used to break her fall. I knew she was too good to be true. Fearing that she might accidentally set me on fire if I allowed her to help, I sent her on a Starbucks run and insisted on cleaning up by myself. This was why I found myself down on all fours, with my rear end sticking out from underneath the desk, and my cheek pressed up against the cold, hard wood, trying to reach the last few pieces of paper, when my phone rang. The embarrassing default country-music ring tone on my new cell still startled me every time. In this instance, it caused me to bump the top of my head into the desk. In doing so, I also managed to bite right into my tongue.

"*Th*it!" I barked at no one in particular, after scrambling to my feet and flipping open the handset. The blood in my mouth was little inconvenience compared to the resulting lisp. All this, combined with the aggressive wedgie from my thong, put me in a less than welcoming spirit when I answered the phone.

"What?" I asked flatly.

A loud guffaw was followed by an amused and husky male voice which said, "For someone who's supposedly learned all about meditation, you don't sound very Zen."

"What?" I barked, annoyed. "I bit my tongue. Who i*th* thi*th*?"

"I'm sorry. This is Nick. From the gym? And my apartment? And the airport? And the wedding?"

Apparently, men can sense vulnerability the way that hyenas smell blood.

"Ooooooh. Hi," I offered, climbing to my seat and examining myself in my handheld compact mirror. I searched for early signs of an oversize bump being circled by cartoon stars and chirping birds. "This is a surprise."

"I wasn't planning on calling you, but I was concerned that I might have come on a little strong at the wedding, and considering that you only recently got back from your trip and everything...I wanted to apologize in case I made you feel uncomfortable."

"How did you get my number?" I asked, rubbing my head.

"From Cristina. I hope you don't mind. I think you and I keep starting off on the wrong foot, and..."

I was in no mood for more emotional Monopoly. "Don't you think we should conferenth in your girlfriend, jutht to make sure we all get *thtarted on the right foot?* Nick, why are you calling me?"

"What girlfriend?"

"Kat."

"You talked to Kat? Is that why you left? What did she tell you? She is not my girlfriend."

"Oh, okay. Let me gueth. She wath one of your thith-ters?"

Sure. And I rushed out for new batteries in the middle of that rainy night last fall because my *remote control* went dead.

"No, she's not my sister."

Well, this was odd. Dishonesty I knew how to deal with. But *honesty?* It had to be some twisted game, and at that point it was getting to be laughable.

"Okay, then. I don't know what kind of kinky crap you and your girlfriend are into, but I'm not interethted in being the meat in your Vina thandwich, okay? Tho whatever you want, go look for it thomewhere elth."

"Vina, please stop for a minute. For the record, Kat is an ex-girlfriend, from law school. She was also a friend of Prakash's, which is why she was at the wedding. She's crazy, a real maniac. She kept throwing herself at me because she hadn't seen me in over a year. I told her I wasn't interested, and I guess no one else would touch her with a ten-foot pole. She probably got pissed off when she saw us talking. I swear I'm telling you the truth, but if you want we can get Prakash on the line to corroborate my story. I understand that the burden of proof is on me, and…did you just say *'Vina Sandwich'?"*

"Thorry." I lowered my head as if he could see me. "Maybe I've been thpending too much time around butch lethbianth and drag queenth who are more feminine than I am. I'm probably being defenthive."

"It's no big deal. I don't normally blurt out something like this, but given our track record, I think the less time I spend beating around the bush the better, before we get our signals crossed again. Do you think you could let your *defentheth* down for long enough to have dinner with me some time?"

Well hel-lo… I paused for a moment to recall the mental snapshots I had taken of him in his kitchen. Within the millisecond it took for me to consider his offer I had weighed everything from the convenience of his having been pre-screened by Prakash to the fragility of my current emotional state. I concluded that getting involved with any man right now would be a mistake. A very tempting mistake that came with the virtual guarantee of fresh-squeezed orange juice in the morning. Orange juice that might trickle down those tight, veiny forearms, onto that six-pack of a stomach, which I could then lick off....

To hell with it. I was ready to face another demon. Maybe he would hurt me, or leave me, or lie to me, or whatever. Maybe I would fail to protect myself, or maybe I would see right through it this time. Or maybe there would be nothing for me to see through. So I was still standing and life was calling. It was a chance I had to take. Besides, it was only dinner.

"That *thoundth* like fun!" I gushed like a schoolgirl trying to sound casual through a mouthful of food, while batting my eyelashes so hard that I could have taken flight.

·· 32 ··

With Christopher and Prakash on their cruise to Belize, I had agreed to cat-sit again. I was watching Booboo nose around happily inside of a Bebe bag I had left out on the floor the next evening when the phone rang.

"Hello, darling. Is this a good time?" asked the body snatcher who had swallowed my mother while I was away. I was still having trouble getting used to the idea that my parents had started to respect my time. It was one of the many things that had changed since they watched helplessly as I boarded a plane headed for the South Pacific.

"Sure, Mom. Yes. Of course it's a good time. What's going on?"

I sank into the couch and began nudging the bag away from Booboo with a toe at different speeds. Convinced that it was alive, he readied himself for the attack.

"I was talking with your Auntie Neela, and she was telling

me that her brother Amit used to have severe, severe anxiety when he was in college."

"Really?" I perked up. "How surprising."

Booboo leaped on the bag, which I yanked away, making his eyes light up more.

"Yes, yes. And it's not so surprising, but we never talked about these things before. Now I have decided that it's a part of life, and so what? We have good things and we have challenges just like everybody else, *na?* So what if our daughter went through a difficult time? Everybody does, and the only difference is that nobody says anything about these things in our circles. So I've told your father that we're not going to hide from anyone. Our daughter is a wonderful girl, and we have no use for anyone who will judge us."

"Okay..."

"So anyway, Neela was telling me that her brother used breathing exercises he learned from some special type of yoga to calm his nerves. Would you like to try that? Maybe we could try it together, if I could find a class in Manhattan? It could help me, too."

I had to smile. Never had I heard anyone trying so hard to speak my language.

"That sounds great, Mom. Will Dad be joining us?" I already knew the answer.

"*Beti*...he will try."

"Thanks, Mom."

"Nothing to thank me for. Don't be silly. I want to spend time with my child."

"I know, Mom. I know."

"And that's why I told your father that he better not dare ask you about business school or marriage anytime soon."

"Really? And how did he take that?"

"He huffed and puffed, but he'll get over it. He's frustrated because there's this surgeon from Cold Spring Harbor who finished up his residency at Stony Brook University, and last week when we met them at the Kapoors' dinner party, his parents asked about you."

"Mom," I said, lowering my voice, "you're doing it again. What did I tell you about my personal life?"

Booboo climbed on top of the bag, resettled himself and listened in.

"I'm not invited." She sounded like a child who had been chastised for playing in the formal dining room.

"That's not how I put it, exactly, but yes. Besides, I'm not sure this is a good time for me to be dating at all."

"Fine, fine. We're not pushing. So what? I've been thinking lately that I am getting sick of always worrying about my daughter's marriage this, my daughter's marriage that. It's all the ladies talk about when we meet for lunch these days. Why aren't the kids getting married? When will they get married? Who will they marry? I told the girls last week at lunch—I'm finished. Let my daughter marry whoever she chooses. I've raised her. I've educated her. She can marry who she marries. All I know is…*I'm married.* And you know what? They all agreed that I had made a very good point."

"No offense, Mom, but I'll believe it when I see it. Besides, does Dad agree with any of this?"

"I didn't ask his opinion. Okay, you must have things to do, *na?* I'll talk to you tomorrow. Good night."

Booboo slammed his eyes shut and turned his head away, no longer able to look at me.

"Don't you judge me," I said to him, after hanging up the phone. "This one date with Nick barely counts, because it's not going to lead to anything. Besides, I'm just not ready to tell her yet."

"It's over." Pamela was standing in my doorway and telling me less than ten minutes later. "I just ended it."

"Come in and tell me what happened," I said, nudging Booboo back into my apartment with an ankle to the face. He wasn't making a jail-break on my watch.

"Just what I said. I did it. Just like that."

"What do you mean, you did it? How?"

"Why does it matter?" she asked, eerily calm in her track-suit and no makeup. "I gave him his keys. His *keys,* Vina. Do you remember how many hints I had to drop before he even gave me those stupid keys?"

"Yes, and I remember the hints were more like sky-written announcements."

"See? That's just it." She plopped down into a chair. "It's the most amazing thing. I feel like I'm thinking clearly for the first time in *years!* All this time I thought I would collapse if I had to give him back his keys. But then I was standing outside his apartment, taking them off my key chain, and they're just keys! They're not a promise of anything, since I had to manipulate him to get them. And he's only one guy.

It's all so stupid. It's as big a deal as I make it. I decided that I…I didn't want to let it be such a big deal anymore. So I broke up with him."

"What did he say?" I picked Booboo up onto my lap and switched off the TV, so I could give her my full attention.

"Who cares! I didn't stick around to listen. It felt so great."

Even Booboo had trouble believing it.

"Honestly," she assured us.

"Wow." I ran my fingers over my face. "I'm proud of you. What do you want to do now?"

She shrugged her shoulders and stuck out her lower lip. "I'm not sure. I still want to get married someday, just not to him. Maybe I should be alone for a while. You know I've never really been single. Then again, I might call you crying tomorrow morning when it hits me that I'm actually single. Right now, that doesn't seem likely. And, I've been thinking about grad school. God, there are so many possibilities now that I think about life outside the context of *William*. If it's me alone, then I can kind of do whatever I want, right? Maybe even get an MBA? That way I could become the director of a gallery. I mean, I don't know if it's a real possibility. But I know I don't have anything to lose. Why? Do you think me getting an MBA is a crazy idea?"

"Pam—" I pondered "—I think that putting the rest of it on hold to be happier with yourself and inside yourself is a fantastic idea."

"Thanks, but I think I could say the same thing to you."

"Maybe we're both growing up."

"Cristy wouldn't approve," Pam joked.

"Yes, but my parents would be very proud of you."

She laughed.

"And so am I."

·· 33 ··

Remember how your mother told you to always wear clean underwear in case you were in an accident? Well, good little girls the world over grew into otherwise rational women who insisted that we could apply the same principle in reverse. If clean underwear somehow made it okay to get into a car accident, since you wouldn't risk losing the respect of the paramedics who were trying to resuscitate you, then unshaven legs were industrial-strength protection against the possibility of a regrettable sexcapade. Because even in the heat of the perfect romantic moment, no girl would let a guy get anywhere near a pair of legs au naturel.

At about seven on Saturday night I was making my way to a French-Ethiopian fusion restaurant to meet Nick. My makeup was flawless, my perfume was tasteful and my legs were a veritable jungle. Damn his inviting smile. Since I was an emotional basket case and Nick was just the kind of man-mountain I would love to plant my flag on, I decided I wasn't taking any chances.

To be fair, I didn't know him very well, and maybe that was part of the attraction. When the evening began, he embodied the entire idea of my putting myself out there and feeling desired again. That was dangerously tempting. I arrived early so that he couldn't watch my entrance. As I crossed Lexington Avenue with the restaurant in sight, I adjusted and readjusted everything from my hairdo to my bra straps, in an attempt to convince myself more than anyone else that I was sexy and charming, despite the knowledge that I was in fact hairy and already unnecessarily smitten with this man.

My eggs were in an uproar the moment Nick came through the door and it almost made me drop my glass of Merlot. I don't know if it was because he could crush every other man in the restaurant like an empty beer can, or because every time I met him he was coming to somebody's rescue or because the cartoon birds previously circling the bump on my head had since flown in through my ears, set up camp and started playing a bluegrass rendition of "Sexual Healing." What I did know was that I had to thank God Cristina had come over while I was getting ready and made absolutely sure I didn't shave my legs that night.

With Nick sitting directly across from me, I couldn't help but let my mind wander. He had a heavy Brooklyn accent, a decidedly non-Upper-East-Side gait and a smile that made me want to give him more reasons to smile. His hands were like meat cleavers and he laughed from the pit of his belly.

I was silently wishing I *was* the slab of Siga Wot beef on the plate before him when he derailed my runaway train of thought....

"Vina, you seem distracted. Are you listening to me?"

"Hmm? Oh, yes, of course. I seem a little out of it probably because I'm still reeling from that bump I got on my noggin."

I hadn't heard one word he had uttered in the prior five minutes, but I had imagined myself biting him in at least three places. *When did I turn into such a frat boy? And did I just say "noggin"?*

"Clumsy me!" I added, as if this would make me seem like any less of a geek.

"Right." He challenged me with eyes that could barely mask his mounting amusement. "Then what was I talking about?"

"Um...right now?" I blushed and batted my eyes in the hopes of flirting my way out of it. Apparently, I wasn't as cute as I thought.

"Yes. Right now." He crossed his chiseled arms across his chest, further adding to my confusion. It was like a woman waving her breasts in a man's face and then expecting him to think clearly. Completely unfair.

"I'm sorry, Nick. I guess I'm the one who's a little off tonight."

"Look, I understand." He leaned halfway across the table with his neck, as if he were about to let me in on when the prison-break was going down. "I read all about your company's problems in the *New York Times,* and Chris and Prakash filled me in on the fact that you've had a rough couple of months."

Now I felt like a predatory and insensitive man. A cad. The sleazy, well-coiffed British playboy in every movie. I had to admit that the fantasy of a muscle-bound personal trainer better suited for a test of physical, rather than mental stamina, had me feeling like a newly minted twentysomething Internet millionaire in a roomful of aspiring models. *Like I could have my way with him, order him up like a stack of pancakes, grease him up with butter, drench him in syrup and let the party begin.*

But now he had gone and said something sweet and understanding, and I felt as though I deserved to be whacked on the hand with a ruler. That sexy, wonderful jerk.

"Anyway," he continued, "like I said, I thought it was impressive that you did that meditation retreat. I would love to hear more about it. I admit I still have trouble believing that someone with such an active imagination could manage to stay quiet for so long. I'm very interested in different cultures and traditions. Basically, I'm fascinated by everything out there. I probably sound like a scatterbrained kid."

"No," I said. "Not at all. It's refreshing, actually. A pleasant surprise."

"Why is that?" he asked, while motioning to the waiter for more wine.

"No reason. I mean, I think it's great but to be honest with you, most typical *American* men from New York who are living this lifestyle are not open to things like that."

"Oh, so you already think I'm typical."

"I don't know that much about you, other than the inside

of your bedroom and what you do for a living, so I don't
want to categorize you."

"No, no. It's fine. I get that all the time—because I work
out I must be a big, dumb lug, right? That, and this
Brooklyn accent means all I know is pizza and beer?"

You poor, misunderstood man. *Let Vina make it better.*

"So now you know that I'm more than meets the eye.
What else do you want to know?"

"Okay." I stalled for time, trying to come up with a question
that would make him feel a bit less objectified. "Tell me more
about your family. Your parents. Where did you grow up?"

"Cleveland. We moved to Brooklyn when I was about
seven after my mother passed away. I'm the youngest of four,
and my dad decided to raise us closer to his family, who were
in New York. That's why family's so important to me, I guess."

"I'm sorry to hear about your mom," I said. "How did
it happen?"

"Cancer, and my parents were together for, like, fifteen
years. So my father never remarried. He decided to focus
on the kids instead. I was lucky, though. We grew up with
lots of cousins and aunts and uncles and everything. And
God knows there were enough women in the house telling
me what to do all the time. Besides that, I think the biggest
thing I learned from having three sisters and no brother is
to pick and choose my battles. Women win, most of the
time."

"Is that why you became a lawyer? To learn how to argue
better so you could win the occasional family argument?"

"That would make sense. But no. My dad's big thing was

that he promised my mom that at least one of us would become a lawyer, like she had wanted to do. She never did, because she got pregnant right after they got married and I think she was twenty years old. She always planned to go back later, but I guess with three kids it's not so easy. In the end, three of us did become lawyers. I never really wanted to do it, honestly, but I saw how disappointed my father was when my second-oldest sister chose not to. So I took out all those loans, went to law school and found out that I enjoyed it."

"So then how did you wind up in this line of work? The fitness industry, I mean."

"Practicing law, as I sort of told you, wasn't as gratifying as I had expected it to be. In fact, I ended up defending some people I didn't feel very good about defending, and I had what you might call a 'crisis of conscience.' I decided to take some time off from the law. Fitness was always a part of my life, and then the director of fitness position became open at my gym, so I tried it out for a while before deciding what else to do. I had some money saved up, and I wasn't happy, so I figured it was now or never. I finally let myself stop feeling guilty about what my mom would want. But anyway, I loved fitness, so I stayed. It was hard initially to make the decision to stop focusing on what everyone else thought made sense for me. Sure, I make less money, but I'm so much happier now than when I was a lawyer. And what's the point of a job that you're not excited about, right?"

"I guess so." I was floored, and for the first time since I could remember, speechless.

"You don't agree? I would have thought you'd be on the same page as me with something like this."

"I think I am, in theory. But practice is something else entirely."

A waiter interrupted us to present a warm chocolate cake dripping in fresh whipped cream and strawberries.

"I hope you don't mind that I preordered this. I just followed my instincts," he explained, while gathering a heaping spoonful and lifting it toward my mouth. "Now don't tell me that you're one of those women who doesn't eat dessert."

"I like your instincts," I replied through a mouthful of chocolatey nirvana. "So when did all of this happen? The career change?"

"About two years ago," he answered, helping himself to the next spoonful. "But to be honest with you the ambition-bug is back in me already. I'm researching the possibility of opening up a gym of my own that I could eventually turn into a chain across the country. The concept is different from anything else out there because people would be working with top celebrity trainers exclusively. Nobody would enter the gym without an appointment with their trainer. We would also have limited membership, like a country club, so there would be a waiting list to make it exclusive. I know it's a long shot, but so was Starbucks, right? Besides, I can always go back to the law. But I might never take a chance like this again. So recently I've been looking into financing for our first location."

I think if I had moved at all, I would have had an orgasm right then and there.

"Okay, I take it back. You're definitely not typical."

In fact, he had morphed into the perfect guy. This posed a problem because it was easy to dismiss a hyper-attractive yet unintelligent man, but for a woman who's got her act together, ambition is the *ultimate* turn-on. And I was pretty sure that I couldn't handle anything more romantically serious at the moment than a fling. Chocolate-covered or otherwise.

"I try to make unconventional choices from time to time. I've got to do *some*thing to distinguish myself, right? How *else* am I gonna get the attention of a gorgeous woman like you?"

"Oh, I'll bet you say that to all the girls." I struggled to steady my trembling hand as it lifted the glass of water to my mouth.

"No, I really don't. You know, it's hard to find a woman with real versatility. Anyone who can take the chances you do, and manage to hold her own with these Wall Street tight-asses, must be something special."

"You're sweet."

"And you're gorgeous." He smiled with a hint of boyish nervousness which made me want to give him a big hug. "Has anybody ever told you that you look Sicilian?"

"Once or twice," I said, and wondered to myself what his mother must have looked like.

"Seriously, you're not typical by any stretch of the imagination, either. It's obvious from your writing. I don't know how passionate you are about your job, but you seem like you've got some things to say. Come to think of it, have you ever thought about pursuing it professionally?"

Maybe I could just climb out of the ladies' room window, run across the street to the drugstore, buy a razor, shave in the bathroom stall and make it back before the check arrived?

The benefit of seeing your life as a movie is that along the way, you get to pick your own soundtrack. The drawback is the overwhelming sense of directorial indignation you'll feel whenever someone fails to take their cue. It was one of those warm New York summer evenings tailor-made for strolling hand-in-hand, lingering in street corner embraces and kissing gently for the first time under the soft glow of the lights from the lobbies of high-rises. As we turned the corner onto my block, Nick and I slowed down a bit, presumably in order to prolong the conversation and heighten our anticipation of the impending good-night kiss.

All was going according to plan. Five hours of engaging conversation had passed us by. It must have been some sort of a first-date record. He had expressed interest in the feelings behind my feelings about the death of my childhood goldfish. I had laughed appropriately at his spring break story, which ended in him waking up alone on the bathroom floor of a Mexican gas station with a tattoo of a cheeseburger on his butt. I was so distracted, in fact, that I completely failed to notice the subway grate. I lost my balance when my favorite red, three-inch, snakeskin Versace heel plunged directly between the metal crosshairs. Eagle-eyed and attentive, Nick must have seen it coming. He swooped in at exactly the right moment, throwing an arm around my waist and scooping me gingerly out of harm's way before I could fall. Disappointingly, he didn't sweep me up into a passionate lip-lock. Nick placed me back onto my own two feet and continued walking toward my door. There were only two possible explanations: either there were a few pages missing from his copy of the script, or he had decided that I was fat.

"I had a really nice time. This was fun," he decided, as if I had been his first attempt at Speed-Dating. Then he came closer for a kiss that my grandmother would've deemed chaste. Well, maybe not *my* grandmother. But *somebody's* grandmother.

"Yes, it was." I laughed nervously. His facial expression melted from warmth into concern and he leaned in close before asking me what was wrong.

"Nothing!" I claimed too enthusiastically, shaking my head as if I could swat the thought away.

"It's not nothing. You're thinking something. What is it?"

"Really! It's nothing." I avoided eye contact by rummaging around inside my purse, as if the answer might have fallen inside. He wasn't about to settle this one out of court. So I gave in and decided to oblige his curiosity with what turned out to be a particularly horrendous display of verbal diarrhea.

New rule: No more Merlot around any man who is sexy, sensitive and able to lift my entire body above his head with one hand.

"I just… It's no big deal… I just… It's weird. Normally, *I* pull away from a guy. I'm the *girl*. That's what I'm used to. And you've been so nice. I don't know if it's manners or being old-fashioned. I'm not complaining. I just… I guess I'm used to a guy being a little more aggressive. But we had such a fun evening, and…oh, my god. I can't believe I'm telling you this."

What the hell was wrong with me? He looked as if I had stunned him with a tazer and he might be about to tip over. I considered moving out of the way, only I didn't know whether a bear fell forward or backward after being shot with a stun gun.

"I guess it's weird to me that you find me so…resistible. Oh, dammit! That's not what I meant to say. That makes me sound so arrogant and that's not what I meant."

Maybe if I concentrated really hard I could dissolve into liquid form and make my getaway through those accursed metal grates or some of the cracks in the sidewalk. Like some sneaky comic book character. A superhero. Or a supervillain. A dating supervillain who ruins romantic moments by saying inappropriate things and then disappears before she can be held accountable! *They will call me The Datinator, and I will wear a red cape with delicate Indian embroidery, and occasionally hit people over the head with a bottle of Dom Pérignon.*

I couldn't stop myself. "Wow. I've made a perfectly lovely evening completely awkward, haven't I? I swear I'm not normally this bizarre. Um…yeah. Listen, maybe we should say good-night."

Finally, consciousness returned, or, maybe *goodnight* was the secret word, because he grinned and decided to put me out of my misery.

"Vina, you are probably the funniest woman I have ever met. And no, for the record, I do *not* find you at all…what was the word you used? *Resistible?*"

"Thanks, but could you please not look directly at me right now?" I resumed groping in my purse for my keys.

"I didn't want to come on too strong," he said and took my hands in his, forcing me to look him in the eye. "At least not unless you gave me some sort of a green light."

He reached a hand along my neck and slipped it tenderly into my hair, pulling my face toward his. Within moments I was kissing him so passionately that I even surprised myself. As if winning a similar intensity from him might make up for the ridiculousness of my outburst, I persevered. And it worked. Thankfully for my ego, he seemed to think this was fun, and we spent the better part of the next half hour leaning against the stone facade of my building, sucking face like a couple of teenagers racing against a curfew. At one point, he pulled away and smiled at me, semibreathless and covered from chin to nose in traces of my lipstick to ask, "Wow. Do all the girls from Long Island kiss like that?"

"I don't know," I blurted without thinking, high on his pheromones and cocky at my face-sucking prowess. "I don't kiss that many of them."

Wait a minute. Did I just imply that I *did* kiss *some of them?* Thank God for men who knew when to shut me up with a kiss. Because for the first time I wasn't thinking about anything other than that moment.

·· 34 ··

I pulled the comforter tight around my body to savor the clash of the warmth with the crisp October morning chill sneaking in through the edges of the windows. Rolling onto the half of the bed that Nick recently left behind, I took a deep breath of something that had started to become so familiar. It was the scent of the pancakes cooking in the kitchen. Chocolate-chip pancakes, to be specific, since it wasn't hard to detect a hint of burned chocolate wafting through the air. There were no chips in the fridge the night before, so the sweetie-pie must have snuck out early to get them before I woke up. On our fourth date, he brought along four roses and asked if we could see each other exclusively. On our three-month anniversary he told me that the only thing he would be willing to accept as a gift was something I wrote just for him, because my heart would be contained inside it far more than it could ever be in any other object. And when the tears streaked down my face as I explained that it would be difficult for me to let him into my heart after having been hurt so deeply before, he listened quietly and literally kissed them off of my cheeks.

Dropping my head back onto the pillow, I gazed in the general direction of the kitchen, and I smiled. Exposing myself had been the right move this time, no matter what happened next. He would never know how much he had healed me. Right about then, my cell phone rang....

"Heeeeeeeey. Are you as hung over as I am?" Cristina asked in a hushed voice.

"*Nobody* is as hung over as you are," I told her. "But we did have an early night. We didn't drink much after the restaurant. By the way, your new boyfriend's amazing."

"Francois is not my boyfriend."

"Does he know that? Considering the way he was nibbling on your elbow last night…"

"I kicked him out an hour ago. I swear, I spent all night listening to him talk, and I didn't hear anything I hadn't heard before, you know?"

"Yeah, yeah." I swallowed to stop my mouth from watering at the scent of the pancakes.

"Isn't Nick annoying like that? Aren't you bored of him?"

"Not really. Maybe he's blinding me with food and sex. Either way, I'm still interested."

"You're such a married couple," she complained.

"I am not a married couple," I said a little too loud, and then smiled at the sight of the framed diploma that always reminded me of the first time I woke up in Nick's apartment. "What are you doing?"

"Nothing. I'm sniffing all the milk in my fridge to see if there's anything that hasn't gone bad yet, so I can have some coffee. How about you? Do you want to get brunch?"

"I literally just woke up. I'm still in bed," I answered, piling one pillow on top of the other behind me. "And Nick's making chocolate-chip pancakes, I think."

"Okay. I'm hanging up."

"No, you're not."

"I know." I heard her roll her eyes. "You're a lucky woman."

"And he's a lucky man."

"And he knows it. Talk about nibbling on *my* elbow. Nick still doesn't seem to notice that there are other women in the room. My prediction? He'll propose within a year."

"Whoa there, trigger-happy! I don't know about all *that*. I'm happy with him, but…"

"But what, *chica?* I don't know what to tell you. You've got your life back. You've got a wonderful new man. And he makes *friggin' chocolate-chip pancakes* for you, even after he saw you in that hideous dress last night."

"Hey!"

"Look, I told you that brown is not your color. It was almost as bad as what we had to wear to Chris's wedding. And if I'm not honest with you, who will be? Anyway, where else are you going to find a guy who's so superficially pleasing, but so not superficial? It's an elusive balance."

"I know, I know."

★ ★ ★

If meeting most women's parents is the emotional equivalent of taking the SAT (no matter how much you've prepared, you'll never know all the answers, so you just thank God that they're judging on a curve), then meeting my parents is the equivalent of the MCAT tailored for trilingual engineers. No one ever passes.

Meeting most men's parents, on the other hand, has been a piece of cake for me. And I've come to pride myself on it, since, aside from being able to limbo far lower than is natural or necessary, there are few things that I can do better than most other women. Christopher thought the fact that I could sense and tell each parent exactly what they wanted to hear made me an emotional prostitute. I thought the fact that he was traditionally attracted to men on the rebound made *him* emotional toilet paper.

Maybe the former girlfriends of my former boyfriends had been such disasters that the parents were simply grateful I wasn't sporting track marks. Or maybe my boyfriends were so bland that the time I spent with them, before meeting their parents, left me starving for the adult conversation. Whatever the reason, I would often delay breakups for fear of losing my rapport with the 'rents. I worked well in an artificial environment—the meetings were always planned weeks ahead, everybody knew everybody else's allergies and *Do-Not-Touch* topics and there was only the example of *the women who had hurt their son in the past* for me to compete with. I shined like a bottle cap resting on top a trash heap in the sun.

The keys to success in winning the hearts of the people whose sons you have bewitched include:

1. Dress for church, or temple, or mosque, or whatever.

Up (like it's an occasion to be excited about), but also conservative (like you always assume God's watching). Nothing below the collarbone or above the knee. Makeup like his mother would have worn at your age, which you should know because you asked him in advance. Jewelry that's classy but affordable. You should be good enough for, but not better than, their son.

2. Give 'em a little bit of your dwarky side. The wider and goofier the smile, the better.

There's a reason why a certain relatably quirky redhead is a hit across all cultures and demographics. Laugh at yourself when you do or say something silly, and his parents will laugh with you. Maybe even glance shyly over at their son for reassurance, and make sure that they see this, but also make sure that they don't see that you see that they see this. It will remind them that he already loves you, and make them want to find reasons to approve.

3. Don't talk too much. Answer their questions and ask more.

His parents aren't interested in falling in love with you. They're only interested in accepting you. The intricacies of your emotions are his cross to bear. Well, his, and your therapist's. One of the parents always wants to be the center of attention. Figure out which one, and help them. Even if you don't give a damn about Dad's stamp collection, or the summer Mom spent in Dijon during college.

Since my parents always assumed I would be meeting men through them, as opposed to the other way around, at least a year of a relationship would pass before I'd even bother to mention my man to them. And if he wasn't Indian, it was a disaster-recovery mission from the start. You assume a certain number of casualties, some carnage, tears and recurring nightmares for everyone involved. That might be another reason why I spared most men the indignity of it for as long as I did. I was hoping to give them as much positive reinforcement as possible in advance, since it was virtually impossible for *some stranger who just walked in off the street, some meathead whose family they didn't even know* (my father identified way too well with the '70s sitcom *All in the Family*) to win the early approval of the people whose offspring he was attempting to steal. He was lucky if he left without his self-esteem deep-fried and seasoned in a doggie bag.

I knew it was a bad idea, but Nick insisted just a few months into the relationship that I allow him to meet my parents. When I called to invite them over for lunch, my mother interrupted to tell me that she had decided not to make any new friends until after my wedding.

"Am I engaged and nobody told me?" I asked, smiling conspiratorially at Nick as he crossed my living room.

"No, darling, of course not. But surely you will be within the next few years."

"Mom…"

"No pressure, no pressure. I am just planning my affairs accordingly."

"So *why* exactly can't you make any new friends before then?" I tried to keep my composure while he lifted my hair and began nibbling on the back of my neck.

"Because," she began as if she were explaining to me for the fifth time why I wasn't allowed to wear my pajamas to school, "any friends I have will be offended if I do not invite them to my daughter's wedding. And limiting guest lists is always a difficult thing to do. Everybody is so petty."

"Why don't you tell everyone we plan to have a very small wedding?"

"Why don't I just go and have a liposuction?" she mocked.

"What?" I rose to my feet, causing Nick to nearly tumble off the couch. *Sorry,* I mouthed, before walking toward the window.

"Vina, you know us better than that. There are certain things which are not done. And what's more, you know things don't work that way in Indian society. We cannot change traditions to suit ourselves. I don't want to make new friends right now, and then have to alienate them within two years because of the wedding."

"Oh, so now it's two years?"

"Vina, calm down. I am only talking, that's all."

"Okay, so what you're saying is that my *not* being married is now directly cramping your social life."

"That is not what I said."

I knew she hadn't.

"Why are we talking about this? Listen, it's time for you and Dad to meet Nick. He has offered to make lunch for all of us at his apartment on Sunday."

"Why?" she asked.

"Because…we might be hungry?"

"Don't make fun, Vina. Anyway, you father is not going to like this. But I'll try to convince him. I think it should be fine. So you are…umm…very serious about this…Nick?"

"Mom." I was as stern and declarative as a grammar-school headmistress. "I am *not* inviting you to this lunch to announce an engagement. You're meeting him. That's all. Calm down. And please tell Dad not to be mean."

·· 35 ··

Grocery shopping with a boyfriend on a weekend afternoon. Does it get any better? It provides all of the gratification of shopping at the mall, but he doesn't have to lie about whether that skort makes you look fat, and you don't have to act as if you didn't notice him steering clear of the diamond store. My hand lightly brushes his as we reach for the same avocado. Inevitable snickering in the fruit aisle over whether a banana can *ever really be too firm.* Groping each other inappropriately amongst the frozen foods to keep warm, until management kindly requests that you *keep the public affection to a minimum, since this is a family place.* It's suggestive enough of nesting to keep your feathers fluffed, without throwing him into a fit of hyperventilation.

At least it is under normal circumstances. However, less than three hours away from my parents' estimated time of arrival at his apartment, Nick was *waaaaaay* too calm for anyone's good. How had he managed to miss the fact that offering to feed my parents the first time he met them was about as casual as a presidential inauguration?

He stood before me surrounded by Whole Foods' fresh produce with both arms outstretched, one holding a cantaloupe and the other a honeydew.

"So which will it be? Ladies' choice." He winked.

"I don't know. The cantaloupe, I guess."

"You guess? You *guess?* Well, that's not good enough." A sarcastic grin spread across his face. "Don't you understand that your parents' entire opinion of me is riding on what they think of my fruit salad?"

Not amused.

"Vina, you know, you should show more enthusiasm. I'm a guy who cooks. Doesn't that make me a great catch, according to all those girly magazines?" He tossed the honeydew onto a pile of lemons beside us, dropped the cantaloupe into the cart and leaned into the push.

"I don't read those magazines," I told his back.

"I know. That's one of my favorite things about you. Well, that and the fact that you've got a really sweet ass. Who knew Indian women were built like that?"

"Everyone who's ever bothered to look." I smiled coyly, catching up. My gaze met that of a young girl riding in a cart pushed by her mother, who glared disapproval at our adult discussion. The girl reminded me of myself at her age, and the woman couldn't be much older than me, which made me feel very, very old.

"That's probably true. Anyway, remind me to thank your mother for that."

"You will do no such thing," I chided, as we turned a corner toward Wines & Spirits. "Okay. What else do we need?"

He waved a couple of bottles of wine at me as if they were bells and I was the only one who couldn't hear them chiming.

"What's this?"

"Uh…a really good bottle of Chardonnay." He played dumb. "According to the price tag?"

"We can't serve this."

"Why not?" He held the bottle at arm's length and squinted. "Was 1999 not a good year for you? For me, *it was a very good year.*"

Not cute.

"No, '99 was a perfectly good year." I felt my forehead.

"Then why can't we serve it? Unless…" His eyes grew wide before he gasped, fixing his stare on my belly, with all the cockiness of a man whose girlfriend insists on condoms even though she's on the pill. "Are we *preg*nant?"

Why do men always do that? Why do they overemphasize the "preg," as if some other sort of "nant" would be lesser cause for alarm?

"*Not* funny." I replaced the bottles on the shelf. "Serving wine at a casual late lunch will make them think that you drink at every meal. This will make them worry if you come from a family of alcoholics, which will make them judge you unworthy of their daughter."

"But you know much more about wine than I do," he protested.

"That's not relevant. I belong to them. And first impressions are critical."

"I thought you belonged to me."

"Not after today I won't if this doesn't go too well." I raised an eyebrow at him but couldn't help cracking a smile.

"Okay, babe. No problem." He raised both hands in surrender. "Relax. We'll serve juice and iced tea. That is, unless you think the fact that it's not chai will make them think I'm *culturally insensitive?* Anyway, it's no biggie."

"But it *is* a biggie. I'm crazy about you, but I swear, the fact that you're taking this so calmly is really stressing me out."

"So you're crazy about me?" He looped his fingers into the belt holes of my jeans, and dragged me toward him. Normally, such a *Me-Tarzan-You-Jane* gesture would have had me goofy and weak in the knees, but in light of the day we had ahead of us…

"Oh, lord. I'm gonna puke." I doubled back, resting one hand on my belly and using the other to pinch the top of my nose.

"Vina," he said slowly and knelt down to look me right in the eye, "there is no reason to be nervous. When my last girlfriend's parents met me, they loved me instantly. Within six months, the father took me aside at a family barbecue and told me that I had his blessing if I wanted to marry her."

"Mmm-hmm. And why didn't that work out, again?"

"We drifted apart. After a while I didn't feel as strongly about her as I thought I did."

"Okay, so the translation of that in my parents' language

is *Love is a fashion trend to you, and so is their daughter.* Maybe that's not the story you should open with."

"Maybe I should start with how we met?"

"Yeah, that would go over well. *Mr. and Mrs. Chopra, your daughter, after waking up naked in my bed, chanced upon three video cameras aimed directly at her, assumed I was an online porn producer and ran screaming for her life. But don't worry, nothing happened between us that night. She was waaaay too drunk at the club for me to even consider trying to get any action. That came later.*"

He laughed and kissed me on the top of my head, told me I was cute, and then headed over toward the juice aisle. I was left standing somewhere between Johnnie Walker and Jose Cuervo, feeling guilty that I failed to impress upon him how totally out of his league he was, when it came to my parents.

I suppose he had no idea how scared I was that a truly disappointed glance from my father might force me to re-consider him entirely. As much as I hated to admit it, no matter how much I separated myself from my family's re-strictions, it would always, always, always matter what they thought. All I could hope for was that he understood, re-spected and continued to relate somehow to my need to please them. I could also do what was possible to help him along. I told him to make whatever he considered to be spicy food, and then add at least three teaspoons of paprika per person. I told him never to refer to either of my parents by their first names until they invited him to do so, which would be never. I told him to ask my mom about her gar-dening and use it as a segue into explaining how he wants a garden of his own one day so that he can grow fresh vegetables to cook. I told him to ask my dad about how he made his transition from engineering to real estate and use it as a segue into explaining every twist and turn of his own career before the real interrogation began. It was all about pre-emptive strikes. This was a war, I had shaken him by the shoulders and tried to make him understand the night before that we were dead in the water without a good, solid strategy. All this, and I bought him a new sweater that I thought they might not deem too expensive, too casual or too fitted for their taste. The less they had to contend with his practically prison-sculpted physique, and what it implied about the carnal interests of their only daughter, the better.

I met Nick's father and sisters for the first time about a month after we began dating. He sprang it on me less than twenty-four hours in advance, and failed to even tell me their first names until we were in the elevator on our way up to the restaurant. Since that dinner, they had always worked their visits with him around my schedule, to make sure that I felt included. His sisters had even started asking him to hand me the phone just to chat whenever they called. And all of this was perfectly normal to him. The poor bastard had no idea what he was in for.

·· 36 ··

This was almost as much fun as the time my mother gave me The Sex Talk.

Don't do it, she explained, waving a finger at my face before leaving me to deal with my hormones and SAT review books.

How could the three people who were supposedly *the most at ease* around me be so *ill at ease* around each other? I knew them all well enough to see what they really meant to say, despite the words that came out of their mouths. Thank God my grandmother had insisted on coming along. She was the only person whose eyes seemed to indicate she acknowledged the enormous and drunken pink elephant in the room.

For example, my mother asked, "So tell me, did your mother teach you how to cook, or did you learn on your own?"

When she really meant: "Is there someone in your family I

can blame for the fact that you think this flavorless mush can pass for food? Or were you born without taste buds of your own?"

And my father said, "Hello."

When the message in his eyes was: "Get away from my daughter, you sketchy, promiscuous American man. She may not see it, but I know that for you she is just a passing fancy. I will eat your food and I will smile at you across the table because my wife tells me that I have no choice. But I've got my eye on you, *meathead.*"

In a way I was guilty of it myself, having asked, "Nick, honey, can you please pass the iced tea?"

When what I really meant was: "Double Dewars. Neat. With a waterback. And please keep 'em coming."

At the moment, my mother was educating Nick about the light sensitivities of particular varieties of orchids, while my father wrinkled his nose with suspicion at the slices of caramelized pear he was chasing around his plate with a fork. I'd told Nick that the pears would make him look like he was trying too hard.

"Thank you for making room for me at the table, Nicholas," Nani attempted, with an injured glance at my mother. "Even though some people told me that I was not invited."

"I'm so glad that you decided to come, Nani. Vina talks about you all the time."

"Of course she does. She is a good girl. They think they can tell me what to do, just because I forget some people's names sometimes. So what? Some people have names which are easy to forget. But I can still go and see my granddaughter whenever I want. And her husband also. I have been alive since before electricity!"

"Mom, behave," my mother interrupted, sensing my father's eye begin to twitch at the mention of the word *husband*.

Nani shot a mischievous grin at Nick, before signaling that she was zipping her mouth. Then she motioned for me to give her some more salad.

"So, Nick, do you think the Pasta Fagiole is ready yet?" I interrupted, reaching for the salad tongs.

"It's fah-*zsohle*, honey," he explained lovingly, holding my face as if to help me mouth out the correct sounds. "And let me check."

Then he bounced happily off toward the kitchen.

Did he just touch me in front of my parents? Like it was no big deal? Was he on crack? He might as well come out of the kitchen butt-naked and smeared in whipped cream, explaining that it was time for a Nicky sundae!

"I know I get a lot of the pronunciations wrong," I said as a meek attempt to distract them from the gratuitous display of affection to which they were forced to bear witness. "Actually, his Hindi is getting to be better than my Italian."

"The only thing that has ever bothered me about your daughter is the way she says *mozzarella*," he added as he walked back into the room, steaming pot and ladle in hand. "*Mott-zuh-reh-luh*. It sounds like a fire-breathing dragon that could incinerate Tokyo. It's *Moot-za-relle*. You gotta roll your *r*s, babe."

"I know, I know," I said, seriously considering jamming my fork into his eye.

"Ahem," Daddy Dearest cleared his throat in a gesture that was more of a roar than the balancing of an air passage. "So where did you earn your law degree, Nicholas?"

Translation: "I don't find any of this the least bit amusing or heartwarming. Let's talk about all the reasons why you're wrong for my daughter."

Way to be the alpha male, Dad.

"Georgetown." Nick perked up, hopeful that they were finally showing overt hints of interest in him.

"And what made you decide to quit?"

Where the hell was a fire alarm when you needed one?

"Sir, I wouldn't say that I had *quit,* exactly. I took some time off. I had moral disagreement with the way that the law was being practiced at my firm."

"Do you mean that your firm was involved in some illegal activities?" My father's interest was piqued at the possibility of incarcerating Nicholas as a sure-fire way to keep his hands off of me.

"No, no. It was that I learned, unfortunately, sometimes the letter of the law can be a far cry from the spirit of it. And anyway, the profession was not as enjoyable as I had hoped."

"That is why they call it *work,* and not *fun.* Morality in one's profession is a luxury that most people cannot afford, you know," he said at Nick, satisfied more with himself than with his point.

"I understand what you're saying completely. The law isn't something I felt very passionate about. I decided to take some time to find a way to blend the things that I enjoy doing with the things that are lucrative. Since I'm not married with children yet, I feel that it's important for me to take chances like this now. It's sort of like Vina's frustrations with her career."

It was like watching a sixteen-year-old Doogie Howser imitator try to convince a bouncer that his name really *was* Juan Gomez. Clearly, my parents would see these as the fanciful ravings of a free-spirited, hippie lunatic who could never really understand true commitment. Or taxes. Or anything else that mattered. And by association, they would conclude, I was buying into his manifesto.

I was fully prepared to resent my Nani for not chiming in, when I turned in her direction to discover that she had fallen happily asleep in her chair.

"Well, of course Vina cannot simply leave her job because things are not enjoyable all the time. Before anything else, she has to get her MBA, anyway," my father continued, hopping happily about on the map of my life in his mind. "She has always said that. There are no two ways about it."

Was I even in the room?

"Or she could become an international bestselling novelist, and then business school might not make as much sense." Nick smiled at me, probably thinking that he was winning them over by displaying how much attention he paid to the details of my life.

Clearly, he expected me to jump on the bandwagon he'd

just erected in my honor. He didn't know that I had found the *Advanced Hindi for Dummies* book hidden in his bedside table that morning, while I was searching for a missing sweater of my own. How could a man who was making so much effort to relate continue to be so unaware?

"She can write. She can always write. Or paint, or sing songs or dance in the streets. But this is more of a hobby. Something she will do on the side. She is too sensible for that romantic lifestyle, anyway. The truth is that she really enjoys her career on Wall Street."

As hurt as I was, I could not bring myself to contradict my father in front of Nick. Family is family.

"Let's change the topic, shall we?" I interjected, refilling everyone's already nearly full glasses of iced tea.

"So, Nicholas, do you still have much family in Italy?" Mom offered, refilling her bowl with more Pasta Fagiole in an attempt to make him feel better. "I recently saw a Channel 13 special program about how the country is doing in modern times. Did you know? They said they had *declining* population growth?"

"Oh, I'm sure that's just an ill-stated statistic." I don't know why I felt the urge to defend Italy.

"Actually, Vina, it's true," Nick interrupted me. "I was talking about it with my uncle the other day. And I think it's a damn shame, pardon my language. I am all for women's rights to enjoy their lives and choose whomever they want to marry. And maybe some of these women never find the right man. I can accept that. There are a lot of jerks out there. But I think the real problem is that people are not willing to compromise for their spouses. Or for their families. These people expect constant romance. But what they don't realize is that without family, there's nothing. Where else does society get its moral fabric? Italy isn't the same now as it was when my father was growing up there. You know, that's what I really love about the Indian culture, to be honest with you. I think it's why I felt so comfortable with Vina right away. Her values make sense to me. She's ambitious and everything, but she comes from a loving family. And I know that she would do almost anything to make you happy, because she knows that at the end of the day, that's what matters."

"And what about the importance of culture?" Dad asked, clinging desperately to the shreds of his skepticism.

"Oh, well." Nick paused, and I knew he was choosing his words very carefully. "I would have to say that I have always felt the woman's culture should dominate the home."

Who was this man? Why was my dad smiling at him? And why was my mother smiling at my Nani? Suddenly, I felt more nauseous than I had all day.

·· 37 ··

The chill that settled over the apartment was instantaneous. After he closed the door behind my family, Nick made for the kitchen without so much as a glance in my direction.

"You did great." I came up behind him at the sink, and slipped my arms around his waist to envelop him in a hug.

"Did I?" he asked, giving the dishwashing liquid a rather aggressive squirt.

"Yes, you did," I answered, loosening my grip and sitting atop the counter to face him.

"Okay."

"Honey, what's wrong?"

"Nothing. Everything's fine."

He was scrubbing a plate to within an inch of its existence.

"Okay, look. I'm sorry for making you put on that show for them." I touched his arm. "I didn't realize it was such a big favor to ask."

The vein on the right side of his neck engorged, and he took a long, deep breath before turning toward me.

"Vina, I have no problem dressing up however you want me to, to impress your parents. I'll speak in Hindi. I'll do an interpretive dance. I don't care. I understand that it's important to you that they accept me. So I did it. Gladly."

"Then what's the problem? It was just one afternoon!"

"That's the point." He ran a soapy forearm across his forehead, revealing eyes which were far more upset than I expected. "For me, it's just one afternoon. But I see now that for you…it's your whole life. It's actually how you live. And I don't know how to handle that."

I blinked. "What are you talking about?"

"Let me ask you this. Is it that you're ashamed of me for not being Indian, or is it that you feel like you have to apologize for having any part of a personality that might be different from what they planned for you?"

"You're not making any sense." I slid off the counter and started for the living room.

"Yes, I am. I make perfect sense." He slammed a soapy melon-baller into the water before following me. "Those are the only possible reasons why you would act less like yourself with them around, than I have ever seen you act in the entire time I've known you. You swallowed everything you wanted to say. You were walking on eggshells, Vina! You never walk on eggshells with anyone!"

"Look…" I launched back into teacher mode, reminding myself to be patient because he knew not what he was saying. "I am a lot further along than anyone I know who has parents as conservative as mine. It's not something that…"

"I know, I know. It's *not something that I would understand,*" he said, mocking me for the first time. "Because I'm just the white boy. Well, to be honest with you, I don't want to understand them. I want to understand you. And I want them to understand you. Or maybe I want you not to care anymore whether or not they ever do! I'm the guy who's with you every day and every night. It's like you think you have to apologize for so many of the things that make you *you*. And I love all of those things! Every single one of them! I don't want you to change them, and I don't want you to apologize for them. I love it that you say what you think even if you know I won't agree with you. I love how complicated you are and how such a confident woman bites her fingernails when she thinks I'm not looking. I love all the different things that you're able to be passionate about, even if they're so different. And I love the way that you wear your emotions on your sleeve with me. I love the whole person I've gotten to know who has already changed my life so much more than she understands. But you turned into another person around them. And it breaks my heart. That's not the woman I love."

I dropped to the couch.

"Vina, I don't see why you can't do everything. Write, work on Wall Street, dance in the streets if you want to, like your father said. I want to see you do everything you secretly think you can do and wonder if you're capable of doing. And I have always believed that you will, when you're ready. But now I wonder if maybe the reason you're holding yourself back is because you feel like you need them to approve *before* you can take your own interests seriously. And I can understand that, a little bit, because I used to do it in my own way for my dad's sake and my mom's memory. But I'm not sure I can handle seeing you do it. Why do they have to cut off any idea of yours that differs with theirs? And more importantly, why do you let them?"

"They never told me to give up writing, completely. It's that they don't really…value it."

"I don't care what they value. They're…they're so dismissive."

I felt quickly protective. "Nick, they're my parents."

"And you're a grown woman. So the important question is, what do you value?"

I realized then and there that it really wasn't their fault. It was mine, because I had never asked myself that question before. And I felt embarrassed, for the first time, in front of Nick. I bowed my head.

"I'm sorry."

He knelt before me. "I don't want you to be sorry, Vina. You are already everything that you should be, and the rest is gravy. I can see it so clearly, and I don't want you to hold yourself back like that. Nobody who loves you would ever want you to."

It was the first time that he had said it, and I knew for sure that it was real. The kind of love that I needed, and that I never would have recognized had I not gone through everything that came before that moment. Salt-and-Pepper had said that love would recognize that I was searching, and want me for who I was as well as for who I wanted to be. If this outburst wasn't evidence of Nick rejecting the idea of me silencing myself, I didn't know what was. From the start I had felt as if he knew me, but I had kept it to myself. Partly because it would have been like pointing out the wetness of the water. But now, expressing it felt like the most logical thing in the world.

So I swallowed, and I smiled, taking his precious soap-splattered face in my hands. And the words seemed like a whisper in comparison to the emotion that was coming from inside me for this man.

"I love you, too."

I paced back and forth in front of the dining table, trying not to be distracted by the bickering in the kitchen. Prakash and Christopher had argued incessantly since applying for adoption of their Chinese orphan last month, probably in an attempt to simulate the stress of the pregnancy they would never have to endure.

"What could possibly be taking Nick so long?" I asked Booboo, who responded by licking his own belly.

In the months since Nick had met my parents, I had secretly submitted an op-ed piece to the *New York Times* every week, opining on everything from sheep cloning to reality TV. I had received so many form-letter rejections from them at that point that I was considering wallpaper-ing my kitchen with them. And eventually the letters got their message across—nobody was interested in what I had to say. That was why, when the *Times* called three days earlier to explain that they were publishing my latest submission, even Nick had trouble acting as if he wasn't surprised. Apparently, my life was more interesting than my opinions, and my latest submission was good enough to print. But my own bemusement gave way to a serious case of neck stress when it occurred to me that the whole world was about to share in my most personal thoughts and feelings. What would they think of me? How would they react? How would I feel about myself, once I saw those words in print? It was a good thing I knew people in Fiji; nobody could find me there. I had sworn Nick to secrecy and sent him out in search of the paper since we didn't have time to stop at my place before coming over to Prakash's that morning.

I pounced on the handle the instant the doorbell rang.

"Oh. It's you." I turned and walked back toward the window.

"Sorry I'm late for brunch, but is that any way to greet one of your best friends? I kind of lose track of time while I'm studying for the GMATs." Pamela removed her scarf and scanned Prakash's loft. "Where is everyone?"

"Huh?" I looked behind her for signs of Nick coming down the hallway. "I dunno. Cristy's on her way. Chris and Prakash are fighting or screwing in the kitchen. I'm not sure which, but I wouldn't go in there if I were you."

"What else is new? And Nick?" she asked, pausing amid the process of mixing herself a mimosa.

I headed back to the door, knowing she wouldn't have thought to lock it behind her. "Oh, he should be here any…"

And just before I could lock the door, it pushed back.

"Here it is, babe." Nick scooped me up into a hug and twirled me around before setting me down.

"Here what is?" Pam asked.

"My baby's been published in the *New York Times,*" Nick announced triumphantly, handing each of us a copy from his pile of at least thirty. "Here. Take a copy."

"Bullshit!" Prakash came running out from the kitchen, having overheard us. "Okay, this means we're gonna use the good champagne for a toast. Not the crap we put out for the mimosas."

"It was not crap." Christopher came out, wiping his hands on his *Breakfast Included* apron and frowning at his husband.

"Oh, come on. Be serious." Prakash went for their liquor cabinet.

Cristy was the next one through the door, and she nearly knocked me over. "Why didn't you tell me? This is incredible! *Chica,* congratulations!"

"Thanks." I blushed. Even though the newspaper was spread out before me, it was still hard to believe, especially since the last time the *Times* paid me any attention was such a disaster. My thoughts, in print, for the pleasure and dissection of *millions of people* the world over. I dropped backward onto the new camel suede sofa that Christopher had forbidden any of us to sit on.

"Okay, but we can't get too drunk," Nick admonished. "I need my Vina to be coherent tonight. We'll be celebrating her debut!"

"Where are you going?" Cristy asked, handing me a champagne flute.

"It's a surprise." Nick kissed the top of my head. "Oh, that reminds me. I have to confirm our dinner reservation."

He disappeared into the kitchen, and Pam and Cristina slid onto either side of the couch beside me.

"Well?" Cristina whispered.

"Well what?" I slurped and then swished the champagne around in my mouth.

"Is tonight a big night?" Pam asked.

"Yeah, sure." I blinked, still fixated on my name in print.

"Don't play dumb," Cristy said. "It's not convincing."

I looked at her, and then back at the miracle in my hands, willing time to stand still.

"Do you think he's going to propose tonight?" her voice climbed about three octaves.

"I don't know." I propped my feet up on the marble coffee table. "I hadn't thought about it."

"Haven't you even looked for the ring while he's in the shower?"

"Nope."

"Why not?" Christopher asked, coming to sit on the coffee table after kicking my feet off it.

"Because I'm usually in there with him?"

"Stop avoiding the topic," Cristina commanded.

"Look guys, I love him, yes. But life's good. And I'm just enjoying watching it unfold."

Brrrring! For once, I was saved by a phone call from my

parents. I flipped open my cell phone, rose to my feet and stepped toward the window, still clutching my newspaper.

"Darling, we did not believe it when we saw our daughter's name in the *New York Times* this morning," my mother gushed before I could say hello. "Our daughter!"

"Really, Vina. *Kamaal keeya,*" my father said. I turned away from the others and leaned against the windowsill. "You have made us very proud. I cannot imagine that my daughter can even think this way, much less write this way. This is truly something noble."

"It's not that big of a deal, Dad." I blushed, watching Nick come toward me with a champagne flute in one hand and a bottle in the other. Behind him, my friends were assembling for the toast they knew he was about to make.

"We are so proud of you," my mother told me. "Now hold on, your Nani is grabbing at the telephone."

So am I, I thought, lifting my glass for a refill as I awaited for my grandmother's voice. *So am I.*

·· My Postscript ··

On the shape of panic, the closet of claustrophobia and the liberation of falling apart

There are an estimated six million claustrophobics in the naked city. I'm one of them. And thank God for that. Until recently I lacked the courage to share that fact with even the closest members of my inner circle. But I'm not writing this piece to come out of my proverbial closet; my closet spat me out by force. I'm writing it to help many of you come out of your own, by choice. Because facing my disorder meant facing some other, more important things about myself. Myself, and adult life in general. Allow me to explain.

I woke up one day a few months ago feeling so disappointed in myself. No, I was not alone in a Dumpster in Connecticut, and no, I was not lying next to a naked stranger wearing a tool belt and covered in raspberry jam. You New Yorkers, with your dirty imaginations. I was disappointed because I finally had to admit that the origin of my problems was staring back at me in the mirror. In the months preceding that afternoon, I had lost nearly everything that mattered to me.

My moment of revelation occurred on the cold, hard floor of a midtown elevator where I found myself in the fetal position after a full-fledged nervous breakdown. I was on my way to a deposition with the SEC. And clarity came in the form of admitting to myself that my career, my relation-ship, and ultimately my faith in my own judgment paid the price for trying to be perfect as others defined it. I had spent twenty-seven years setting myself up to fail. And I began to wonder, in the weeks and months that followed, why I would have done that to myself, and if it were possible that I could be the only one. Somehow, I didn't think so.

Most claustrophobics experience an intense, often socially and professionally debilitating disorder that begins without benefit of emotional stimuli, and prevents them from feeling comfortable in enclosed spaces. In the most severe cases, people will literally begin to hyperventilate at the prospect of even entering a subway, a small room or an elevator, for fear that diminishing oxygen will cause them to suffocate to death. Mercifully, mine was a milder form, which triggered responses only when coupled with mounting external emotional distress. Routinely, my claustrophobia pushed me close enough to peer over what I had come to recognize as my emotional edge. But what I didn't realize until after the day of my breakdown was how much worse I was making the disorder for myself. Because while I had experienced emotional distress in close quarters many times before, that afternoon in the elevator was the first time that it pushed me over the edge to a panic attack and subsequent breakdown. And now I realize why.

The core of claustrophobia, regardless of its severity, is a fear of losing control. And like many otherwise rational adults, I was carrying around the ridiculous notion that I had some. The idea was that by my late twenties, I ought to have had my life figured out. To know what I was doing, where I was headed, and why the world spun the way that it did. It wasn't enough to be good at my job, or to try my best with my relationships. I desperately needed to believe that nothing had been left up to chance. That I knew what I was doing, and I made my own destiny.

Like I said, thank God for my claustrophobia, because I had become good at balancing on that high-wire above reality, and I had every intention of staying there on my tippy-toes forever. Alongside many of you. It was a carefully crafted illusion that I "had it together," and it was comforting. Then something wonderful happened. Everything fell apart. Finally, on the floor of that elevator, so did I. After the dust settled on the investigation I was cleared of any wrongdoing. The SEC charges of insider trading were dropped, and those who had deceived me were forced to accept responsibility for their lies.

While I was vindicated, I found that I was far from free. Some nagging questions remained, the loudest one being *Why did I miss all the signs?*

So I cried, and I hid, and I thought and I meditated, and the only answer that came to me was this: *Because I chose to.*

That's when all the pieces began falling into place. The last time I could remember living in a world without anxiety was somewhere around age four. Curly-haired, chubby-cheeked, eating a bowl of chocolate ice cream and wearing a T-shirt claiming Here Comes Trouble, I was usually wiggling to the sound of the tunes in my head, swinging my legs off the side of my chair and completely at peace with a hug and a smile from my mom. Where had that girl gone?

Like the happy child inside of most people, she was buried under years of trying to please everyone around her. Buried under the weight of pressure, age, cynicism and shame, all emotions with which she had been so happily unfamiliar. By subscribing to the notion that I ought to aim for perfection, I chose to internalize the pressure to know everything. I began to hold myself to standards no one would ever have expected of a child. And I became my own worst enemy, once I forgot about that girl entirely. I muted her voice while living my life for all of the others.

And it took my breakdown to show me how far it had gone. After a while, so much was resting on the illusion of my own control, that second-guessing myself was not an option. So consciously or subconsciously or in some vein between the two, I ignored the warning signs. I refused to ask questions or to take a step back. I no longer allowed myself to squint and discern the fine line between my instincts and my defense mechanisms. I was so afraid to have any of my ideas or choices contradicted that I refused to allow dissension even from within.

Sound familiar? I'm sure that it does. Because we all do it, to different degrees. We lie to ourselves all the time, *Shh-hhhhhh*ing that inner voice until it is no longer even audible above the roar of the lives we build above it. Hence my disappointment in myself. Since then, I've discovered something wonderful. It turns out that the inner voice never goes anywhere. It just waits patiently until it can be heard once again.

The calm after my breakdown was palpable, which is why I recommend it to everyone. And as for my claustrophobia, I'm not ashamed anymore. The funny thing is, the minute you try to let go of the delusion of control, without knowing it, you start letting go of your anxieties and your phobias, and you begin to distill what's important.

My claustrophobia has taught me that I was suffocating as much inside of my own expectations as I was inside of my disorder. That true strength was being humble enough to second-guess myself. That I never had any control to begin with. And knowing that was the most tremendous gift.

I see now that the claustrophobic in me was in large part a manifestation of the phobic in all of us. I don't mean to imply that claustrophobia in most cases is not a legitimate and clinically diagnosed disorder. All I know for sure is that the last year of my life changed everything because I suffered the kind of crisis that I hope only comes around once. I know that I am fragile, and fallible, and so is everyone else.

So I choose to aim for improvement rather than perfection, and to appreciate the effort as much as the results. Because it's not about perfection, or ego, or anything else. It's about that girl I tried so hard to bury. It's about appreciating that my instincts may be the echoes of her voice. It's about raising a glass when it's time, raising an objection when it's necessary and raising my self-awareness to the point where I will never again fail to do what's best for me. And it's about knowing that as long as I live that way, my four-year-old self will be smiling back at me from across the table, ice-cream bowl in hand, innocently rooting me on.

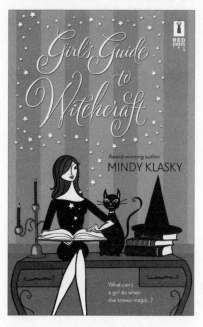